"He said he'll have another drink," Joel said, his tone calm, but firm, as he stood there with his carbine held casually before him.

"You're makin' a helluva mistake, mister," Ansil Bowers finally spoke up. "I ain't gotta serve none of you Rebel trash."

"You're gonna serve this one," Joel told him, "and the sooner you get on with it, the sooner we'll be gone."

Emboldened by Lige Tolbert's presence, Bowers replied, "The hell I will." In the next instant, he suddenly jerked backward, startled by the sharp crack of the carbine and the crash of broken glass as the lamp behind the bar was shattered. It was followed at once by the sound of another cartridge inserted in the chamber, and a moment later, by the gasps of the startled bystanders.

Joel motioned with the Spencer and said, "Pour him his drink, and be quick about it. I'm losin' my patience."

SILVER CITY MASSACRE

Charles G. West

A SIGNET BOOK

SIGNET
Published by the Penguin Group
Penguin Group (USA) LLC, 375 Hudson Street,
New York, New York 10014

USA | Canada | UK | Ireland | Australia | New Zealand | India | South Africa | China
penguin.com
A Penguin Random House Company

First published by Signet, an imprint of New American Library,
a division of Penguin Group (USA) LLC

First Printing, January 2014

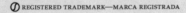

ISBN 978-0-451-46656-3

Printed in the United States of America
10 9 8 7 6 5 4 3 2

For Ronda

Chapter 1

It had taken him a long time to make up his mind, too long, he figured, but at last he deemed it time to put this senseless war behind him and get on with the rest of his life. Joel McAllister could look himself in the eye, knowing that he had given all that he had originally pledged to the Missouri Volunteers and .General Joseph Shelby's Confederate cavalry. He had fought under Shelby's command for over two years, distinguishing himself in countless raids and skirmishes, enough so that he was awarded a battlefield promotion to the rank of lieutenant.

It had been more than two months since Lee surrendered at the little Virginia town of Appomattox, but Joe Shelby had defied orders to surrender his cavalry, saying he would never live under Yankee rule. Like several hundred of Shelby's volunteers, Joel had followed the fire-eating general when he left Shreveport and marched into Texas, determined to take his troops to Mexico. A sense of loyalty to his general had been the reason Joel had made that decision.

After some troublesome nights of serious thought, however, he found himself on the bank of the Brazos River near the little town of Waco, questioning the choice he had made. It was a hard decision to make, for he had felt it his duty to follow his superiors and not ask whether or not their orders were right or wrong. Over the last two days, he had labored over the question and he realized that he was ready to say good-bye to war. Choosing to leave with some honor, he had informed his company commander, Captain Grace, that he was departing in the morning, having decided that his future did not lie in Mexico. The captain was disappointed but assured him that the general would understand and wish him luck, just as he had with the majority of his command who had departed for home when the unit was in Shreveport.

"Where are you heading?" Captain Grace asked.

"About as far from this war as I can get," Joel answered. "I've been thinkin' it over, and I've decided to light out for Idaho Territory."

"Idaho?" Grace responded, obviously surprised. "What in hell is in Idaho? That's halfway across the world. You might as well go to California or Oregon."

"That's a fact, I reckon," Joel replied. "But maybe it's far enough away so there's no North or South, and this damn war ain't the only thing on everybody's minds. That ain't my only reason, though. I've got a brother out that way, and I reckon he'd be glad to have a partner to help him work his place. I've been thinkin' it over, and I ain't cut out for a career in soldierin'. I've got nothing to go back to in Missouri. The only family I've got left is my brother."

"Well, I wish you luck, McAllister. You're a fine soldier and a damn good man. I wish I could let you take your horse with you, but the general said any man who quits after we cross into Texas will leave on foot. I'm sorry. I surely am."

"I understand the general's feelin's on the matter," Joel assured him. "Our horse stock is needin' some help right now, so I didn't expect it any other way. I've got no problem with that. I'll turn my horse out with the others tonight."

"That's mighty understanding of you," Grace said. "I know the general will appreciate your attitude. You say you're planning on leaving in the morning?"

"Yes, sir, right after breakfast."

"Good," Grace said. "I'm sure the general will want to have a word with you before you go. Maybe he'll make an exception of his order and let you take your horse."

Joel smiled and nodded. They shook hands then and the captain turned and walked back toward his tent. Joel watched him walk away, remaining there on the bank until Grace entered the tent. He then returned to his own tent and the chestnut gelding tied beside it. The horse had been with him since his first day assigned to the regiment. It had more or less picked him to partner with. On the day they met, the gentle gelding left the herd of extra horses and walked right up to him when he approached them, bridle in hand. At the time, Joel had had no particular preference, so he accepted the chestnut's easy invitation, and there had been no reason to regret the decision ever since. Concerned about the horse's performance in battle, Joel had been pleased to find the chestnut willing and able during a cavalry charge, and fleet of foot when-ever a quick retreat was ordered. That characteristic of willingness inspired Joel to name him Willing, which he soon shortened to Will.

The captain had been right when he said the Idaho Territory was half a world away from Waco, Texas. But being the practical man that he was, Joel had no intention of walking that distance, and certainly no thought of leaving Will behind. He figured the regiment owed him a horse at the least, and a packhorse to boot, which he planned to liberate from the herd of extra horses grazing in the narrow valley as soon as darkness set in a little more. There was a strong possibility that Grace was right in thinking Shelby would let him take the horse. But Joel preferred to bank on a sure thing, so he planned to leave that night, in spite of what he had told the captain.

He was about to enter his tent to finish packing up his saddlebags and bedroll when the familiar figure of Sergeant Riley Tarver suddenly appeared in the diminishing light of evening. Even in the poor light, there was no mistaking the squat, solidly built Tarver as he approached on short legs, appropriately bowed for a cavalry trooper. Joel paused to await him. The sergeant was always found close to his lieutenant whenever the regiment was in battle. Joel was not oblivious of the fact that Tarver seemed to have taken a responsibility upon himself to ensure his safety. He had to chuckle when he stopped to think about it—Riley Tarver had selected him to watch over much the same as Will had. And while he had never voiced it, he sincerely appreciated the sergeant's apparent devotion to him.

"Evenin', Sergeant," Joel greeted him. "You lookin' for me?"

"Evenin', Lieutenant," Riley returned. "Yes, sir, I was thinkin' on havin' a word with you, if you don't mind."

"All right," Joel replied, thinking he caught a sense

of concern in the sergeant's manner. "What's on your mind?"

Tarver hesitated while he sought to organize his words. "Sir, can I talk kinda frankly?"

"Why, sure you can, Riley. Nothing ever stopped you before. Is something botherin' you?" It occurred to Joel that he was going to miss the burly sergeant.

Riley pushed his campaign hat back far enough to enable him to scratch his curly white hair, still hesitant to come out with what he had come to say. Finally he spat it out.

"Lieutenant, you know, we've been in some pretty tight places over the past two years, and I hope you won't think it disrespectful if I say I've come to know you pretty well."

Joel stifled a chuckle. He was well aware of the sergeant's admiration. "Not at all," he answered. "I reckon we both know each other pretty well."

"Well, sir," Riley went on. "It looks to me like you've been thinkin' pretty heavy on somethin' for the last week and a half—like maybe that somethin's botherin' you. And if I was to take a guess, I'd say you ain't too damn keen about goin' down to Mexico." He paused when he saw that his comment had caused Joel's eyebrows to rise, but Joel made no reply, so he continued. "It ain't none of my business, but I just wanted to tell you that I ain't lost nothin' in Mexico. If you're thinkin' about musterin' out of this army anytime soon—and you could tolerate a partner—why, hell, I'm your man. I'm ready to be done with this war, and the farther I can get away from it, the better."

Joel was stunned. Had he been that transparent? Or was Riley so devoted to him that he had learned to read his mind? He had given absolutely no thought toward having a partner on his long journey up the face of the country. It made for an interesting suggestion, however, one that called for his consideration. After he'd thought about it for a few long moments, it suddenly struck him as an amusing proposition, considering the timing. And he had to admit that if he were to pick one man with whom to partner, it would have been Riley Tarver.

Joel's lengthy pause caused Riley to worry. "If I've spoke out of line," Riley quickly offered, "I wanna say right here and now that I didn't intend no disrespect."

Joel needed no more than another moment to reply. "How soon can you be ready to go? 'Cause I'm leavin' tonight."

Riley's jaw dropped in surprise. "You mean I can go with you?"

"If you can get your gear together to leave tonight," Joel answered, "'cause I ain't figurin' on ridin' another day closer to Mexico."

"Glory be!" the sergeant exclaimed, scarcely able to believe it. "I knew there was somethin' workin' on your mind. I was wonderin' why you pitched your tent kinda off here by itself. Yes, sir, I'm ready to go right now." His grin was so wide that his face could scarcely contain it. "Where you figurin' on headin'? Not that I care one way or the other."

"Idaho Territory," Joel answered.

"Idaho?" Riley responded, as much surprised as Captain Grace had been, but unlike the captain, he thought it was a grand idea. "Well, now, there's a piece of luck, I'd say, 'cause I've spent some time up that way, back before this war. I followed the rest of them fools out to California lookin' for gold." He paused for a little chuckle when he recalled, "I didn't find enough to buy tobacco for my pipe."

"Maybe you'll have better luck this time," Joel said. "My brother's sittin' on a claim out there near a little town called Silver City. At least that's what his letter said, but I didn't get the letter until six months after he sent it. I reckon he's still in the same spot. That's what I'm countin' on, anyway. I can't say for sure what we'll find when we get out there. My brother mighta moved on somewhere else."

"I didn't know you had a brother," Riley said.

"Yep, Boone's two years older than I am. He went in the army about six months before I did, got his leg torn half off by a load of grapeshot at Vicksburg—crippled him up pretty bad, so his soldierin' days were over. Boone ain't the type to let anything stand in his way, though. So when there was news that folks had found gold in Idaho Territory, he decided he'd go, too. Accordin' to his letter, he thinks he's sittin' on a mountain of it. He said there were a lot of folks who went to California that came back to prospect in Idaho. There may not be any gold left to find when we get there, but I figured I might as well go out there and see the country for myself. So if you're sure it'll suit you, then welcome aboard."

"It suits me just fine," Riley assured him. "I'm ready to go. We've done lost this war."

"There are a few things we have to take care of tonight if we're gonna get outta here before anybody knows we're gone," Joel told him. "How do you feel about horse stealin'?" He went on to remind him about General Shelby's policy regarding the horses. "I told Captain Grace that I wasn't leavin' till after breakfast tomorrow, 'cause I'm plannin' to borrow another horse to use as a packhorse tonight. I kinda gave him the idea that I was gonna turn my horse in with the others tonight and leave on foot after breakfast. Looks like we'll need two more now, and I wanna be long gone from here before reveille."

"Yes, sir," Riley exclaimed, excited now with the prospect. "Horse stealin' runs in my blood, on my mother's side, and I can get my possibles ready in no time. I'll go see if I can get us a little extra bacon and beans from the mess sergeant while he ain't lookin', and I can rig us up a couple of packsaddles for them horses we're gonna need." He paused to give his new partner a grin. "It'll most likely be a little easier to steal a couple of horses from that herd if there's one of us to distract the guard."

"I reckon," Joel replied with a matching grin. He reached out to accept Riley's extended hand, and the two parties sealed the partnership. "We'll need a couple of stout packhorses, 'cause I'm plannin' on loadin' 'em down with weapons and ammunition."

One thing the regiment had was plenty of both. After the surrender of the Confederacy, there were any number of arms stored at various magazines across Texas, and General Shelby had taken advantage of the opportunity to proceed to Mexico well supplied. Riley understood the lieutenant's thinking. The arms would be useful as trade goods to exchange for whatever supplies they might need along the way; plus, there were a lot of Indians between here and where they were going.

Joel wanted to make sure that Riley had considered all the risks involved, so he paused to ask a question. "Are you sure you wanna make a long ride across this territory when it's just the two of us? You know there have been reports of Cheyenne and Arapaho raids all over parts of Colorado since that massacre at Sand Creek about a year ago, and the Comanches ain't ever been peaceful."

"Yessir, I'm aware of that, but I figure we'd be watchin' our asses pretty careful, and we'll have plenty of firepower to make it costly for any Injuns that light into us. Besides, I got me a strong hankerin' to see those Rocky Mountains again."

"All right, then. Get your stuff together," Joel directed, "and bring it to my tent after the camp settles down for the night. Then we'll see about gettin' ourselves a couple of horses."

"I'll see you in about an hour," Riley said. He paused just before lifting the tent flap. "I reckon you've figured on how long it'll take us to get to Idaho Territory. It's almost September now, and we ain't likely gonna be able to do much travelin' when the snow starts."

"Yeah, I know," Joel replied. "But I reckon I've got the rest of my life to get there, so I ain't worried about whether or not I make it before spring."

"Me, too," Riley said.

True to his word, Riley Tarver returned when the campfires had died down among the lines of tents in the narrow valley. He was leading his horse, a dark sorrel, with several canvas sacks and half a dozen rifles to add to those Joel had already managed to acquire. They were tied on loosely behind the saddle. He found Joel packed as well, and ready to go.

"I didn't wanna wait too much longer," Riley said. He nodded back the way he had come. "It looks like about a quarter moon lyin' low on the prairie, and I figured we'd best get our business done before it gets high enough to give out much light."

"I expect we'd better lead these horses on up the river a ways and tie 'em up in the bushes while we go after the packhorses," Joel said.

"You plannin' on strikin' that tent?" Riley asked.

"No. The sentry's already passed by here once, and I reckon he'd wonder what was goin' on if it was gone the next time he came around," Joel replied as he looked hurriedly around him in case he might have overlooked anything. "And it's damn near time he showed up again, so let's get goin'."

No more time was wasted as the new partners led their horses down a gentle slope toward the line of trees and shrubs that bordered the river, picking their way carefully to avoid any holes that might cause the horses to stumble and create a noise.

"This oughta do," Riley said when they came to a bunch of tall bushes. "How we gonna do this thing?" he asked when their mounts were secured. "Damn!" It suddenly occurred to him. "I got the packsaddles, but I didn't get no bridle."

"I didn't get an extra one myself," Joel replied, unconcerned. "I've got rope, though, so we'll make bridles."

"Good thing," Riley said, "'cause I didn't even think about bringin' rope." He shook his head and joked, "I guess that's why you're an officer and I'm just a sergeant."

Carrying nothing but the coil of rope, they went back down the river for a hundred yards before leaving it at a spot that put them even with the herd of extra horses standing peacefully in the treeless valley. They paused there waiting to locate the guards, before moving on in toward the horses. The sentries were not obvious against the dark background of the milling horses, but after a few minutes, Joel spotted a solitary figure slowly pacing his post. They continued to watch until the figure met up with another figure near a large clump of sagebrush. The two sentries paused there for a short while to exchange conversation before parting to reverse their steps. "That's where to catch 'em," Riley said. He turned to Joel. "Who's gonna do the stealin', and who's gonna do the talkin'?"

"I expect I'll steal the horses," Joel said. "You've got a better chance of distractin' the guards. They're more likely to chew the fat with you. If I did it, they'd be tryin' to act real alert and watch everything goin' on."

Riley agreed, so they waited until the guards completed another circuit of their posts and met again at the sagebrush, before scurrying out across the narrow valley.

"Hello, the horse guard," Riley called out as he approached the two soldiers.

"Who goes there?" one of the guards demanded, and both men reacted alertly.

"Nobody but ol' Tarver," Riley answered, "just takin' a look around the camp—makin' sure everything's all right."

Both men relaxed when they recognized the stumpy, bowlegged sergeant. "Evening, Sarge," one of the men greeted him. "What are you doing, wandering around out here in the dark?"

"Like I said, just keepin' an eye on things, makin' sure you boys ain't takin' a little nap out here. Anything goin' on?"

"Nary a thing," the other guard replied. "Quiet as a whore in church."

"That's always good, ain't it?" Riley said. "Maybe one of you boys has got a match, so's I can light my pipe."

The two sentries were content to pass a little time with the sergeant, giving his accomplice ample time to select two stout horses and fashion bridles with his rope. Happily distracted, they took no notice of the lone figure leading two horses away from the herd, even when he was obliged to stop and chase a few horses back when they started to follow. After finishing his smoke, Riley took his leave and the two sentries resumed their responsibility. A little over an hour later, the two horse thieves rode up the bank of the Brazos and set out for Idaho.

Chapter 2

Traveling slowly but steadily, so as to get as much distance as possible behind them before having to rest the horses, they followed the course of the river to the northwest. Just after daybreak, they rode through a grove of cottonwoods close by the riverbank and dismounted on a sand flat near the water's edge.

Joel figured that they had gained a reasonable head start on any patrol the general might have sent after them, especially since he felt certain no one had seen them leave. The odds were slim that Shelby would delay his troop movement south to chase them, anyway. With these thoughts in mind, the new partners were comfortable in giving the horses a good rest and cooking a little breakfast for themselves.

"I wanna do a better job of packin' these horses," Riley said as he pulled the packs from the horse he had been leading. "I was in too much of a hurry when we loaded 'em back yonder. I'll unload yours, too, Lieutenant, soon as I get this'n off."

"Might as well settle something right now," Joel said as he pulled the saddle off the chestnut. "We ain't in the army no more, so there ain't no more lieutenant or sergeant. We're equal partners on this deal, and I'll be splittin' the chores with you fifty-fifty. So don't call me 'Lieutenant' anymore. All right?"

"Yes, sir, *Joel*," Riley replied, grinning broadly when he emphasized the name. He wouldn't have expected anything different from the broad-shouldered young officer, but he knew he would continue to regard him as his leader. The man had far and away earned his respect with his conduct under fire.

"I know I plan to get outta this uniform first chance I get," Joel went on, "and find some decent clothes. By the time we get to Idaho, we're gonna be needin' something a helluva lot warmer than these ragged uniforms."

The last comment was without doubt, because at his guess, they would be lucky to get to Silver City before spring, and it would be cold in the high mountains.

"I expect you're right about that," Riley said, having already thought about the country they were heading for, and the winters he had seen for himself when out there before. "Makes me crave a cup of hot coffee just thinkin' about the way that snow piles up in them mountain passes. I'll make us a fire and we'll cook us some breakfast."

The morning passed uneventfully, with no sign of pursuit, so after resting the horses, they started out again. They divided their cargo of twelve Sharps carbines and extra ammunition between the two packhorses. That, added to their food supplies, cooking utensils, coffeepot, frying pan, coffee cups, bedrolls, and other useful items, made for a reasonable load for the horses to carry.

As for their personal weapons, both men carried Spencer carbines in their saddle scabbards as well as Navy Colt revolvers holstered on their belts. The Spencers, captured from Union outfits, were favored by both since the weapons were repeaters and designed to take a .54-caliber metal cartridge, while the Sharps took a combustible paper cartridge. The problem during the fighting was the lack of the metal cartridges to fit the Spencer, which the Confederates didn't have. But their unit had been lucky enough to capture a Union supply train, so they now had an ample supply of ammunition. Joel was of the opinion that the Spencer packed a more powerful punch than the Sharps, which he planned to utilize in hunting for big game.

The first full day of travel found them still following the general direction of the twisting and turning Brazos, aided by the existence of a well-worn trail that reminded them that they were riding in Comanche territory. The river managed to maintain its contact with the travelers, although it often took leave to turn away from them before coming back again. The country looked the same, with no indication that it would ever change in appearance, the gently rolling prairie broken only by the occasional line of hills.

On the second day of travel, upon entering a wide valley bordered by a long ridge on their right, they came upon a recent campsite that Riley determined to be Indian.

"Not more'n a day old," he told Joel as they both tested the ashes of the campfire.

"I agree," Joel said. "I expect we'd best keep a sharp eye."

He walked around the clearing among the cottonwoods, inspecting the tracks, seeking to get an idea of the size of the hunting party. It was plain to see that they had come upon a popular camping spot, for there were many older tracks as well as the remains of a couple of other campfires, long dead. He returned to focus his attention on the fresh tracks.

"They're Indians, all right. None of these horses are shod. Doesn't look like a very big party, maybe three or four at the most—may not be that many—could be one or two and extra horses."

"Maybe they'll take off in some other direction," Riley speculated. He was not overly concerned about a fight with hostile Indians, if these were indeed hostile. Depending upon how well armed the Indians were, they would most likely be able to ward them off.

"From the looks of these tracks, they left here in the same direction we're headin'.'"

"But like we said," Riley replied, "they're most likely a day ahead of us."

"We'd best keep an eye on their tracks anyway," Joel advised. "Maybe they'll turn off in some other direction." They climbed back into the saddle and continued on. After a few miles, the Comanche's tracks turned back toward the east.

They encountered no more tracks on that day, and no more than an occasional sign of Indians during the next few days. Still they knew better than to relax their caution. There had been word of increased Comanche attacks on the little settlements and ranches in northwest Texas in recent weeks.

For two more days they continued to follow the Brazos until late one afternoon they arrived at a point where the river seemed to change its course back more to the west. Accustomed by then to the many turns and twists of the river, they decided to stick with it, so they made camp there at a wide bend, with plans to start out again in the morning. Weary of the open sameness of the country, they welcomed the nightly fare of bacon and coffee.

"Damned if I ain't ate so much bacon I'm gonna turn into a hog if we don't see somethin' to shoot at before long," Riley complained. They had occasionally seen sign of deer, but no sightings of the animals themselves. "I swear, I'm about ready to think about butcherin' that packhorse."

"He looks a mite tough," Joel teased. "Maybe you'd do better butcherin' Dandy."

"Couldn't do that," Riley responded, chuckling. "Ol' Dandy might come back to haunt me."

"How'd you come up with a name like Dandy for that horse, anyway?"

"On account of the way he acts around the ladies," Riley informed him. "See, he don't know he's been gelded—acts like a damn stallion every time he gets near a mare. Thinks he's a real dandy when it comes to courtin' the ladies. I feel real sorry for him if he ever finds out he ain't got nothin' to work with."

The next morning found them in the saddle before sunup, and they continued to follow the drunken course of the river until stopping to rest the horses an hour or so before noon.

"I think we shoulda left this river back yonder where we camped last night," Joel said.

Coffee cup in hand, he stood by the tiny fire they had built to cook their breakfast and stared thoughtfully off toward the distant hills to the west. He turned

then to address Riley, who was poking around in the
fire to encourage it to continue to burn.

"How far do you figure we've rode this mornin'?"

"Fifteen, sixteen miles, I'd say," Riley answered.

"And it's been due west, or maybe a little bit south,
the whole time," Joel complained. "And it doesn't look
like it's ever gonna turn back the way we were headin'.'"

"I was thinkin' the same thing," Riley said. "I reckon
you're right. We'd best turn around and head back to
the north. I don't know if there's a short route straight
up through the mountains in Colorado Territory, but if
we keep to the east of the high range we oughta be able
to find Denver City. And I've been there before. I can
find the old Oregon Trail if we go north from there up
to South Pass. Won't be no trick a'tall, maybe a piece
farther, that's all."

That made sense to Joel, so they struck out on a
northwestern course, relying solely on the probability
that when they had traveled far enough into Colorado
Territory, Riley would eventually recognize country
he was familiar with.

Joel wasn't concerned by the fact that he was passing
through country he had never seen before. He didn't
discount the possibility that Riley's memory might
have faded a little over the years. Even if it had, he figured they would sooner or later find someone who
could head them in the right direction. If that failed, he
was confident that they could simply ride due north
until they hit the old Oregon Trail and then follow it
west. Boone had told him in his letter that the trail west
crossed the Snake River at Three Island Crossing. And
once he reached that point, someone should be able to
tell him how to get to Silver City. So they continued on
across a rugged stretch of Texas plains, pushing the

horses from one nearly dried-up river to the next. It was on the fourth day after leaving the Brazos that they encountered the first real trouble.

"If I had to guess," Riley commented when they struck the first sizable river they had seen for a long while, "I'd bet this is the Canadian."

"Maybe so," Joel replied, not really caring what river it was. "It's the first river we've seen in a spell that ain't so dried-up you could spit across it." Even so, it was obvious that this river was suffering the same dry summer as the smaller ones they had crossed, for the water was drawn away from the banks a good ten or twelve feet. "There's still a good three hours of daylight left, but I'm for campin' here for the night. The horses can use the rest, and I wouldn't mind peeling these clothes off and takin' a bath."

"That sounds good to me," Riley said. So they picked a spot in the shade of a group of cottonwoods on the bank, pulled the saddles off their horses, and unloaded the packhorses. Once that was done, both men jumped in the river, clothes and all, figuring the uniforms needed washing as well.

After the long ride over the last few days, it was tempting to horse around in the cold water in an effort to keep warm, even for a usually somber man like Joel. Before long a water battle began, with Riley starting the duel, splashing Joel with his hand. In response, Joel fired back with a double-handed blast. Like two schoolboys, they churned up the river water as they battled to drown each other, until Joel became aware that Riley was no longer fighting back. Instead, the grizzled old sergeant was staring at the opposite bank, his face drained of the youthful grin of moments before. Joel turned to see what had captured Riley's eye.

"Where the hell did they come from?" Riley muttered.

Sitting their horses, a line of twelve Comanche warriors stared in silent fascination at the strange actions of the two white men. Startled, Joel could only stare back at them while he speculated on the possibility of retreating. He could only guess at the amount of time it would take to get to his rifle back on the bank before the Indians decided to shoot. He didn't care much for the odds. At least they were on the other side of the river. In the brief seconds he had to size the situation up, he could see that there appeared to be but a few rifles among them. That helped, but there was still the possibility of getting shot full of Comanche arrows. Still the warriors made no move to attack, seeming instead to bide their time, observing the bizarre behavior of the white men. Finally Joel whispered to Riley. "What's the Comanche sign for *friend*?"

"Damned if I know," Riley murmured in reply.

"I thought you knew something about Indians."

"I never told you that," Riley shot back.

"Well, just hold your hands up," Joel said, "and start backing outta here real slow-like." He then held up his right hand and waved it slowly back and forth in front of his face, as if making a solemn signal. The gesture caused the Indians to exchange puzzled expressions before returning their stony gaze to the two white men, now stepping carefully back from the knee-deep water. The obvious retreat caused no outward concern to the warriors. They continued to sit patiently on their ponies while Joel and Riley left the water and backed up the bank to reach their weapons.

Having regained some measure of confidence now

that he held his Spencer carbine in his hand, Riley wondered aloud.

"Whaddaya s'pose they're waitin' for? Why don't they move?"

His question was answered in the next moment when they heard one of their horses nicker. Reluctant to take his eyes off the menacing line of warriors still sitting silently across the river, he looked quickly back toward the horses.

"Oh, shit," he muttered softly when he saw an equal number of Comanche warriors slowly walking their ponies through the line of cottonwoods behind them. "Whadda we do now?"

"There ain't a helluva lot we *can* do," Joel replied. "Just don't act like you're scared."

He picked up his carbine and cradled it across his arms, then turned and walked boldly toward the line of Indians in the trees. In the center of the line, his face a chiseled mask of open contempt for the two white men, a magnificent specimen of Comanche manhood watched Joel with curiosity, content with the obvious advantage he held. Joel naturally presumed him to be the leader.

"Do you talk white man?" Joel asked.

The Comanche responded with a questioning look before calling to another member of his party in his native tongue, "Black Otter!"

A younger man came up beside the one Joel had addressed. "I talk white man," he said. "My name is Black Otter." Before he could say more, the fierce-looking Indian spoke again. His tone was sharp and agitated. When he had finished, Black Otter translated. "He is Little Hawk. He asks what you are doing in

Comanche country, and why we should waste time talking to you."

"Is he a chief?" Joel asked, aware of the sound of Indian ponies crossing the river behind him now.

"No," Black Otter replied. "He is a medicine man. He leads this war party. We will take your guns and your horses."

"That would be a mistake," Joel told him. "We have heard of Little Hawk of the Comanche. We have come many miles to find him." Riley looked at him quickly, questioning. Joel continued. "If you try to take our guns and horses, many of your warriors will die, for we have the medicine rifles that shoot many times." Little Hawk's eyes blazed in anger as Black Otter translated. Joel went on. "We heard that Little Hawk is a wise man, so we have come to show him the army guns that load from the breech. We bring two of these guns as gifts. If you like them, we can bring many more." He turned to Riley then. "Get a couple of those Sharps out of the packs and some cartridges." He waited then for Black Otter to finish translating before continuing. "My partner will demonstrate."

"These white men lie, like all white men," Bloody Hand, a warrior who commanded respect among his band, spoke up. "I think they didn't come to find us. They didn't know we were even here before we surprised them. They have two horses with packs, maybe more of these guns. I say we should kill them and take all their guns."

His words brought forth several comments from the others, some in support of his position, but most in favor of following Little Hawk's advice.

"Bloody Hand is angry because the soldiers killed

his brother," Little Hawk responded. "I think it is right that he should feel this anger. Maybe what he says is the right thing for us to do. But these soldiers wear the clothes of the Gray Soldiers, so they are the enemies of the Blue Soldiers who attacked Bloody Hand's hunting party. I think these white men tell the truth, and if that is so, we have a chance to trade for many more guns than what they can carry on two horses. That is all I say." His words were enough to quell the small wave of disagreement.

Aware of the discussion taking place among the warriors, but with no way of knowing what it was about, Joel and Riley hesitated, wondering if it was something that should worry them.

When the Indians appeared calm again, Riley pulled two carbines out of the pack, being as careful as he could to avoid exposing the others they had brought. He approached Little Hawk and handed one of the empty rifles to him so he could examine it. Then he loaded one of the paper cartridges in the other carbine and turned to aim at a tree across the river. As rapidly as he could, he fired, reloaded, and fired again, leaving a reasonable-sized pattern of three bullet holes in the tree trunk. His demonstration brought a wave of excited murmuring among the warriors surrounding the white men. The few rifles they carried were old muzzleloaders. Little Hawk was outwardly impressed with the speed with which Riley reloaded.

"Tell Little Hawk that we have many more of these guns at our fort in Colorado, and we will bring a wagonload back to trade for animal skins," Joel said.

"Little Hawk wants to know if he can trust you to do as you promise," Black Otter said.

"We want to be friends with the Comanche," Joel assured him. "He knows he can trust our word because we give these two rifles as gifts."

Little Hawk spoke again through Black Otter, saying he would like to shoot the rifle himself. "Certainly," Joel responded. "The sergeant will show him how."

Little Hawk slid off his pony and handed the carbine to Riley. Riley showed him how to load the cartridge; then the medicine man aimed at the same tree Riley had peppered and fired the first round. It was a solid hit, in the center of the trunk. Riley showed him how to eject the spent cartridge and reload the next shot. He fired, hitting the tree once again. No longer trying to maintain his stern countenance, he smiled broadly, pleased with his marksmanship with the weapon. He spoke to Black Otter, and Black Otter translated.

"How many skins do you want for a gun such as this?"

Joel glanced at Riley, who shrugged in response, so Joel continued with his hoax. "One buffalo or three deer hides," he said, having no notion what a rifle should trade for if he really was bartering.

Black Otter agreed immediately without consulting Little Hawk, which led Joel to believe his price had been a lot less than the Indians were expecting. "Little Hawk wants to know when you will bring these guns," he asked.

"One month," Joel replied. "Tell him one moon, and we'll be back with a wagonload of guns and ammunition."

Black Otter looked at Little Hawk, who nodded when told of Joel's promise. "Go in peace," he said. "We return to our village now. In one moon's time, we will return to this place with many skins to trade."

"Good," Joel said. "We will come back to this place."

Riley got a box of the paper combustible cartridges from the packs and handed them to Black Otter. "You're gonna need these," he said.

The Indians turned their horses back toward the south, preparing to leave. Little Hawk nodded solemnly to each white man, then made one more comment to Black Otter before nudging his pony to step smartly away, his new carbine in one hand, held high over his head. Joel looked at Black Otter, questioning.

Black Otter shrugged. "He said you'd better build a fire to dry your clothes."

"I expect that's so," Riley said, standing beside Joel as the Indians departed the grove of trees. After the Comanche disappeared as suddenly as they had arrived, he turned to face Joel. "Damned if you ain't the best liar I've ever met, and I've known some good ones, myself included." He chuckled at the thought of having been at the mercy of a party of Comanche warriors, yet still standing with their scalps intact. "We'd best saddle up and get the hell away from here while we got a chance. That one feller looked like he'd just as soon shoot us and be done with it."

Joel hesitated and thought about it. "I don't know," he said then. "I think if they were gonna jump us, they would have done it while we were standin' in the middle of all of 'em. If they start to think about whether or not they got skunked, they might sneak back to see if we skedaddled. I think we'll be all right to stay right here and leave in the mornin'." He turned away then and started back toward the packs. "Besides," he added, "I'm wet as hell, and I need some coffee. There ain't but about a couple of hours of daylight left, anyway." He started again, then halted to say one more thing. "I'll tell you one thing, though. We've got to be a helluva lot more careful about lettin' anybody sneak up on us like that."

"Why?" Riley joked. "You can just make up another story to tell 'em." Another thought occurred. "Damned if we weren't lucky as hell there was one Injun in that bunch that could talk American."

After a supper of beans and bacon, Joel and Riley sat on their bedrolls, drinking coffee, completely naked except for their boots, which they had had the sense to take off before jumping in the river a few hours before. Their clothes, including the underwear, were hung on crude screens fashioned from willow branches and drying on the other side of a healthy campfire. Both men had an extra shirt and underwear, but they figured they had to wait for their pants to dry anyway, so they decided to save the extra clothing. Riley got up to test the progress of the drying uniforms.

"That evenin' breeze is starting to feel a little bit nippy on this old hide," he said. "Maybe I oughta move these clothes a little closer to the fire."

"If you move 'em any closer, you're likely to set 'em on fire," Joel said, although he, too, was beginning to feel the nip in the air.

The two Comanche warriors who had moved silently up to a small clearing a hundred yards from the camp by the water slid off their horses and tied them to a small tree. With their bows ready, they moved a little closer before pausing to consider the two naked white men by the fire.

"They must be crazy," Bloody Hand said softly, his

words filled with contempt. "They have no shame to show their nakedness. Little Hawk was fooled by their promises of many guns. They are clearly insane."

"He will be angry with us for killing the white men," Lone Bear said.

"Little Hawk is getting old," Bloody Hand spat. "The others will see we were right when we come back with the guns the white men carry, the medicine guns that shoot many times. They are better than the guns they promised to trade for skins."

"We must get a little closer, so we don't miss," Lone Bear said.

Bloody Hand nodded, and the two warriors left the clearing behind to make their way through the trees bordering the river. Intent upon drawing close enough to ensure their accuracy, they worked their way within thirty yards of the fire before their presence was detected by the horses.

At the first whinny from Dandy, Riley dropped to his knee just as an arrow whistled by over his head. Also instantly alert, Joel rolled away from the fire, grabbing his rifle from the blanket as a second arrow glanced off the sandy riverbank just beyond his bedroll. Cursing the horses for alerting the white men, the warriors nocked another arrow and charged the camp.

Caught on the opposite side of the fire from his bedroll and his rifle, Riley crawled as fast as he could to get to the carbine. Bloody Hand was upon him before he was halfway around the fire, his bow fully drawn. Before he could release the arrow, the sharp snap of Joel's Spencer rang out, slamming him in the chest and causing the arrow to be released harmlessly into the fire as he sank to his knees.

Seeing the muzzle flash, Lone Bear reacted quickly, but not quickly enough to loose his arrow before Joel's second shot ripped into his belly. The impact of the .54-caliber slug caused the startled warrior to stagger a few steps backward before sitting down hard on the bank. Stunned, he sat there, staring at the man crawling to his bedroll until another shot from Joel's carbine tore into his chest.

Still in a panic to get to his weapon, Riley reached it only seconds before a fourth shot from Joel's carbine knocked Bloody Hand over on his side. Riley scrambled to his feet, weapon ready at last, to stand over the Comanche warrior and make sure he was dead.

"Glory be!" Riley gasped. "That was too damn close for comfort!"

Joel did not respond. He was already moving cautiously toward the horses in case the two warriors were not alone. Finding the horses undisturbed, he searched the trees beyond the clearing before returning to the fire.

"Looks like these two were on their own," he told Riley. "They left two horses tied back there on the other side of the trees." He was a little more than peeved to have been surprised by the attack. "That's the second time we let those damn Indians slip up on us. Maybe now we'll get serious about keepin' a sharper eye. If it wasn't for that horse of yours, we'd most likely be lyin' there on the ground while those two were goin' through our packs."

"Yeah, but we ain't," Riley said, "so somebody must be lookin' out for us, even if it ain't nobody but Dandy." He was still in awe of the lightning-fast reactions of his partner when there really had been no time to react.

"You move pretty damn fast when you're naked as a jaybird."

As if just remembering then, Joel looked down at himself. He was wearing a coating of sand from having rolled off his bedroll.

"Damn," he swore, "I'm gonna have to go in the river again."

"I don't know about you, partner," Riley stated. "But I'm thinkin' I'd like to get my clothes back on and get the hell outta here, even if it is in the middle of the night. I swear, this damn spot is bad luck."

"I won't argue with you this time," Joel declared, thinking that he should have gone along with Riley's suggestion to leave the camp before. "Those two might not be the only ones thinkin' about payin' us a visit."

Their uniforms were still not totally dry, but they put them on just the same, packed up their camp, and put out the fire. Then they went back beyond the trees to collect the two ponies left there by the Comanche, stripped the Indian saddles off, and left them on the ground. The two extra horses might prove to be an additional bother, but they decided they might as well take them since they could be used to trade for supplies or ammunition. The horses, one a paint, the other a gray, weren't particularly anxious to go with the white men, and tried to pull away when Riley approached with a rope. He figured it was most likely the strange smell of the white men, so Joel threw one of the Indian saddle blankets over the paint's head, rubbing it gently on the horse's face until it calmed down. The same treatment worked on the gray as well, at least well enough to enable them to fashion a lead rope to be tied to each of the packhorses. All this was done as quickly

as possible, with each man frequently pausing to scan
the stand of cottonwoods behind them. When all was
ready, they left the river, heading out across the dark
prairie in the same direction they had followed for the
last several days.

Sometime during the wee hours of the morning,
they reached another river winding through the
almost flat terrain. It was a rough guess, but they estimated that they had ridden about twenty miles from
the Canadian, so they decided to make camp and rest
the horses. The spot where they struck the river offered
little in the way of firewood, since the banks were
crowded with berry thickets but no trees. Concerned
more with catching a little sleep, however, they chose
to roll up in their blankets and worry about a fire in the
morning.

Daylight brought a clear sky and the sun peeking up
across a prairie that appeared as wide and flat as a gigan-
tic skillet. But as far as Joel could see, and that seemed
like forever, there was no sign of any other being.

"I don't reckon there was any more of them Injuns
that decided to come after us," Riley announced when
he returned from the bushes with an armload of dead
branches. "Good thing, 'cause there ain't a helluva lot
of places to hide."

"We'll fix some breakfast and head on outta here,"
Joel said. "I wanna take a better look at those Indian
ponies we picked up next time we stop."

The captured horses seemed to have settled in with
the others, and no longer resisted being led. They rode
for half a day before stopping again to rest and water
the horses. After some bacon and coffee, Joel and Riley
looked their newly acquired stock over carefully and
came to the conclusion that they had gained two pretty

good horses, neither one more than about four years old. Joel especially liked the gray.

"When we get a little more of the dust of this prairie behind us, I think I'd like to see if I can throw a saddle on that one."

For the present, however, the two Indian ponies were led behind the packhorses as they set out for Colorado Territory.

Chapter 3

Almost two weeks had passed since they left the Canadian River when they made camp outside Denver City. The journey would have taken less time, but they had the good fortune to come upon a herd of deer near the Arkansas River, and were able to catch them at a shallow crossing. Both men managed to get off two clear shots, resulting in four carcasses to skin and butcher. By this time, they had concluded that there were no Comanche following them, so they took a few days to smoke-dry the meat and rig packs for it on the backs of the Indian ponies. The fresh venison was a welcome change from the steady diet of bacon that Riley had been complaining about for some time, and there was now a good supply of the dried meat to take the salt pork off the menu for a while.

"All a feller needs now is a good drink of whiskey," he opined. "And since we'll be goin' to town to get some supplies, I'm set on havin' one."

"I expect I'll join you," Joel said. "It has been a while."

Both men had little more than the money from their last payday in the army, and that was Confederate scrip, worthless beyond being used to start a fire. With rifles and extra horses, however, they were confident that they had plenty to trade for what they needed.

With the towering peaks of the Rocky Mountains to the west of them, they had continued their trek north across the high plains until reaching the creek below the thriving mining town. An abandoned mining claim with part of an old sluice box still standing seemed like a good spot to make camp. From the look of it, the prior residents had spent some time there before giving up and moving on.

"Most likely found a little bit of dust to make 'em stay so long," Riley speculated, "enough to buy grub, maybe. I'll bet for every miner that strikes it rich, there's a thousand workin' for grub money." That triggered another thought he was curious about. "You reckon that brother of yours is gettin' anything outta that claim of his out in Idaho?"

"I've got no idea," Joel replied. "Tell you the truth, I haven't thought much about it."

He was truthful in his answer. If there was gold to be found, it was all the better, but the driving force behind his decision to go west was a strong hankering to see that part of the country. He would decide what he was going to do once he got there, whether it was raising horses and cattle or maybe even sheep. He didn't care, he just felt the mountains calling him, and he was determined to see them before he got sidetracked somewhere else.

* * *

Although there had been a considerable portion of the Denver City population that had been Confederate sympathizers, and militia units had been organized to fight on the side of the South, the war had gone in favor of the Union. The Confederate troops were now disbanded, but there was still no sign of uniting the territory under one flag. It was into this fragile state of divided loyalties that the two ex–Confederate soldiers rode into town early one Monday morning, leading horses loaded down with army carbines and dried deer meat. As they were passing the bank near the south end of the town, they saw the bank manager just unlocking the door.

Curious to know if the Confederate money the two of them carried might still be of any value in this part of the territory, Joel pulled Will to a stop in front of the door.

"Good mornin' to ya," he called out.

The banker, upon turning to see who had greeted him, was startled to discover the two trail-weathered riders in the faded Confederate uniforms. His first thought was of the possibility that his bank was about to be robbed. Oblivious of the banker's fears, Joel asked his question.

"Me and my partner, here, are still carryin' our pay from the Confederate army. I was wonderin' if we could find out what it's worth if we exchange it for Union money."

Relaxing at once, since it was now obvious the strangers were not planning to rob the bank, the manager answered.

"I'm afraid I have to tell you that your money is worthless. You see, Confederate money was printed and

issued by the states—not like Union currency. So what
it amounts to is there might be a small exchange rate in
some states—no more than pennies on the dollar at
that. Most states and territories don't give you anything
for it. Colorado Territory is one of them."

It was not really surprising news to Joel. He figured
as much, but he thought it had been worth asking, just
in case.

"We're needin' to pick up some supplies," he said.
"We've got stuff to trade. Maybe you could point us
toward someplace that'll do some tradin'."

"The man you want to see is Guthrie," the banker
replied. "He'll sell or barter." He turned to point
toward the north end of the street. "Right next to the
saloon—there's a big sign over the door—Guthrie's
General Store. He was here before the town, ran a trading post, dealing with the Indians mostly, so he's used
to trading."

"Much obliged," Joel said, and nudged Will with his
heels.

They continued up the street toward the general
store, both men fairly amazed at the number of people
they passed, men and women, going about the business one would expect in a busy town back east. It was
not what Joel had expected of a mining town. There
were several men lounging on the boardwalk before a
saloon that proclaimed itself to be the Miner's Rest,
and Riley turned to give Joel a grin as they rode past.
Next door to the saloon, they dismounted and tied
their horses to the hitching rail. Riley licked his lips as
if already able to taste that drink he was bent on having
as soon as their business in the store was completed.

"Don't forget," he felt compelled to remind Joel, "we
need to have some cash money to boot."

Joel chuckled. "I won't. Else you might trade one of the horses for a shot of whiskey," he teased.

"Mornin', fellers," Ed Guthrie greeted them when they walked in. A short, stocky man that struck Joel as the spitting image of Riley if he had had hair on his shiny bald head, he came out from behind the counter. "You fellers just hit town?" he asked, making no effort to hide his frank appraisal of the two Confederate soldiers. Not waiting for an answer for his question, he asked another. "What can I do for you?"

"We'll be needin' some supplies," Joel answered, "some coffee, some sugar, flour, dried beans, some salt, and a few other things, soon as I can think of 'em."

Riley, who had walked over to a counter on the other side of the store, piped up then. "Some pants and shirts, too," he said. "These damn uniforms is about to fall to pieces."

Guthrie nodded. "It'd be a pretty good idea, even if they weren't," he said. "Folks around here are lookin' to forget about the Blue and the Gray. There's been too much trouble between the two sides, and we'd just as soon forget about the war and get on with life." He walked over to Riley. "You fellers thinkin' about tryin' your luck pannin' for gold?"

"Nope," Riley replied. "We're just passin' through on our way to Idaho country, so we need some stout clothes that ain't gonna turn to rags first time they get wet."

"Well, I can fix you up with anything you need," Guthrie said. "What are you usin' for money? Dust? Paper?" He paused a moment, then: "You know, I can't do no business with Confederate scrip."

"Feller at the bank told us you'd barter," Joel said, stepping in. "We've got trade goods that are worth a good bit of money."

Guthrie scowled, apparently disappointed. "Skins?"

"Well, we've got a couple of deer hides if that's what you want," Joel said. "But we're talkin' about things you can sell, like brand-new Sharps carbines, and boxes of ammunition to go with 'em, and two fine horses we'd let go at the right price."

Guthrie's frown disappeared immediately. "Brand-new?"

"Brand-new," Joel confirmed, "never been fired."

"Maybe we could work out a trade," Guthrie said, "dependin' on how much stuff you're lookin' to buy." He cocked his head back and added, "Course I'll have to take a look at the guns before we even get to talkin' trade."

"Sure," Riley said. "I'll go get one." He walked out to the packhorses while Joel looked over Guthrie's stock of woolen trousers. In a few minutes, Riley was back with one of the Sharps and handed it to Guthrie. "There you go. Like we said, ain't never been fired. Weapon like this would cost you about forty dollars or more."

"Well, I suppose so," Guthrie allowed as he looked the carbine over. "Course that'd be the price back east at the factory. There's a helluva lot of these army weapons showin' up now, so the value might not be worth the price of a new one."

Joel glanced over at a couple of old shotguns leaning against the wall behind the counter. "Don't look like many have been showin' up here," he said. "I don't see anything you've got to sell but those old shotguns. Seems to me that a shiny new Sharps carbine would be worth a lot more than the original price back east."

"And I'll guarantee you, there's four deer hides out there on our horses that were shot from a helluva long ways farther than a shotgun could hit anything," Riley said. He didn't feel it necessary to explain that the deer were shot with their Spencers. The principle was the same.

Guthrie couldn't help grinning. "All right," he conceded. "Let me figure up everything you're buyin' and then we'll see if we can work a trade."

The trading went on for the better part of an hour, but it was finally settled to both parties' satisfaction. Guthrie's price for the supplies they gathered on the counter came to a little more than forty dollars. Bargaining for some extra cash money to boot, Joel and Riley finally agreed to let Guthrie have one additional carbine and a box of cartridges to go with each. He stood outside with them while they loaded their purchases on the packhorses. When he got a glimpse of the extra weapons that remained, he began bargaining anew, but the most Joel and Riley would do was to let him buy two more for the equivalent of sixty dollars in gold dust. The trading finally done, Riley announced, "Now, since I've got a little money, I'm gonna have myself a little drink to wash all the lying outta my throat."

"Well, it was a pleasure to do business with you boys," Guthrie said, then hesitated before deciding to say more. "I might give you a little advice if you're fixin' to go into the Miner's Rest. Ansil Bowers, the feller that owns that saloon, is a strong supporter of the Union, and back before the war was over, folks that was loyal to the South didn't do their drinkin' in the Miner's Rest."

"Well, it's all over now, and the Union folks oughta be satisfied. They came out on top," Riley said. "Let bygones be bygones is what I say."

Joel laughed. "You're so anxious to get in that saloon,

you'd better go on. I'll be in in a minute after I finish tyin' these packs down."

"You talked me into it, you silver-tongued devil," Riley snorted joyfully. "I'll try not to drink it all up before you get there."

Guthrie lingered a few moments longer after Riley disappeared through the saloon door, watching as Joel tightened the last knot on the packs. Joel sensed that the store owner wanted to say something more but was still making up his mind.

"You know," Guthrie finally said, "you fellers seem like decent men, and you didn't ask my advice, but I think you might enjoy your whiskey better if you went on down to the Gold Nugget. Fred Bostic owns that saloon. He backed the Union, same as Ansil Bowers, but he thinks pretty much like you boys. The war's over, so let's all bury the hatchet. But Bowers lost his only son in a battle against Rebel troops near Springfield, Missouri. The boy was fightin' with a regiment of Kansas volunteers, and Ansil never got over it. You and your partner do what you want. I'm just tryin' to give you a little friendly advice."

"I understand what you're sayin'," Joel said. "I 'preciate it. We're sure as hell not lookin' for any trouble."

Guthrie stepped back up on the boardwalk, then turned to say one more thing. "It mighta been better if you had shucked those Confederate uniforms and put on your new clothes."

"You're probably right. I'll go see if I can keep Riley from gettin' in trouble."

Ansil Bowers glared at the stocky man in the rumpled gray uniform with sergeant stripes on the sleeves. He answered Riley's friendly greeting with a sour grunt, which Riley ignored before ordering a shot of whiskey. Showing his obvious disgust by his unfriendly attitude, Bowers put a glass on the bar and picked up the bottle, hesitating before pouring.

"What are you using for money? I don't take that Rebel money. It ain't nothin' but trash."

Riley's hackles went up just a little, but remembering Guthrie's comment about the owner of the Miner's Rest, he was determined to avoid any unpleasantness. He pulled his money out and slid it toward Bowers.

"Good ol' federal dollars," he said, and forced a smile.

Still undecided on whether or not he should refuse to offer service to a Rebel soldier, Bowers reluctantly poured the drink. Then he took the money and went to the end of the bar in an obvious move to put some space between himself and the unwelcome customer.

Seated at a table close to the end of the bar, two men played a casual game of two-handed poker. The exchange between Bowers and the stranger caught the attention of one of the cardplayers, Lige Tolbert, a sometimes miner, sometimes deputy sheriff, and full-time town bully. Engaged in none of those pastimes at the present, he saw an opportunity to relieve the boredom of the late morning. He had no particular loyalties to any cause, Blue or Gray included, but he knew the passion with which Bowers hated Confederate Rebels, so he decided to amuse himself as well as the few others in the saloon at that hour. With a grin for his card-playing partner, he stood up, pushed his chair back, and ambled over to the end of the bar across from Bowers.

"Damn, Ansil, what's that awful stink? I swear, I never noticed it till just a couple of minutes ago. Smells like a dead rat run into the place. You smell it?"

He made sure his voice was loud enough for everyone in the saloon to hear. The room went suddenly quiet, as the conversation among the few patrons ceased and all eyes were drawn to the stocky grayhaired man in the weathered uniform.

The implication was not lost on Riley. He looked over at Lige, who was grinning contemptuously. It was not necessary to spend much thought on the purpose of the man's comments. Riley had seen more than a few troublemakers like Lige in more saloons than he could remember. He decided to ignore the comment and see if nothing more came of it. Lige, however, was not content to let it go without some reaction from the stranger.

"You can smell it now, can't you, Ansil? It's worse than a skunk, I swear."

It was obvious to Riley that his antagonist was going to keep at it until he got some response from him. He knew that he could simply turn tail and slink out the door, which was probably what the bully expected, but it was not his nature to do so. Tapping his empty glass on the bar, he nodded to Bowers and said, "I think I'll have another little snort." Then he turned his attention to Lige and, with a knowing smile on his face, commented, "Couldn't help hearin' what you said about the smell in here. I think I caught a little hint of that stink when I walked in. And now that you mention it, you're right. It got a helluva lot stronger when you walked closer to the bar."

The leering smile instantly disappeared from Lige's face. "Why, you old son of a bitch, you came to the wrong place to pick a fight. We don't allow no Rebel trash in here, do we, Ansil?" Ansil responded with no more than a shrug. "So now I'm tellin' you to get your worthless ass outta here before I throw you out."

Unfazed, Riley remained at the bar, ignoring the bully, who had now taken a couple of steps away from the bar, preparing to follow up on his threat if Riley refused to leave. The crusty old sergeant refused to meet his gaze, looking at Bowers instead. "I'll have that other drink now, if you please," he told him.

"You'll have what!" Lige exploded, scarcely able to believe the old man's gall. "I'll show you what you'll have!" He had taken only a step toward Riley when he heard the sound of a rifle cocking. As all eyes had been trained on the confrontation at the bar, no one had noticed the lone figure standing in the saloon door.

"He said he'll have another drink," Joel said, his tone calm, but firm, as he stood there with his carbine held casually before him.

"You're makin' a helluva mistake, mister," Ansil Bowers finally spoke up. "I ain't gotta serve none of you Rebel trash."

"You're gonna serve this one," Joel told him, "and the sooner you get on with it, the sooner we'll be gone."

Emboldened by Lige Tolbert's presence, Bowers replied, "The hell I will." In the next instant, he suddenly jerked backward, startled by the sharp crack of the carbine and the crash of broken glass as the lamp behind the bar was shattered. It was followed at once by the sound of another cartridge inserted in the chamber and, a moment later, by the gasps of the startled bystanders.

Joel motioned with the Spencer and said, "Pour him his drink, and be quick about it. I'm losin' my patience."

He did not discount the probability that the shot had been heard by a sheriff, or marshal, whoever represented the law in town. Bowers did not move, so Joel pulled the carbine up and aimed it at the large mirror behind the bar.

"Wait! Hold on!" Bowers screamed. "I'm goin'!" He moved at once to fetch the bottle.

Thinking the confusion had distracted Joel's attention from him, Lige dropped his hand on the .44 he carried, but thought better of it when Joel said, "That would be your last mistake today."

The barroom was gripped in stony silence as Bowers poured whiskey in Riley's glass, his hand shaking so with rage that he spilled a good portion on the bar. He set the bottle down and took a step to his right. Motioning with the weapon again, Joel waved him back toward the end of the bar, thinking that Bowers might have tried to position himself where he kept a shotgun behind the counter. The consternation on Bowers's face tended to convince Joel he had been right.

"Let's hurry it along, Riley," he said. "I'm beginnin' to get a feelin' we ain't really welcome here."

"Don't you want one?" Riley replied, seeming to be in no particular hurry.

"I kinda lost the mood right now. Tell you what, take the bottle. Pay the man, so he won't be out any money, and we'll be on our way."

Riley tossed his drink back, grabbed the bottle, and backed toward the door, one hand resting on the pistol he wore. "Gimme a minute," he said, "and I'll untie the horses."

Joel continued to back carefully toward the door after him, alert to any motion from any quarter. "You're lucky to get outta here alive, mister," Bowers fumed.

Emboldened by Joel's retreat, Lige took a step

toward him, and when Joel didn't seem to react, he took another. This was the moment when postmaster Sam Ingram, craving a drink, walked into the saloon, completely unaware of the tense situation inside. Surprised, Joel had to step quickly aside to keep from being bumped into by the equally surprised postmaster. Lige saw the confusion as his opportunity to act and charged Joel, drawing his pistol as he ran. His mistake was in misjudging the reflexive actions of the man holding the carbine, and his .44 barely cleared the holster when the butt of the Spencer slammed against his nose and dropped him like a stone on the barroom floor.

Joel watched him for a few seconds, but when Lige didn't move, he kicked the dropped pistol away from his hand and continued to back slowly out of the saloon. In the doorway, he stopped to give one last warning.

"So far, nobody's had to die over this, but know one thing for certain I will shoot the first man I see come out this door. That, I promise you."

He paused a second longer to make sure everyone understood him before suddenly stepping outside, where Riley was waiting in the saddle, holding the chestnut's reins. Joel ran to jump into the stirrup and they were off before he swung his other leg over, thundering off down the street toward the north end of town.

Behind them, the cloud of silence that had gripped the saloon during the tense moments before suddenly erupted into a noisy kettle of excited conversation.

"Who the hell was that?" Sam Ingram asked as Bowers and the man Lige had been playing cards with knelt down beside the injured man. No one bothered to answer him, curious as they were to see how badly

Lige had been hurt. They rolled him over, causing him to groan in pain, his face covered with blood.

"Well, he ain't dead," Bowers stated, "but damned if his nose ain't spread all over his face." He sent a boy who worked in the saloon to the pump to get a pan of water and a washcloth. "Maybe we can clean you up a little," he said to Lige, whose brain was still rattled and who was not sure what had happened. When the boy returned with the pan of water, Bowers sent him to get the doctor. "Better tell the sheriff while you're at it," Bowers called after him. "I don't know why he ain't here already. He musta heard that gunshot."

Gradually, Lige came around. As he gained consciousness, he realized the pain even more as it had come to grip his whole head like a vise. He winced with each gentle stroke of Bowers's washcloth, unable to breathe without gasping for air through his mouth. When his head was clear enough to remember, he murmured painfully, "He's a dead man. He'll pay up for this."

"Maybe you'd better just forget about it," Bowers said. "He's already long gone, and you don't look like you'll be in shape to ride anytime soon."

"We'll see about that," Lige grunted, pushed Bowers's hand away, and struggled to get to his feet, only to stagger over to a chair to sit down and wait for the doctor.

Bowers gave his flattened nose a long look before making a sarcastic comment. "I don't reckon you'll notice the stink if he comes in here again," referring to Lige's original remarks that had caused the altercation. Lige was about to retort when Doc Calley walked in.

"I thought your boy said he was shot," Doc remarked to Bowers as he went over to examine the injured man.

His tone was almost one of disappointment. There were many in town who considered Lige Tolbert a bully the town would be better off without.

"I think it's broke," Lige said.

"I think you're right," Doc replied sarcastically as he tilted Lige's head back and peered at the results of Joel's rifle butt. "He damn sure flattened it." He continued to study it for a few minutes, then told him there was very little he could do to fix it. "I can push some of the bone back to where it was, but you're gonna have a flat nose from now on. I'll try to fix it so you can breathe a little easier through it."

"Just be quick about it," Lige said. "I've gotta ride."

"I don't expect you'll feel much like riding by the time I'm through," Doc told him. "You've already got a lot of swelling starting up and pretty soon your eyes are gonna puff up like toadstools. But I'll do what I can."

"Hurry up, Doc. I ain't got time to sit around here all day," Lige said, with as much bluster as he could manage through his aching head. He had a reputation as a bully that he was forced to defend, and he was already aware of the look of amusement in the faces of some of the spectators. "Tommy," he said to Bowers's boy, "go down to the stable and tell Buck to saddle my horse. I'm goin' huntin' for a damn Rebel."

"All right," Doc sighed patiently, and went to work on him. "But my advice is to take it easy and let it heal." He turned to see Sheriff Jack Suggs coming in the door.

"Took you long enough," Lige complained.

Suggs was another man Lige didn't get along with. He was only the acting sheriff, until the elected sheriff came back from Cheyenne, but Lige was still sore over the town's decision to give Suggs the job instead of him.

"I was eatin' my dinner," Suggs said. "Who got shot?"

"Ansil's carnival glass lamp," one of the spectators replied with a chuckle.

Suggs turned to him and asked what had happened, and listened while he watched Doc work on Lige's face. When he had heard what the man had to say about the altercation, and his story was confirmed by the head nodding and agreeing grunts from the other witnesses, Suggs shook his head impatiently at Lige.

"Sounds to me like you stuck that nose into somethin' that it'da been best kept out of. He flattened the hell out of it, all right."

Already tired of hearing how flat his nose now was, Lige demanded, "Ain't you goin' after him? He cut loose with a damn carbine in here."

"No, I ain't," Suggs said. "From what I hear, it warn't nothin' but a barroom brawl and you come out on the bottom. And I ain't got time to chase after somebody in a bar fight." Finished with the issue then, he turned to Bowers. "Might as well pour me a drink, long as I'm here." He walked back to the bar, leaving Lige to seethe, well aware of the injured man's hatred for him, but smug in his thinking that Lige was helpless to do anything about it. When Bowers poured his drink, Suggs asked, "Who started this thing, Ansil?"

Bowers shrugged, as if the answer was obvious. "Lige," he answered. "He was rawhidin' a friend of that feller. They were both wearin' Confederate uniforms."

"That's what I figured," Suggs said, and tossed his drink back. Satisfied that he had an accurate account of the disturbance, he felt there was nothing he should do about it. "Well, I'll get on back to the office," he said, cast one more quick glance in Lige's direction, then walked out.

"Nobody gets away with this," Lige grumbled. "I'll get that son of a bitch."

"Hold still," Doc told him, "or you're gonna have this bandage wrapped around your neck."

Lige held still, but he was thinking that Doc could show him a little more respect.

Maybe after I track those Rebels down, I might come back and take some of that sass out of you, he thought.

As his mind cleared, he became more inflamed with the desire for vengeance. To add a little incentive to his desire to catch up with the two Rebels, he remembered then that someone who saw the two men leave town said they were leading four horses, two of them with packs. "I can track as good as any Injun," he boasted. "I'll find those bastards."

"I hope you do," Doc said. "I hope you do. Make us all proud of you." The sarcasm was lost on the simple being who was Lige Tolbert. It only confused him.

Approximately twelve miles north of Denver City, Joel and Riley sat by a fire on the bank of a small stream. Unaware that the man bent on tracking them was already in the saddle, even with his face swollen from injury, they were drinking coffee made from the beans they had purchased in Guthrie's store. Joel had taken his drink of whiskey before changing to coffee, primarily because Riley insisted upon it.

"Weren't fair that you didn't get the chance to have a drink back there in the saloon," he said.

Not sure whether there would be anybody coming after them for the disturbance in the saloon, they had taken precautions to hide their trail. Their path had led them to a river not more than a mile from town, but the water seemed too deep to ride in for any distance

upstream or down. So they crossed over and continued on until reaching a wide stream that just served
the purpose. Entering the water, they rode upstream,
closer to the mountains, for about half a mile before
leaving it to head due north again. Feeling it a good bet
that they would have lost anyone thinking of tailing
them, they relaxed to enjoy the coffee.

"That feller ain't likely to forget you for a long time,"
Riley remarked. He had gotten a brief glimpse of Joel's
encounter with Lige through the open door of the
saloon. "Dang, that musta smarted somethin' fierce.
Laid him out cold, I reckon."

"Well, he didn't get up," Joel replied with a shrug.

"I expect we've seen the last of him," Riley said.
He felt very pleased with the situation. He had
already known of Joel's character in a regiment-sized
skirmish, and he had wondered how his young partner could handle himself in a barroom fight. Now he
knew he could count on him in most any situation.

"I reckon this is as good a time as any to shuck this
uniform," he said. "Much longer and it'd be fallin' off
by itself." He pulled his boots off in preparation for
disrobing.

"I expect you're right," Joel said, and started coming
out of his uniform as well. "It seems they ain't much
good for anything but startin' trouble."

Riley suggested it would be a fitting final ceremony
to close the war officially by burning the tattered uniforms. Joel agreed, so they cast the remains onto the
fire. The grimy uniforms almost put out the fire, and
Riley had to tend them using a stick for a poker until
he could feed portions of the heavy cloth little by little.
An undesired result of the ceremony was the creation
of a black smoke column that rose from their camp.

"That ain't good," Riley remarked, and pulled the uniforms from the fire. He and Joel stomped the smoldering material until the flames were extinguished. "Everybody in the whole damn territory will know we're here."

"I expect you're right," Joel said. "We'd best move on outta here. The horses are rested enough, anyway."

Chapter 4

Lame Foot stood at the top of a rocky mesa, barren of all but a few trees.

"There," he said to his companion, Hunting Owl, and pointed toward a thin black column of smoke drifting up on the western side of a low line of hills.

Hunting Owl climbed up beside him to see. He said nothing for a few moments while he considered the thin column wafting straight up before being sheared off by the breeze drifting across the crown of the hills.

"White man," he said, for it would be unusual for an Indian to build a fire out of something that would make that much smoke unless he was trying to signal someone. "Wagons, maybe."

"Let's go see who it is," Lame Foot suggested. "It might be soldiers."

"Should we tell the others first?" Hunting Owl asked. The rest of their hunting party was at least a mile behind the two scouts, on the return to their camp on the South Platte.

"Let's go see who made the fire. Then we can warn the others if there is danger," Lame Foot advised.

When Hunting Owl agreed, the two Arapaho warriors jumped on their ponies and rode down from the mesa, then galloped across the narrow valley to the line of hills beyond. Leaving the horses on the side of the hill, they crawled to the top, making their way to a spot where they could see the camp by a stream. The camp, which was almost completely hidden by a bank of willows, might have been overlooked had it not been for the smoke drifting up through the tops of the trees.

"It is hard to tell," Lame Foot said, "but I think it is only one or two men. I can see part of one horse between the willows and the stream."

"That is good," Hunting Owl said. "That means they can't see us if we move up on the other side of the willows."

Both warriors were surprised to find a party of only one or two white men in this Arapaho and Cheyenne territory. These were troubled times between white man and Indian since the cowardly attack at Sand Creek by Colorado volunteers, and consequently, white people seldom passed through unless they were heavily guarded. This bit of luck might result in the acquisition of guns, and that was very much on their minds as they decided how best to approach the camp.

"Maybe we should split up. You can sneak up from downstream," Lame Foot suggested. "And I will approach from upstream and make them think I am alone and come in peace."

"They may shoot at you," Hunting Owl said.

"I'll be careful. If they start to aim their guns at me, I'll escape into the trees. I think there's a good chance they will want me to come closer, and you can slip up behind them with your bow."

Hunting Owl nodded in agreement. It was a good plan. Lame Foot was older than he and was wise in the ways of combat.

"Give me a little time," he said, for he would have a greater distance to go to be in position. They split up then and descended the hill, one angling downstream, one upstream.

When Lame Foot reached the willows by the stream, he was about forty yards from the camp. He could see two horses in the trees between him and the camp. He could also clearly see one white man, sitting by the fire.

Is there another one? Maybe in the bushes relieving his bowels, he thought.

He edged a few yards closer. There was still no sign of another man. He could see the white man clearly now. He had a strange look about him that puzzled Lame Foot for a moment. Then he realized there was a bandage wrapped around the man's face.

He has been wounded. Maybe he is running from a battle. Lame Foot decided then that the man was probably alone, so he stepped out of the shadows of the trees and called to him.

"Hey, white man, I come in peace."

His shout caused the white man to scramble to his knees and reach for his rifle.

Ah, Lame Foot thought, recognizing the Henry, *he has the medicine gun that shoots many times.*

Knowing he must be careful not to make the white man shoot, he called out again, "No need to worry. I come in peace. I am hungry. I saw your fire and I think maybe you share some food."

Wary, the white man finally spotted his visitor. "Yeah," he called back, "come on in. I'll give you some food."

Come on in a little bit closer, he thought, *and I'll give you some lead to eat.*

He got up from his knees then and stood watching the Indian approach, his rifle held casually across his thighs.

When Lame Foot advanced to within fifteen yards, the white man sneered. "You come in peace, huh? Well, there ain't no peace between me and a damn beggarass Injun."

He brought his rifle up to his shoulder, but before he had time to aim, he was stunned by the solid impact of an arrow in his back. He turned to face his assailant only to be staggered by another arrow. The air was split then by the war cries of both warriors, and he was struck by two more arrows. Staring in horror at the thin shafts driven deep into his stomach, he dropped to his knees and fumbled with his rifle, which suddenly seemed foreign to his hands. He remained in that position for a few moments until Lame Foot walked up and kicked him over on his side.

Lige Tolbert, his broken face sagging even more after his scalp had been taken, lived for thirty additional minutes of pain before death decided to have mercy on him. Left on the bank of a nameless stream, a meal for buzzards, or wolves, whichever found him first, he would not be missed in Denver City, although his name might come up occasionally when there was a discussion of sons of bitches at the Miner's Rest.

Their plan was simple, keep riding north along the base of the mountains until reaching South Pass, where Riley was certain he knew the way to Idaho from there. After they'd left the stream north of Denver City, two days of steady riding brought them to a wide creek that caused a spark in Riley's memory.

"I swear," he exclaimed, "I've been here before. I know this place—Crow Creek. I tracked a deer down this stream from the South Platte, back in 'forty-nine." He gave Joel a self-satisfied grin. "I told you I knew this part of Dakota Territory. Hell, I kilt buffalo not too far from here."

"I wish we'd see some buffalo now," Joel said. "I'd like to skin one and make a buffalo robe."

The days were already getting colder, and he was beginning to think the coat he had traded for in Denver City wasn't going to be enough when the real winter hit. The last couple of days, while they had held to a steady northern track, with the Rocky Mountains to the west of them, seemed to see the temperature drop with each mile gained.

"We ain't even past summer good," Riley said. "What month you reckon it is?"

Joel paused to think for a moment. "I'm not sure— end of September, maybe first of November." He gazed over to his left at the mountains, and the mantle of snow covering the tallest peaks. "I'll bet it's pretty damn cold up there."

"You're right about that," Riley quickly agreed. "Wait till you get to my age. When your bones get older, winter gets in 'em a whole lot quicker, and it takes longer to warm 'em up in the spring."

They decided to follow a fairly used trail along Crow Creek, thinking to follow it to its confluence with the South Platte. They had not ridden more than a few miles when they came upon a log cabin built close beside the water. Thinking it a homesteader at first, they then realized it was a trading post of sorts, although it seemed a lonely spot to have one.

"You reckon he might have some whiskey?" Riley wondered, having long since finished the bottle they had bought at Denver City.

"I'd sure as hell be surprised," Joel replied. "I'm wonderin' if he might have some coffee beans."

They still had a supply of coffee beans, but he wouldn't pass up the opportunity to buy some more if they were available. Based on the remoteness of the country they had been traveling, he wasn't sure they'd see another town anytime soon, and he knew he'd miss his coffee a lot more than whiskey.

When they were within fifty yards of the log structure, they saw an Indian woman step out from behind a porch post and go inside the building. She had evidently been watching their approach for some time.

"Wouldn't be a bad idea to make sure that carbine is settin' nice and loose in your scabbard," Riley cautioned.

In a couple of minutes, however, a man came out the door and walked into the clearing in front of the cabin. Joel and Riley continued their approach. As they neared the cabin, the man suddenly threw up his hand and yelled, "Welcome, strangers! Come on in."

They could see that he was a white man, although from a distance he might easily be mistaken for an Indian. He was dressed in animal skins and wore his long hair pulled back in a braid, Indian-style, and he was clean shaven. They acknowledged his wave with one of their own and rode on in.

"I swear, Little Robe said it was two white men, but I didn't believe it till I saw you with my own eyes." He craned his neck, taking inventory of his visitors and their possessions, trying to determine what manner of men they were to be traveling alone in Indian country. "I don't see many white men out this way," he went on. "The name's Seth Burns. This here's my store, but most of my trade is with the Arapahos."

He motioned toward a short hitching rail beside the porch.

"Joel McAllister," Joel said as he stepped down, "and my partner here is Riley Tarver. I reckon we're as surprised to see you as you are to see us. We could use a few things if you happen to have 'em." He looped Will's reins over the rail. "Would you happen to have any grain for the horses?"

"No, I ain't," Seth replied. "I sure ain't." He craned his neck to look at the horses again. "Them two horses in the back look like Injun ponies. They do better on grass than them others. I can see your other horses are needin' the grain, all right. I'm right sorry I can't fix you up with some." He shrugged and announced, "I can fix you up with some other things, though, like beans, flour, coffee, things like that. You got here at the right time. I just got back from Fort Laramie with a wagonload of supplies last week." He walked around to their packhorses to take a closer look. "Seems like you fellers are packin' a pretty good load. Is that for tradin', or you thinkin' about cash or dust?"

"I reckon it depends on which you'd rather do," Joel told him. "Maybe we've got some things you could use."

"Like what?" Seth asked.

"Like some brand-new Sharps carbines and cartridges to go with 'em," Joel said. When he noticed a definite spark of interest in Seth's eyes, he continued. "I expect you could do a lot of tradin' with your Arapahos for a weapon like that."

"That's a fact," Seth allowed. "But you might be lookin' for a helluva lot in trade for a new rifle like that."

"Maybe, maybe not," Joel replied. He had been eyeing Seth's fringed buckskin trousers and shirt with some interest. "What would it take to get a buckskin shirt like the one you're wearin'?" Riley cocked an eyebrow at that, surprised by Joel's interest in the trader's clothes.

Seth shrugged. "Why, it wouldn't take much. I've got a right sizable stack of skins already dried and softened. My wife is a Jim Dandy seamstress." He spread his arms to show them. "She made this shirt, and every other'n I own. Just take a couple of days, dependin' on how much fancied up you wanted it."

"How long would it take her to make me one without all the fancy fringes?"

"Both of you?" Seth asked, glancing then at Riley.

Joel shifted his gaze toward his partner also. The idea sounded sensible to Riley, so he nodded. Joel turned back to Seth and said, "Yeah, both of us."

Seth turned to his wife, who was standing on the porch, watching the discussion. He spoke to her in Arapaho, after which she took a step to the side, better able to estimate the extent of the project. When she advised her husband, Seth turned back to his customers.

"Little Robe says two days, maybe three. She says she's got some nice soft doe hides all ready to make me a new shirt."

"Whaddaya think, partner?" Joel asked Riley.

"Hell, fine by me—sounds like a helluva idea," Riley responded. "While we're at it, maybe he's got some buffalo robes, too."

Enthusiastic over the prospects of a good trade, Seth

said, "Well, come on inside and take a look. I might have some other things you need. Little Robe can make some coffee, and maybe find you a little somethin' to eat. You can camp right here on the creek." He turned to lead the way inside. "Maybe you can show me one of them carbines you're lookin' to trade. Where are you fellers headin', anyway?"

"Silver City," Joel said as Riley went back to fetch one of the Sharps.

"Where's that?" Seth asked, having never heard of it.

"Over on the Snake River, Idaho Territory," Joel replied.

Seth turned his head to level a questioning gaze. "Damn, that's a fur piece. Kinda late in the season to be startin' out for that country, ain't it?"

"You could say so," Joel said. "I reckon we'll get as far as we can—see how our luck holds out."

"Well, your partner is right, you're gonna need some good buffalo robes where you're headin'."

They made their camp a few dozen yards upstream from Seth's store while they waited for their buckskin garments. Little Robe was a cheerful soul, who seemed to enjoy sewing the clothes for the two white men. In addition, she took time out to prepare food for her guests. The evenings were spent exchanging tales between Riley and Seth.

"How'd you pick this spot to build your store?" Riley asked one afternoon.

"Until a year ago, I had a place on Dry Creek," Seth said. "One day a couple of white fellers came ridin' in with a fifteen-man soldier escort. I thought they was lookin' for some wild bucks that raided a white settlement on the South Platte. But they said they didn't know nothin' about no Injun raids. Them two civilians said they worked for the Union Pacific Railroad, and they was scoutin' the best route for the railroad they said would be comin' this way in two or three years. Well, they picked this spot on Crow Creek for a crossin', so I figured the thing for me to do was move my store right here, and if the railroad showed up, I'd have me a front-row seat. Even if it don't show up, I like this spot better."

After the bargaining was concluded, and the sewing job done, Joel and Riley said farewell to Seth and Little Robe and set out from Crow Creek, clad in new buck-skin outfits, riding well-rested horses. The clothes just recently purchased in Denver City were stowed away on their packhorses, hardly broken in. Seth Burns was content with his acquisition of two new Sharps carbines and two boxes of cartridges.

The trading took a total of four days out of their already tight travel time, but they considered it worth the delay. They used the time to saddle-break the two Indian horses to the cavalry saddles. Both horses seemed faster than their regular horses and they accepted the strange new saddles without much of a fuss. Joel decided to ride the gray and lead his chestnut. Feeling a slight guilt for choosing the unshod horse over his longtime partner, he justified it in his mind by telling himself that Will deserved the rest. For his part, the gelding showed no sign of complaint, and probably appreciated the rest, for Joel was a sizable man.

A trip that Riley had estimated to be about six days turned out to take a full week. But they finally reached South Pass, a thirty-five-mile-wide saddle of sagebrush and open prairie between the Wind River Mountains and the Oregon Buttes. They made camp beside the

Sweetwater, a river that many wagon trains had followed across the country's midsection on their way to Oregon. They had had no contact with anyone, nor seen sign of any Indian activity during the whole trip from Seth Burns's trading post. But Indians were unpredictable. They might be friendly one day and set on destruction the next, so Joel was happy not to have encountered any hunting parties.

Upon reaching the Sweetwater, they saw the obvious ruts from countless wagons to confirm Riley's claim that he could find the Oregon Trail. They figured their trip to Silver City to be at least halfway accomplished, even though Riley warned that there was some rugged country ahead of them after they reached the Snake River. As if to emphasize his warning, a light dusting of snow roused them from their bedrolls the next morning.

"Not enough to worry about," Riley said. "It's just the Rockies lettin' us know we ain't that far from winter."

Leaving South Pass, they pushed on away from the mountains with Riley pointing the way. Joel couldn't help noticing the air of excitement in his elder partner, as Riley relived the first time he followed that trail. Although quite a few years ago, there were wagon ruts still evident along the way. The next five days found them following a path through a series of shallow valleys with mountain ranges in the distance that seemed to be lined up one behind the other. But the threatening snow never came and the horses were all in good shape, so they made good time while the weather cooperated. Actually, Joel worried very little about the possibility of bad weather. Like Riley on his first journey across the Great Divide, he was too awed by the majesty of the rugged mountain peaks to worry about winter closing in. He enjoyed the confidence of knowing that whatever befell them, he would deal with it.

With the mountains behind them now, they ascended to a wide, almost flat plain, and Riley said that the traveling would be easier for a good spell, at least until they reached the Snake River Plain.

"We'll be comin' on Soda Springs," he said. "We stopped to rest up here. There's hot springs all over the place, bubblin' up like you ain't never seen."

Joel agreed that the prospect of a hot soak wouldn't be bad at all. Within a short time, however, his thoughts were directed toward another confrontation with hostiles, for he suddenly heard gunshots in the distance. He reined the gray back and he and Riley stopped to listen.

"They're a fur piece off," Riley said, and Joel nodded his agreement. "Could be a huntin' party—huntin' buffalo, maybe."

It was difficult to tell exactly which direction the shots came from, because they were partially muffled by a ridge to the northwest of them.

"I expect we'd best keep a sharp lookout to make sure we don't ride up on a huntin' party," Joel said. They continued on the same track they had been following since morning.

They had just entered the edge of the broad, open valley that Riley said was called Soda Springs when Joel spotted smoke rising lazily in the distance. Without speaking, he pointed. Riley nodded.

"Yeah, I saw it, too," he said.

Cautious now, they continued to ride along the valley, angling slightly south of the fire until they could identify the source, leaving room to retreat to the hills if necessary. Gradually closing the distance, they were at last able to make out two wagons set ablaze, the obvious explanation for the gunshots they had heard earlier.

"Injuns," Riley said. There appeared to be none around at the time. "Looks like they've done their deviltry on some poor folks and left the wagons to burn."

"There ain't no sign of anyone," Joel said, fearing the worst. "From the look of that fire, it couldn't have happened too long ago."

As they drew closer, they could see several lumps on the valley floor that were no doubt the bodies of the unfortunate owners of the wagons.

"Kinda risky business, ridin' this trail with just two wagons," he remarked solemnly.

"They musta got hung up somewhere back along the trail. Maybe they were tryin' to catch up with the rest of their wagon train. Let's ride on in and take a look. Might be somebody left alive."

He turned the paint's head toward the burning wagons. Joel followed.

They had approached to within a hundred yards when they were suddenly surprised by the sharp snap of a rifle ball as it passed between them. It was followed almost immediately by the report of the weapon.

"Whoa!" Riley exclaimed loudly, and jerked hard on the reins, almost colliding with Joel's horse. "Hold on!" he yelled, when the shot was not followed immediately by a second. "We're friends. Hold your fire, damn it!"

"All right, friends," a suspicious female voice came back, "come a little bit closer, so I can get a better look at you."

"Well, don't go shootin' that rifle at us," Riley answered. "We just wanted to see if we could help. If you don't want any help, then, hell, we'll just be on our way and leave you be."

"Come on in," the woman replied.

There was still a hint of caution in her voice. When they approached within thirty yards of the burning wagons, she stepped out from behind the front wheels of the one wagon that was only halfway consumed by the flames. Dressed in a man's trousers and shirt, and wearing a heavy woolen coat, she held a breech-loading, single-shot Remington rifle ready in case her visitors made a suspicious move. She relaxed her stance a little when they came closer.

"I couldn't tell for sure," she said. "Dressed up in those animal skins like you are, I thought you were some more of those damn Injuns comin' back for another try."

Joel looked around the scene of the attack, astonished that the woman had been able to survive. The lumps they had seen from a distance were, in fact, the bodies they had suspected. And there were more on the other side of the wagons, most of them white, but there were also two Indians among the dead.

"Ma'am," Joel said, "looks like you've had some awful bad luck. Are you the only one alive?"

"That's right," she answered, with no hint of emotion in her voice. "Those red devils killed my sister and her husband and my uncle. They killed Peter Ferris, his wife, Ethel, and their two boys. They snatched up Ethel's daughter, Ruthie, and ran off with her."

"My God," Joel said, amazed by the woman's composure with no sign of the grief he would have expected. "I'm right sorry we couldn't have gotten here a little sooner. Maybe we coulda helped."

"How did you manage to come outta this alive?"

Riley asked. As it did to Joel, it seemed to him an unlikely happening.

"I don't rightly know," she replied. "They came up to us like they were real peaceful, so they could see what we were carryin', I reckon. David—that's my uncle—said he knew Injuns, and we could give 'em some food, and they'd leave us alone. It looked like he might be right, but all of a sudden, one of 'em pulled a pistol out of his belt and just started firin' away. The others cut the horses loose. My sister and her husband tried to run to the wagon to stop 'em, but they shot both of 'em before they got more'n three steps. Then all of 'em started shootin'. Some of 'em cut Peter and Ethel down, and when the boys tried to defend their folks, the Injuns shot them. One of 'em tried to shoot me, but his rifle misfired, and I grabbed my uncle's rifle and killed that son of a bitch. I crawled under the wagon and reloaded. When another'n tried to grab me by the foot and drag me outta there, I let him have it right between the eyes. I reckon they decided it wasn't worth it tryin' to get me, so they backed off, yellin' and howlin' like a bunch of coyotes. I held the rifle on 'em, like I was goin' to shoot if they came near me again, and I was hopin' and prayin' they didn't, because my rifle was empty. The cartridges were inside the wagon and I was afraid to make a try for 'em. I don't know when they set the wagons on fire, because they looked like they were in a hurry to get away from here."

"Damn, lady," Riley softly exclaimed. "You've been through a terrible time."

"The thing that hurts my heart," she said, "was I couldn't save Ruthie. I called for her to crawl under the wagon with me, but before she could, one of those devils snatched her up and rode off with her."

"Maybe we can still catch up with 'em," Joel said. "Might not be too late for the girl." He looked up toward the sun. "There ain't all that much daylight left. They oughta be stoppin' to make camp, if they ain't got a village nearby."

"Easy enough to track," Riley said, examining the hoofprints leading away from the wagons. "How many were there?"

"We counted seven when they first caught up with us," she said, "so that leaves five not countin' those two." She nodded toward the bodies.

Riley finally asked the question that had first occurred to him. "What in God's name were you folks doin' out here by yourselves?"

"When we left Fort Laramie, we were part of a train with twenty wagons. Two days out, the Ferrises' wagon broke a wheel, so they had to take it back to get it fixed. The rest of the train wouldn't wait, 'cause we were already so late in the season, so we volunteered to wait with them, figurin' on catching up with the others later."

"That was bad luck," Joel said, and then he thought to introduce himself and Riley. "My name's Joel McAllister and this is Riley Tarver. We're on our way to Silver City, but we're gonna see if we can follow those Indians first, and hope we're lucky enough to find the girl unharmed." He glanced at Riley to make sure he was thinking the same, and he quickly nodded his agreement. "How old is the girl?"

"She's goin' on thirteen."

"That might explain why they rode off with her. If she was a little older, they mighta killed her on the spot. Sometimes they keep the young children captive." He looked at Riley and shook his head. The old sergeant nodded in return, signifying that he was ready to ride after the hostiles. Joel looked back at the woman. "What's your name, ma'am?"

"Elvira Moultrie," she answered.

"Well, Elvira, we can't ride off and leave you by yourself. Can you ride bareback? We've got a horse for you, but we don't have an extra saddle."

"Hell yes, I can ride bareback. It was how I learned to ride on my daddy's farm in Nebraska."

"Good," Joel said. "I'll put you on that chestnut there. He's gentle enough, and I expect he'd like to have the company. I think we'd best not tarry if we wanna catch up with those Indians."

He watched while she gathered the few possessions she had managed to save from the Indians, at the same time paying more attention to the manner of woman they had picked up. She looked strong physically, and there was no doubt that she was mentally tough as well. Otherwise she would have been weepy and in despair after what she had just gone through. He suspected there was much more to learn about the fiber that ran through Elvira Moultrie, but at a later time. Now it was time to go after the girl.

The tracks left by the Indian raiding party led off across the valley floor in the direction of a range of mountains to the east. Riley wasn't sure he remembered what mountains they were, but the fact that a good portion of the hills were covered with pine, fir, and spruce made him guess they were the Caribou Mountains. It was reasonable to assume the Indians sought a place to camp with good coverage where they wouldn't be discovered. This caused further speculation that the party was raiding in territory claimed by some other tribe. Joel thought at once of the Blackfoot.

"Those two Indians Elvira killed back there," he asked Riley, "could you tell what they were?"

"Damned if I know," Riley answered. "I don't know one Injun from another."

"Blackfoot," Elvira said, overhearing the question. "At least, that's what David said they were."

"It don't much matter, does it?" Riley said.

"I reckon not," Joel answered.

By the time they reached the foot of the mountains, the sun was already perched atop the higher peaks of a distant mountain range to the west.

"In an hour or more, we're gonna be trackin' in the dark," Riley speculated.

"We'll stay with it for as long as we can see the tracks," Joel said, but it soon became obvious that their time was rapidly running out.

After crossing over a small stream, they came upon a game trail that appeared to circle the base of the mountain. In the final seconds of daylight, they were able to determine that the raiding party had followed the game trail.

"We may be in luck," he told Riley. "Looks to me like they're following this trail now. We can't see their tracks anymore, but I think it's worth the gamble to stay on this path. Whaddaya think, Riley?"

"Makes sense to me," Riley replied.

"Me, too," Elvira said, surprising them both. It was only the second time she had uttered a word since leaving the wagons. It was still too soon to tell, but Joel was already forming an opinion that Elvira was accustomed to having a say on most any subject.

The game trail soon became too dark to follow comfortably on horseback as it wound through a thick forest of firs, so they dismounted and led the horses.

Making their way silently over the narrow path, they walked for what Joel figured to be close to a mile when he suddenly stopped and signaled Riley and Elvira to be quiet. When Riley moved up beside him, he pointed to the faint image of sparks floating up through the tops of the trees.

"Looks like we found their camp," Joel said. "Let's go take a closer look."

Leaving Elvira and her Remington there to take care of the horses, Joel and Riley continued cautiously along the trail until reaching a point where it descended to a narrow stream, most likely the same one they had crossed a little way back. From there, they got a good view of the camp. Their horses, including four that were still wearing wagon traces, were on the other side of the stream, while all five of the Indians were seated around the fire. Unable to locate the girl, Joel scanned the area of the camp that he could see in the firelight. Fearing at first that they had decided to kill the girl somewhere along the way, Joel had to fight the urge to raise his carbine and start shooting. He felt a tug at his elbow and turned to see Riley pointing toward the bank of the stream. He stared for a few moments before he finally made out the form of the frightened girl, her hands tied behind her back, and a rawhide noose around her neck. The noose was tied to a spruce limb.

Now that the girl was located, they had to form a plan of attack. Afraid that when the shooting started, the girl might catch a stray bullet, Joel suggested that he should get her out of harm's way before they opened fire on the warriors.

"I oughta be able to go up this mountain a ways, make my way around the camp, and come up from behind her. They're not expectin' anybody to come after them, so I should be able to sneak her away without them even knowin' it." Riley nodded while Joel continued. "Maybe you'd best pick your spot somewhere on this trail between the Indians and the back trail, to make sure none of 'em get away and wind up in Elvira's lap."

"Whatever you say, Lieutenant," Riley replied without thinking.

"I'll take the first shot," Joel told him. "So when you hear it, cut loose, because that'll be my signal that the girl is safe."

He checked his carbine then and started climbing up the side of the mountain, leaving Riley to stand between the hostiles and Elvira.

In a matter of minutes, he had circled above the camp and begun to make his way down through the trees until he reached the stream. Moving silently along the bank, he reached a point where he could clearly see the frail body of the girl, Ruthie, silhouetted in the firelight beyond her. He paused there for a moment to make sure he knew where each of the warriors was, and that they had not moved since he circled above them.

When he was certain that all remained peaceful, he moved a little closer, to within ten yards of the captive girl. Not willing to chance a startled cry from the girl, he slung his carbine on his shoulder and inched up behind her. When he was close enough to hear the soft sounds of her terrified weeping, he drew his knife from the scabbard he wore and moved up close to her. Sensing someone there, she started to turn, but not in time to cry out when he clamped his hand over her mouth.

"Don't make a sound," he whispered. "We've come to get you."

He felt her go limp as he cut the rawhide line binding her to the tree, and he was just able to catch her before she collapsed.

With the unconscious girl lying helpless across his arms, he backed slowly away, keeping a sharp eye on the five warriors gathered about the fire, lest they became aware of what was taking place. Still concerned that she might regain consciousness at any moment and cry out, he hurried to find someplace to leave her where she would be safe. Unnoticed by him, her eyes fluttered, then opened wide.

"Who are you?" she asked, still not certain what was happening.

Though not loud, her voice was heard by the warriors seated around the fire. One of them got to his feet and started walking toward them. He had taken no more than a few steps when he realized that she had somehow gotten loose. He immediately began to trot toward the place where he had left her.

There was no time to waste. Seeing a shallow gully behind him, Joel dropped the girl into it and pulled his carbine off his shoulder.

"Stay there!" he ordered, and turned to meet the warrior, who was now charging, his skinning knife drawn.

The shot was fired at point-blank range, knocking the warrior backward as his feet continued to run out from under him. Joel heard Riley's rifle only seconds after his, and one of the four remaining Indians keeled over. Four more shots followed rapidly, two from each of them, and that quickly, what amounted to little more than a mass execution was all over. Joel chambered another round just in case.

"Come on in, Riley," Joel called out. "I think they're

all done for." He turned then to discover the girl still cowering in the gully. "You can come outta there now, miss. Nobody's gonna hurt you."

She did as she was told, but with an obvious show of hesitation. She was still not sure where she had ended up. She looked toward the fire, seeing Riley walking up to make sure the Indians were dead, then looked back at the man who had snatched her away and told her to stay in the gully. Seeing how the two men were dressed, not unlike the Indians who had carried her away from her parents, she was not at all sure she had been rescued. Seeing her consternation, Joel tried to put her at ease.

"Ruthie, ain't it? Elvira sent us to fetch you back. She's back up the trail a piece."

The girl still seemed to be in shock. Joel supposed she had not yet accepted the fact that she had indeed been rescued, so he walked back toward the rise where he and Riley had hidden while they scouted the camp.

"Come on in, Elvira," he shouted. "It's all over!"

He was not sure she could hear him, but in about ten minutes' time, she appeared at the top of the rise, leading the horses.

The sight of the gregarious woman striding down the path, leading half a dozen horses, was enough to bring Ruthie out of her uncertainty. The woman and the girl both cried out a joyous greeting, and Ruthie ran to the open arms of the woman she had come to think of as an aunt. Her sense of relief lasted for a moment only before the cold reality of the hostile attack came back to her.

"Mama and Daddy?" she asked.

Elvira shook her head sadly. "They're gone, child, your brothers, too. Same as my sister and Ed, and my uncle David. Me and you are the only ones left, and we wouldn't be here if these two fellers hadn't come along."

Elvira cradled the weeping girl in her arms while Joel and Riley checked the bodies to see if there was anything useful to salvage.

"I thought they were gonna kill me," Ruthie murmured tearfully.

"I know," Elvira said, "but they didn't get the chance—same for me. Ain't no use tryin' to figure out why things happen, but it looks to me like the good Lord has got more work for me and you. So let's put it behind us, and get on with our lives."

Ruthie nodded, determined to do as Elvira suggested. Still she was unable to match the older woman's bravado. "I don't know what to do now. What's going to happen to us?"

"We'll just see as we go along," Elvira assured her. She held her at arm's length and looked her in the eye. A wide smile spread across her broad face. "You've got your ol' aunt Elvira to watch over you. We'll be all right." She glanced over at their two rescuers, now engaged in checking out the extra horses the attack had provided. "We were damn lucky these two fellers found us. They seem like decent men, and if they ain't, I'll do some ass-kickin' to straighten 'em out." She gave Ruthie a mischievous wink.

Chapter 5

The question before Joel and Riley now was what to do with the two survivors they had saved from the Indian attack. Riley suggested that they could escort them to Fort Hall and leave them to decide what they were going to do from there.

"They closed the fort down a few years back," he said, "but I expect there's still some kinda settlement there, maybe a town. Hell, the old Oregon Trail went right through there."

"Maybe so," Joel replied.

He already knew that he didn't care much for the added responsibility for taking care of two females. There was also the recent expansion of their horse herd to be considered, for they now had a total of seventeen horses to move along to Silver City, counting the horses they rode and their packhorses. Nine of the horses were Indian ponies. In all fairness, Joel reminded his partner, four of the horses rightly belonged to Elvira and Ruthie. If they left the females at Fort Hall, along with their horses, it would be no great loss to Joel. The unshod Indian ponies had proven to be of stouter quality, and much more suited to living off the short grass of the Rocky Mountains.

"We'll have to leave it up to the ladies," Joel said. "We'll see what Elvira has to say about what they wanna do. But for now, let's get away from here and get back to the wagons, 'cause I expect they'll wanna do some buryin'."

"I'd done forgot about that," Riley said. "Damn, that's a lot of bodies to bury." He was not especially keen on manning a shovel and pick, but he knew it was important to the two who survived to have their loved ones properly laid to rest. "Maybe that big ol' woman will give us a hand. She looks like she could handle a shovel as well as we can." They walked back to where the women were standing by the fire, and Riley put the question before them. "I reckon if we was to get started right away, we could most likely get to Fort Hall before noon tomorrow. You girls feel ready to ride?"

Elvira didn't respond immediately. Instead she took a few long moments to study Riley's face before commenting, "Fort Hall's been closed down for ten years. We knew that when we left Nebraska. I expect everybody did."

She paused again to watch the reactions of the two men, not certain if they were simply trying to wash their hands of the responsibility thrust upon them. Judging by the look of surprise on both their faces, she considered it a possibility that they were simply ignorant of the fact.

"Nobody never told me Fort Hall was shut down that long ago," Riley said. "I knew they was talkin' about closin' it, but I figured there'd still be a sizable settlement there."

"We have to lay Ruthie's family in the ground before we go anywhere," Elvira said then. Her tone left no room for negotiation.

"Why, sure," Riley replied. "We figured that." He looked at Joel and shrugged helplessly.

"That's what me and Ruthie are gonna do, anyway," Elvira continued. "If you fellers ain't got time to wait, then you can go along, and we'll come along when the buryin's done." She was confident that it was not in the nature of either man to ride off and leave them unprotected, so she graced Ruthie with a satisfied smile when both of their protectors immediately assured her that, of course, had been their intention.

"I wonder if that ol' gal has ever had a husband," Riley remarked to Joel when they went to pick out a horse for Ruthie to ride. "If she did, I'll bet I know what happened to him. She most likely worked him to death. Them dead folks back there don't give a damn if they was buried or not. Besides, if some more Injuns come along, that'll just tell 'em we were here, and how long ago to boot."

Joel stifled a chuckle. "It's important to womenfolk to know their kin are properly buried," he told his fretting partner. "And a little pick and shovel work won't hurt either one of us."

He had to admit, however, that his thinking wasn't far from that of Riley's. He didn't mind the work of digging graves as much as taking the time to do it. And it was already snowing by the time they got their little troop together and rode back up the game trail to the point where it first crossed the stream. Thinking the ladies would prefer not to use the Indians' camp, they made a new camp there, planning to ride back to the wagons to take care of the bodies in the morning.

It came as no surprise to either of the men when Elvira produced two shovels and a pick from the partially burned box under the wagon bed, but they gained new respect for the woman when she took the pick and began testing the ground.

"Here," she said. "Shouldn't be too hard to carve out a couple of graves over here. Might be a little too rocky over there where you are."

She nodded toward Riley, standing a few yards away, the point of his shovel in the thin coat of snow that had fallen during the night. Without waiting for discussion, she spread her feet to take a wide stance, spat on her hands, then proceeded to take the pick and attack the ground with a vengeance.

"Yes'm," Riley said, "that's just what I was about to say, ground's too rocky right here."

He watched her hacking away at the hard ground, expecting her to give up in a minute or two. When she continued breaking up the ground with no signs of weakening, he shook his head, amazed, walked over to her, and said, "Here, let me take a turn with that pick." She surrendered the pick, but immediately took one of the shovels and went at it again.

They worked away at the graves for several hours before preparing a suitable resting place for all of the two families' dead. When it was done, and nothing remained but the bodies of the two warriors Elvira had killed, Riley couldn't resist a little tease.

"What about these two? Ain't we gonna bury them, so they can go to the happy huntin' ground?"

"To hell with them," Elvira said. "The buzzards can

fly them to the happy huntin' ground." She reached down and took Ruthie by the elbow. "Come on, darlin', your folks are in a better place. It's best if we see about where we'll be now." Turning back to Joel, she asked, "What are we gonna do now?"

"Like I told you before," he said, "Riley and I are on our way to Silver City to help my brother, Boone."

"What about us, Ruthie and me?"

"Well, like I said, we thought it would be a good idea to take you to Fort Hall, and let you decide what you were gonna do when you got there." The woman had a way of looking at him, almost accusing. In fact, he began to feel that she held him responsible for her and the girl's misfortunes. He looked at Riley for support, but Riley looked away, wanting no further part in the discussion. "Maybe we'll strike a little town on the Snake with some folks who could take care of you better'n me and Riley." Riley nodded at that.

"We'll go to Silver City with you," Elvira said. "That'll be the best for all of us."

Riley couldn't understand how that could be best for Joel and him. "You don't wanna go with me and Joel," he protested. "Why, hell, we're just bettin' on a long shot. Ain't we, Joel?"

"Riley's right," Joel replied. "It's been half a year since I heard from my brother. I'm not real sure he's still there. And from what he told me then, Silver City wasn't much of a town at all. I'm not sure it's a place where two ladies like yourselves would wanna wind up. From what I hear, it's a pretty wild town that sprang up after they found gold in the mountains around it. If we find a nice little settlement somewhere between here and Silver City, you could most likely hitch up with another wagon train comin' through next summer. There might even be some women there."

"Yeah," Riley said. "And maybe you'll get to Oregon, where you was headed in the first place. You probably got some folks out there waitin' for you?"

"Nope," she replied.

"You musta been headin' someplace out there," Riley insisted.

"Just Oregon," Elvira said. "We figured we'd find us a place when we got there, but there wasn't nothin' special about it. One place is as good as another. It doesn't have to be in Oregon, and me and Ruthie ain't lookin' for the same place anymore—not since all our menfolk are gone. I ain't hankerin' to go to farmin' without a man to help out."

"I'll help you, Aunt Elvira," Ruthie volunteered.

"I know you will, darlin', but we'll look around and see if somethin' else is more to our likin'. Hell, we might try our hand at pannin' for gold, maybe right there in Silver City. It might not be as wild as they say."

Joel cast a worried glance in Riley's direction. He couldn't say that he was enthusiastic in the least to take the two females all the way to Silver City, and he knew damn well that Riley was against it. He tried to appeal to Elvira's feminine side to fully consider the hardships that might befall her and Ruthie, but it was to no avail. He was ready to conclude that the woman had no feminine side.

Elvira listened patiently until he had finished before she had her final say. "I understand what you're sayin', but we've decided we'd rather go to Silver City this year, instead of waiting to go who knows where next year." She turned to Ruthie. "Ain't that what you say, Ruthie?"

"I don't care anymore," the girl answered. "I just wanna go with you wherever you go."

Elvira turned back to Joel. "I know what you're thinkin'. You don't need a woman and a little girl to worry about, but you don't have to worry about takin' care of us. I'll take care of Ruthie and me. And in the bargain, you'll get a cook and an extra hand with those horses you've picked up. I've been workin' with horses since I was old enough to walk. Me and Ruthie will go with you to Silver City, and if we find out there ain't nothin' there, we'll pick up and go somewhere else. We're mighty obliged to you for comin' along when you did, but we don't expect you to adopt us. We'll just travel with you, if you don't mind."

"Course we don't mind. We're glad we can help, but it's a long way to Silver City from here," Joel tried again. "To tell you the truth, I don't even know for sure that we won't get caught by the winter and have to hole up somewhere till spring. And you don't know anything about us."

Elvira smiled. "I know you're a decent man, Joel McAllister. I saw that right off. Otherwise, Ruthie and me woulda been on our way to Oregon by ourselves before now. Same goes for you, Riley. I doubt I could find anybody I could trust more than I trust the two of you. Somebody was lookin' after Ruthie and me when they sent you two."

Joel couldn't think of anything else to say to discourage the woman. He shrugged and looked at Riley. "Whaddaya think, partner?"

"Looks to me like we're all goin' to Silver City," he said sheepishly.

"Good!" Elvira said. "Let's get started, then. We're burnin' daylight."

* * *

Thanks to Elvira's fierce defense of her uncle's wagon, the Indian raiders had not gotten the opportunity to plunder it. So she was able to save the cooking implements that she and her sister had used but that she had not taken with her when they had hurried off to rescue Ruthie. Most of the possessions that were burned were not of necessity to her now, including all but a few pieces of her clothing. Most of what she carried away with them were her brother-in-law's clothes, which she found more suitable for the task ahead of her.

The wagon of Ruthie's parents suffered the most fire damage, leaving the young girl with little more than what she was wearing when she was captured. Elvira told her that she would improvise suitable clothing for her from the trunk of clothes that belonged to her sister.

"We'll be all right," she assured Ruthie. "What I can't make, we can buy." She gave her a mischievous wink of her eye. "Damn Injuns didn't have enough sense to steal our money."

Before they set out, there was a short discussion between Joel and Riley to decide if it was necessary to go to Fort Hall anyway, even after learning the fort was no longer there. Ruthie and Elvira had no interest in staying there. That much was certain.

"Sure as hell, there must still be a tradin' post there if we need anything in the way of supplies," Riley said. Upon considering that which they had gained from the misfortune of Elvira and her friends, they decided they were well supplied. "Hell, we've even got us a coffeepot now—won't have to boil it in that bent-up pot no more. And we can save a little time if we head west through those mountains runnin' alongside us instead of ridin' on into Fort Hall. If I ain't lost my recollect altogether, there ain't no more mountains for a long spell on the other side of those we're lookin' at. So we can follow that valley right to the Snake."

That seemed agreeable to everyone, so they started out toward an obvious pass in the mountain range to the west. Joel and Riley drove their little herd of horses ahead of them. Without being asked, Elvira pushed the chestnut up on the flank and kept the herd going in the right direction. Riding one of her father's horses, Ruthie followed along behind. Riley looked at Joel and grinned.

It ain't a big herd, but it is a herd, he thought.

Riley's memory was reliable. When they found their way through the mountain chain, they rode out on a gentle valley floor. After camping at the foot of the hills for the night, they started out again the next morning, holding a northwest course until finally reaching the Snake River on the evening of the second day.

"They weren't foolin' when they said it wasn't an easy river to cross, were they?" Joel murmured to himself.

Overhearing him, Riley said, "No, especially if you're talkin' about crossin' it with a wagon and a team of horses. You ain't seen this river at her meanest yet. About a hard day's ride west of here, it don't even look like the same river, a place where somebody named it Shoshoni Falls, after the Injuns, I reckon. Damnedest waterfalls you've ever seen—and fish, this river is full of fish—best place to catch salmon is at the falls. You see, the falls are too high, the fish can't swim up it, so they're just waitin' there for you to catch 'em. The easiest place to cross is about three days from here at a spot called Three Island Crossin', and it ain't an easy crossin', just the best one."

"Do we need to cross over at all?" Elvira asked.

"Well, most trains did," Riley replied. "It's a sight easier travelin' on the north side of the river—better water, grass, and game, too. The south side's the dry side." He glanced at Joel. "You're most likely thinkin' we could just swim the horses across, but it would be easier on them at Three Island after we pass the falls."

"Well, that ain't exactly what I was thinkin'," Joel said. "I don't think we need to cross the river a'tall. Best I remember, Boone said Silver City was back in the mountains, south of the Snake. And we'll be sayin' good-bye to the trail to Oregon when it crosses over to the other side. So we might as well head the horses on up this side till maybe we find somebody who can tell us how to get to Silver City."

Riley's talk about the spectacular waterfalls farther along their path was sufficient to generate a genuine craving on the part of all four to sample the salmon he bragged about. The weather had been especially cooperative as far as snow was concerned, although the temperatures were dipping lower as each day passed. Since they could now anticipate the end of their journey coming up soon—they were surely no more than a week or more from Silver City—all agreed that they could afford to delay their journey a day to fish.

They drove the horses along the cliffs that formed the bluffs for the river below them, following a road driven many times before by settlers and their wagons. It was late in the afternoon when they made camp near Shoshoni Falls in a grassy glen with a strong stream running through it. The girls, and Riley as well, were in a festive mood, eager to see the falls. While just as much interested to see them, Joel could not forget that there were still Indians to be concerned with, so he told the others to go on; he would stay and tend to the horses.

Circumstances had resulted in providing him with a small string of horses, and driving them the past couple of days had started him thinking about possibilities other than gold mining. Knowing Boone as well as he did, he wouldn't be surprised to find his brother thinking along the same lines. That thought caused him to picture Boone the last time he had seen him. Cheerful, as if riding off to the county fair, he joked that he would have the war won before Joel got around to enlisting. Joel was with General Shelby in Louisiana when Boone came home from the war with a shattered leg. He wondered how much of the boyish spirit remained.

The war was hard on everybody, he thought, *but nobody can hold the McAllisters down for long.* He smiled at the thought. It would be good to see Boone again. *I wonder what he'll think when I show up with a woman and child.* That caused him to chuckle.

Joel had a fire going and coffee in Elvira's gray coffeepot sitting in the coals when his little *family* returned, carrying two of the largest fish he had ever seen.

"Hope you're hungry for some fish!" Riley called out when they walked into the camp.

Joel was amazed. "What in the world did you catch 'em with?"

"Caught 'em with a stick," Riley replied, grinning from ear to ear.

"The Indian caught them," Ruthie said.

Elvira explained. "There was this feller down there

fishin'," she said. "He said he was a Bannock. They've got a village not far from here. He showed us how to catch fish. There are so many of them in that river, and he got 'em with a spear. So he obliged us by spearin' a couple of big ones for our supper."

"Bannock, huh?" Joel responded. He thought he recalled hearing somewhere that both the Shoshoni and the Bannock in this area had typically been friendly to the wagon trains that passed through. "Well, that was mighty neighborly of him. Was he the only one you saw?"

"There were some others on the other side," Ruthie volunteered, "but they were too far away to talk to. They didn't seem as friendly as Red Shirt." She looked up sadly at Joel and said, "He asked us where our wagon was."

"Red Shirt, huh?" Joel responded. "He spoke pretty good American, did he?"

"Real good," Ruthie said. "He wanted to know if Aunt Elvira was my mother."

"Well, let's get busy cleaning this fish," Elvira sang out cheerfully, hoping to prevent the young girl's mind from revisiting the loss of her parents and brothers.

Realizing Elvira's intent, Joel said, "What are we waitin' for? Let me build that fire up a little. I can't think of a better way to celebrate striking the mighty Snake River than to have a feast of Snake River salmon—if that's what it is."

Riley gave him a puzzled look. "I reckon that's what it is. That Injun didn't say."

It was a pleasant evening. The two large salmon provided meat enough for everyone to have their fill, and then some. The big coffeepot was refilled with fresh spring water from the little stream and charged up again with the strong ground beans that were recovered from Elvira's wagon. Joel imagined it to be very much like a settler's family on their trek west.

"Well, I expect I'd best turn in," Riley finally announced. "We'll be on our way again come sunup." Elvira and Ruthie were soon to follow.

"I'll take a look at the horses," Joel said when the two females returned from a visit to the serviceberry bushes on the other side of the stream.

He picked up his bedroll and walked downstream where the horses were gathered peacefully near the water. Instead of returning to sleep by the fire with the others, he spread his bedroll and settled in for the night near a little stand of pines.

As darkness spread her cloak across the peaceful valley, he could hear the sound of the falls, nearly a quarter of a mile away, crashing down from cliffs standing more than two hundred feet high. Ordinarily, a night such as this would bring him peace, but sometimes he had a feeling everything wasn't exactly as it should be. He didn't know why, but he had one of those feelings tonight, even after the pleasant afternoon and evening. He thought back about the conversation around the campfire, and the generous Bannock fisherman.

Hell, he thought, *these ain't Comanche or Cheyenne. They're Bannock, friendly Indians.*

It had been more than two years since the last trouble between the U.S. Army and the combined Shoshoni and Bannock Indians had occurred, a winter campaign known as the Bear River Massacre. More than four hundred members of Chief Bear Hunter's band of Shoshoni were killed. Relations were reported to be peaceful now, although Joel could well understand a reluctance on the Indians' part to forgive and forget. He reminded himself that he and Riley had been surprised by Indian raiders twice before, simply because they hadn't expected to be attacked.

But even Riley said this Bannock they met down by the falls showed no signs of anything other than friendship and courtesy. Still he had that feeling. *You worry too much,* he told himself, pulled his blanket up closer under his neck, and drifted off to sleep.

He wasn't sure what had wakened him—a sound from the horses, the call of a night bird, or the sounds of the falls. Lying comfortably in his bedroll, he did not move, but opened his eyes to peer up at a three-quarter moon peeking through a break in the clouds overhead. He was about to close his eyes again when he was startled by a shadow moving slowly along the young pine trees that stood between his bed and the horses. He felt the muscles in his forearms tense as he forced himself to remain still, even as his natural reflexes told him to react. His visitor was on the other side of the pines, and had evidently not detected Joel's presence as yet.

Careful not to make a sound, Joel moved his hand down to rest on his carbine, wrapping his fingers around the trigger guard. Before taking action of any kind, he decided to find out just what he was dealing with—a bear, or mountain lion, or was he about to shoot one of the horses that might have strayed away from the others?

As quietly and as slowly as he could manage, he rose on one elbow and looked toward the clearing. The shadow was past the stand of pines and Joel could clearly see that the visitor was neither bear nor cat. It was a man, crouching low as he approached the horses.

It appeared that he was alone, but Joel had to be sure. He strained to turn his head as far as he could in both directions, but there was no one else to be seen.

Our friendly Bannock, Joel thought ambiguously as he slowly rolled out of his bedroll and got up on one knee. *Gave us enough fish to fill our bellies so we could go to sleep while he steals our horses.*

He pushed on up to his feet and walked quietly after the unsuspecting horse thief, not sure what he was going to do about him. He could not say he was honestly angry at the intruder for attempting to steal the horses, at least not angry enough to kill him.

Hell, that's what Indians do, he told himself. *To them, it's something that brings them honor. Well, he can look for his honor someplace else, with somebody else's horses.*

The thief's attention was focused entirely on the horses, which were beginning to move about at the sight of the approaching figure. Joel left the cover of the trees and walked quietly behind the Indian, his rifle up before him, ready to fire. The Indian was not aware of the white man moving with him, step for step. His interest was concentrated upon the paint pony that Riley had been riding. Joel watched him as he moved up to the horse and stroked its neck and face. Joel figured that was about as far as he was willing to let it go. He was about to say as much when the thief took the paint by the bridle and started to lead it away from the stream. He turned to find himself facing Joel and a Spencer carbine aimed at his belly.

Both men froze, but one, clearly at a disadvantage, searched frantically for his options for escape. There were none. His only weapon, his bow, was strung on his back, even had there been time to nock an arrow before the .54 slug tore into his belly.

"Gott damn," he finally muttered in halting English as he assessed his awkward situation and waited for the impact of the bullet.

But the bullet never came. Joel wasn't sure why. Maybe it was simply because the Indian did not react with a violent attack when surprised, seeming instead to brace himself for the penalty he must pay for having been caught. The Bannock had not come with killing in mind, evidently. To the contrary, he appeared to have the theft of only one horse in mind. What to do with him? These were the thoughts that swirled through Joel's mind in that span of a couple of moments.

Joel finally broke the tense silence. "Why do you steal our horses?"

"Because you have horses," Red Shirt replied, speaking slowly as he thought about his answer.

"That ain't no reason to steal ours," Joel said. "I didn't come lookin' to steal your horses."

Red Shirt shrugged. "I got no horses."

"Not even one?" Joel asked, and Red Shirt shook his head, still waiting for the bullet to come. Still perplexed over what to do with the thief, Joel said, "I oughta shoot you down right now." He raised his carbine, threatening, but the man looked so helpless he couldn't bring himself to execute him just for trying to steal a horse. "Why should I let you live?"

"Because I not steal horse," Red Shirt said solemnly, "I trade fish for horse."

"Ha!" Joel snorted. "A horse is worth a helluva lot more than two damn fish."

Red Shirt had to think about that for a moment. He had nothing more to offer. And then an idea occurred to him. His eyes brightened with hope as he offered, "I know where to find Silver City. I take you there."

His offer caused Joel to pause to consider. He was confident that Silver City would not be hard to find, not with news of a gold strike. But for a fact, he didn't really know exactly where in the rugged mountains to even start looking, or for that matter, how far away it was. It would be handy if they could be led straight to the town without having to follow the Oregon Trail along the Snake any longer. But it made little sense to trust a thieving Indian.

"Huh," he grunted softly to himself when he recalled that he and Riley had started this journey as a couple of horse thieves. *Maybe this damn Indian belongs with us,* he thought. "Why should I trust you? Hell, I just caught you tryin' to steal our horses."

"One horse," Red Shirt immediately corrected him.

"That still don't mean I can trust you," Joel said.

"I make promise," Red Shirt insisted. "I swear on rock."

"You swear on a rock?" Joel responded, his weapon no longer raised, ready to fire. "What the hell good is that?"

"Rock sacred, big medicine." He reached inside his shirt and pulled out a polished hunk of quartz that was hanging around his neck. "I, Red Shirt, swear on medicine rock, no steal."

The Indian seemed so sincere in his oath that Joel was inclined to believe that he meant it. But he was not ready to accept his word completely. The man was still caught with the paint's bridle in his hand. Not only that, but Joel was responsible for the lives of Riley, Elvira, and Ruthie. He couldn't afford to be careless. On the other hand, an Indian guide would be a mighty handy addition to the party, and they could afford to give him a horse for his services.

Lord help me if I'm a fool, he thought. "I'm gonna trust

you, Red Shirt. I'll give you a horse if you'll guide us to Silver City. Is that a deal?"

"That's a deal," Red Shirt replied happily.

"Swear it on that rock," Joel insisted.

"I swear, it's a deal," Red Shirt said solemnly while holding the piece of quartz firmly between his hands.

"All right, then," Joel said. "You go on back to wherever you're camped and come back here at sunup. Then we'll get started to Silver City. And just so you know, I don't ever go to sleep at night. All right?"

Red Shirt nodded thoughtfully, then asked, "How I know I trust you? I come back in morning, maybe you gone."

Joel stifled a chuckle. "Well, now, there's that possibility, ain't there? But I'll be here because I say so, and my word is steel."

Red Shirt considered that. Then he nodded again. "You got women. I think they don't go before sunup." He started walking back the way he had come into the camp.

Joel watched him for as long as he could see him, then moved back on the other side of the pines that had first shielded him. There he remained for the rest of the night, watching. He thought about his little party of travelers, sleeping peacefully, totally unaware that a new member would be joining them in the morning.

Two horse thieves, two females, and one Bannock Indian, he thought. *Lord help us.*

About one hundred yards away, Red Shirt gathered dry sticks to build a small fire in a gully by the stream. He unrolled his bedroll to spread by the gully with everything he owned laid upon it, everything he needed to hunt food and prepare it, and the few primitive weapons he depended upon for his survival. The

white man he had not seen with the others who came
to the river seemed to be a fair man, a man of compassion as well. For Red Shirt would surely be dead at this
moment had the man not been compassionate.

We will see what the morning brings, he thought. *If the
white man keeps his word, I will have a horse again. A man
without a horse is a dead man. I will be alive again.*

Chapter 6

"What the hell . . . ?" Riley blurted, and walked to the edge of the firelight to get a better look at the figure approaching from the upstream end of their camp. "Now, what the hell does he want?"

"It's the Indian who gave us the fish," Ruthie said when she turned to see what had caught Riley's attention. Her comment caused Elvira to pause over the coffeepot before filling her cup. Like Riley, she wondered what the Indian had in mind.

Hearing the comments, Joel, kneeling on one knee while tying his bedroll in preparation to ride, announced dryly, "That's just Red Shirt. He's goin' with us to Silver City."

He had not bothered to tell them earlier. He wanted to see if the Bannock actually showed up, unaware that Red Shirt had been watching them for most of the night. An awkward silence followed as Riley and the girls stared in jaw-dropping astonishment at the news of another member joining the party.

"You got a cup?" Joel asked, and Red Shirt nodded. "Well, pour yourself a cup of coffee, and then we'll fix you up with a horse."

Red Shirt smiled graciously, dug his hand inside a deerskin parfleche he carried, and came out with a cup.

Riley was burning inside, but holding his tongue, waiting for the opportunity to talk to Joel alone. Elvira, on the other hand, could hold her silence no longer. She picked up the coffeepot again, walked over to meet Red Shirt, and motioned for him to hold his cup out. While she poured, she expressed her curiosity.

"You know, I wasn't payin' much attention to the conversation that went on last night at supper. I ate too damn much, and when my stomach gets full like that, I sometimes miss half of what everybody's talkin' about. I musta been more flighty-headed than I realized, 'cause I swear I missed the part when we was talkin' about this young feller joinin' our party."

"I reckon I did, too," Riley said, "come to think of it."

Not certain how to interpret the remarks, Red Shirt took a step backward, his face a picture of confusion. Seeing his reaction, Joel couldn't help being amused, but he figured it was time to explain the arrangement he had agreed to while the three of them were sleeping.

"I suppose I shoulda told you last night, but I didn't wanna disturb your sleep. Me and Red Shirt made a trade last night. I swapped him a horse in exchange for him guidin' us to Silver City."

"You did?" Riley exclaimed. "I thought you and me was partners, and we split everything fifty-fifty."

"We do," Joel replied. "I'm tradin' him a horse outta my half of the stock, so you'll own one more of 'em than me. Red Shirt says he knows the mountains all around here, so he can take us to Silver City a lot quicker than if we have to keep followin' the settlers' trail to find the cutoff that leads back into the town. Like I said, it's my deal, but you folks are welcome to follow Red Shirt and me, and no extra charge." He looked at Ruthie and grinned. "And maybe he'll show you how to catch fish with a spear."

Riley, although still skeptical, shook his head and chuckled. "Hell, I reckon it's all right with me. Welcome, Red Shirt." He then cocked a wary eye at the confused Indian. "What if we get attacked by a Shoshoni war party? Whose side you gonna fight on?"

Red Shirt shrugged and declared humbly, "I not fight against you."

"That's good to know," Riley said.

Elvira was not yet ready to give up all her caution. "I suppose we'll all get along just fine," she said, directing her words toward Red Shirt, "just as long as you don't behave like a wild savage and get to thinkin' you wanna scalp somebody." The perplexed Indian simply stared in disbelief at the formidable woman confronting him for no reason he could think of. He was further mystified when she did an apparent about-face and asked, "Are you hungry? There's some bacon left that nobody's et yet."

He shook his head, then turned to face a smiling Joel. "Come on, then, and we'll pick out a horse for you," Joel said. "I noticed you took a likin' to that little paint last night, but that one belongs to Riley. There's some good horses in that bunch, though." He motioned for Red Shirt to follow him, and started walking toward the small herd.

Red Shirt was very pleased with his selection of a broad-chested bay horse from the small herd by the stream. Joel expressed his regrets for not having saved the Indian saddle the horse was wearing when they had captured it. "No matter," Red Shirt said. "I make saddle."

When the camp was packed up and ready to get started, Joel turned to Red Shirt and said, "We're ready to ride, so lead us out." The Indian nodded and jumped on the bay's back, then led them back to the Oregon road by the river.

Once they struck the trail again, and turned to follow it west, Riley couldn't help remarking to Joel. "Well, back on the old wagon trail, same as we was before. Hell, I told you there's got to be a pretty plain road to Silver City, what with all the folks has gone there lookin' for gold. I believe you mighta cost yourself a horse just to find out there ain't no other way to that town."

Since they were close enough to their guide for him to hear Riley's comments, Red Shirt reined the bay back to answer Riley. "We follow wagon trail along river till we get to place wagons cross. Then we leave trail, stay on this side of river, head into mountains—wild country. Without Red Shirt, you get lost. Get to Silver City quicker."

"I wouldn't stay lost for long," Riley responded indignantly. "I can always find my way outta the mountains. I got us this far without no guide."

Joel gave a chuckle. "That you did, partner, and I know you'da got us to Silver City, but ol' Red Shirt was born in these mountains, so he's gonna show us a shortcut."

Red Shirt nodded. "I show you shortcut—get there quicker." He nudged the bay forward.

Riley reined back to let the Indian get a little ahead. When he felt sure Red Shirt was out of earshot, he complained to Joel. "I don't know, partner. I don't see what the hell we need a guide for. Sure, we may get to Silver City a day or two quicker, but then what the hell are we gonna do with him?"

Joel shrugged. "I didn't make any deal with him except to lead us to Silver City. That's all. He can go his own way from there."

"Uh-huh," Riley grunted sarcastically. "It was a helluva deal for him—a horse, just for takin' a few days' ride."

Joel decided there was no sense in telling Riley that the Indian was going to steal the horse if he hadn't been awake. At least this way they'd get something for the horse, even if it was just a shortcut to Silver City.

"Accordin' to what he told me," Joel replied to Riley's comment, "it's liable to be more like six or seven days, and that's providin' the weather holds."

Joel estimated they had traveled about fifteen miles when they decided it best to rest the horses. The place they selected was at a bend of the river just before an area of strong rapids. Always looking for an opportunity to vary their diet from the salt pork that served as the standard, Elvira remarked that it would be nice if they could catch fish to cook again.

"I catch you fish," Red Shirt immediately said. "Salmon running now."

"How come you know so much about catchin' fish?" Riley asked. "Most Injuns I ever run into don't know nothin' about fishin'."

As they had already come to expect, Red Shirt shrugged before answering, "I born here. I am *Agai-deka* Bannock warrior. This is what they call my people."

"*Agai-deka?*" Joel asked. "What's that mean in white man talk?"

"Salmon eater," Red Shirt replied with a grin.

Riley laughed. "Well, let's go fishin'. Sounds to me like you oughta be an expert. Elvira, better get your skillet ready, 'cause the man's guaranteed fish for dinner."

Riley's remarks were meant to be chiding, but Red Shirt lived up to the reputation he claimed. There was salmon enough to sate everyone's appetite in short order, much to the amusement of their Bannock fisherman.

After a couple of days following the river, the trail veered away from it to skirt around a deep gorge where the mighty river carved a trough through steep canyon walls. They would travel for most of a day before coming back to it at Three Island Crossing.

"This is where we crossed!" Riley exclaimed upon approaching the most dangerous river crossing on the entire Oregon Trail. "Ben Plummer lost his wagon and everything he owned when his team got skittish and caused it to roll over out there in the deep part. My pa knew what to do. He had me ride beside our lead horse, and I held him by the bridle all the way across. I'll never forget that day. But, hell, you had to cross. If you didn't, it was a hard, dry route to take on this side. All the water and decent grazin' is on the north side."

"We not cross river," Red Shirt said. "We go that way." He turned and pointed toward the rough, rocky ground on the south side of the river.

"Damn, that's right toward the mountains," Elvira said, and she stood looking toward the towering peaks, which appeared to be stacked one behind the other forever. "How are we gonna find our way through all those mountains?"

"That's what we got a guide for," Joel told her. He looked at Red Shirt then. "Ain't that right, Red Shirt?"

The somber Indian shrugged. Joel turned back to Elvira and shrugged as well, imitating Red Shirt. Then, chuckling, he said, "Let's get started."

There were only a few hours of daylight left, so Red Shirt led them on a track that generally followed the river, advising Joel that he thought it best not to push into the mountains until the next day. That was agreeable to all because the waiting mountains looked to be a formidable challenge. They made their camp by a steady stream that fed into the Snake. The men tended the horses while Elvira and Ruthie prepared supper. Since she had a little more time than usual, Elvira decided to use some of her flour and lard and bake some biscuits. They made the dull repast of beans and bacon seem like a banquet, especially when washed down with strong black coffee.

They set out at first light in the morning, Joel and Riley having decided it best to ride for a spell, then stopping to rest the horses and eat breakfast. Red Shirt told them it was best to stay close to the Snake because of the dry country south of the river.

"Maybe two, three hours' ride, come to creek. Stop there to rest and eat."

So they did as he suggested and came to the creek in a little over two hours. After resting the horses there, they set out again, still following the river. At the end of the day, they found themselves crossing a sandy desert area that made them wonder if they were going the right way.

The days that followed were enough to convince the travelers that the dangerous crossing back at Three Islands was by far the proper choice for the Oregon Trail riders. By the time they reached the high mountains, everyone was happy to see pine and spruce partially covering the slopes towering high above their heads.

Red Shirt led them through narrow mountain passes that appeared to go nowhere, following game trails that somehow found passage from one mountain to the next. By this time, there was no choice other than to trust the stoic Bannock guide completely, for none of his white companions were sure they could find their way back to civilization. Joel suspected they were getting close to their destination when they came across several mining claims.

"Looks like they didn't have much luck in this hole," Riley commented when they stopped to water the horses at one of the abandoned claims. Looking around him at the camp, he concluded, "They didn't stay here long, from the looks of their leavin's." Farther down the slope, they found another site, similar to the one above. "I'll bet it was the same ones that worked that claim above. I reckon they finally gave up on the whole stream and lit out for some other spot."

"My brother said the gold strike brought prospectors in from everywhere," Joel said. "He said a lot of those folks who passed through this country, lookin' for gold in California, came back here when they heard about the strike." He looked at Red Shirt then and asked, "How much farther is Silver City from here?"

Red Shirt shrugged, then pointed to a tall mountain slope several miles distant. "Other side that mountain, down in valley."

His words caused everyone to perk up a little. "I swear," Elvira proclaimed. "I don't believe it. You mean there really is a place called Silver City? I was beginnin' to think it was just someplace Joel and Riley dreamed up one night in a saloon."

The word *saloon* triggered Riley's thirst, for it had been a while. "Hell, maybe we oughta quit pokin' along, and we might be able to get to that town before nightfall."

"There ain't enough daylight to get to that mountain he pointed to, let alone go down to the valley on the other side," Joel said.

"We at least oughta give it a try," Riley insisted. He looked at Red Shirt for support. "Whaddaya think, Red Shirt? We can make it, can't we?"

"No," was the Indian's simple answer. "We be there tomorrow."

"There, you see," Elvira injected. "That's your official answer from our guide, you damn drunk. We'd be stumblin' around these mountains in the dark, break a leg on one of the horses. Then where would you be?"

"If I had a drink of likker, I wouldn't give a damn," Riley answered.

Joel winked at Ruthie before commenting, "You know, you two have got to jawin' at each other like an old married couple. Ain't that right, Ruthie?"

"Yes," Ruthie giggled.

"Married couple!" Elvira exclaimed. "Why, I'd sooner be married to that horse standin' over there."

"Now, watch your tongue," Riley responded. "You wanna go and spook the horses?"

"I'll spook you in a minute," Elvira came back, causing Ruthie to giggle again, and drawing a hearty chuckle from Joel.

In another minute, they were all laughing, with the exception of Red Shirt, who was somewhat astonished, unable to understand their mirth. Joel, on the other hand, understood the sudden release of tension that had built up over the last several days of hard travel through some rugged country, and the feeling that this town they sought was never going to be found. He was glad to see them laughing. Tomorrow, they would reach Silver City. Then someone could tell him how to find his brother.

It was going to be great seeing Boone again after so long a time. He wondered if his elder brother had changed much since he last saw him. The war changed a lot of men, himself included. Of course, the obvious change in Boone would be his crippled leg. Joel hadn't seen him since that happened, but he knew his brother's resolve when facing any problem was to go right on in spite of the obstacles.

Joel was eager to know the situation Boone was involved in, and what he and Riley could contribute to expand the venture. He had spent many an evening speculating about the future and what he wanted to make of it. Boone had a mining claim, but he had also claimed a parcel of mountain land that would be suitable for raising horses and cattle. And Joel had to admit that was something he was more interested in than panning for gold. In his letter, Boone said there were already several sizable mining companies working the hills around Silver City, and the town itself had attracted the usual flock of prospectors as well as merchants, saloons, and bawdy houses. It seemed to Joel that somebody was going to have to feed all these people, and that's where he hoped he and Boone would come in.

We'll find out tomorrow, he thought. "I expect we'd best get mounted," he sang out. "We've still got a few hours of daylight left."

It was a little bigger than he expected. From Boone's letter, he had gotten the impression that the town was little more than a few rough buildings and a row of tents. He had to assume that the row of buildings on two sides of one main road were a testament to how rapidly the town was growing. He turned to speak to Riley when he rode over the crest of the hill to join him and Red Shirt.

"Well, there she is, Silver City. Whaddaya think of her?"

Riley didn't answer at once, but took a moment to scan the rough buildings. His eyes stopped on one that had a sign over the door, proclaiming it to be a saloon.

"Looks fine to me," he said then. "Seems to have everything a man could need."

Knowing well what his partner meant, Joel, however, was of a different mind. He looked over the slope behind the stores for a suitable place to put the horses while he was seeking information about his brother. The grassy spot behind what appeared to be a blacksmith's looked to be the best.

"We'll bunch the stock over behind that forge," he told Red Shirt. "That look okay to you, Riley?" Riley said it did, so Joel turned to talk to Elvira. "Soon as the horses are took care of, I'm goin' to see if anybody knows where my brother's place is. What do you wanna do?"

"That looks like a general store next to the saloon," she said. "I think I'll go in and look around, see if there's anything I need. It's handy to the saloon, so me and Ruthie can help pick Riley up out of the street when they throw him out." She chuckled then and waited for his response. It wasn't long in coming.

"They're more likely to elect me as mayor, once they see what a fine gentleman I am when I've had a decent drink of likker," he said.

"I stay with horses," Red Shirt said.

"If we're lucky, we'll be ready to ride out pretty quick," Joel said, making sure Riley and Elvira remembered that he planned to find Boone's place before dark. He pulled the gray around to get in behind the horses again, and he and Red Shirt, with Elvira's help, drove them down into Silver City while Riley rode straight to the saloon.

Toby Bryan looked up from his bench when he heard horses filing in behind his shop. Surprised, he got up and went to the back of his forge to see four riders, one of them an Indian, and one that looked to be a young girl. The girl and one that could be a woman each led a packhorse. They drove about a dozen horses into the field behind his small corral and dismounted. Seeing no one he recognized, Toby stood watching them. After a minute or two, they parted in several different directions. One, a tall man, dressed in buckskins, headed directly toward him.

"Mornin'," Joel called out as he skirted the small corral and entered the back of the shop.

"Mornin'," Toby returned. "Somethin' I can do for you?"

"Is it all right if I leave those horses there for a little while, till I get some information?" Joel asked.

"It's all right with me," Toby said. "I don't own that piece of land."

"I'll need to have four of those horses shod, but I might wait till I find out where I'm headin' from here. Maybe you can help me find a fellow who has a claim around here somewhere."

"Oh?" Toby replied. "Who are you lookin' for?"

"Boone McAllister. You know him?"

"McAllister?" Toby repeated, raising one eyebrow. "Yeah, I know him."

"Can you tell me where to find him?"

"Out at his place, I reckon."

"And where might that be?" Joel was beginning to wonder if he was going to have to prod the man with a stick to get the information he wanted. Maybe it had been his luck to pick the town's idiot for directions.

Instead of answering Joel's question, the blacksmith asked one of his own. "Are you one of Beauchamp's new crew?"

"No," Joel answered. "I don't know any Beauchamp. I'm just tryin' to find Boone McAllister's claim. I reckon I'll just go ask in the saloon. Maybe somebody there can tell me how to find Boone." He turned to leave, but Toby stopped him.

"Hold on, mister," he said. "If you ain't workin' for Beauchamp, are you a friend of McAllister's?"

Impatient now, Joel answered, "I'm his brother."

"Oh," Toby responded, and paused before continuing. "In that case, I'm pleased to meet you." He extended his hand. "My name's Toby Bryan."

"Joel McAllister," Joel said, and shook his hand.

"The best way to get to your brother's place is to follow the creek north outta town." He took a few steps over to the back of the forge and pointed. "That's Reynolds Creek. Just follow the trail beside it for about eight miles till you come to another trail that leads up the mountain. It's marked by a little pile of rocks with a tree limb that looks like a cross stickin' up in the middle of it. McAllister's cabin is about halfway up that mountain. That trail will take you straight to it."

"Well, that sounds easy enough," Joel said. "Much obliged. I'll bring those horses in to get new shoes in a day or two." He turned to leave, then stopped at the edge of the corral to ask one more question. "Who's Beauchamp?"

"Ronald Beauchamp," Toby replied. "He owns Beauchamp Number Two, one of the three biggest mines in Silver City." He paused a moment before adding, "And he owns Blackjack Mountain, just north of your brother's property." He looked as if about to say more but thought better of it.

"Well, nice to meet you, Toby," Joel said in parting. "I'll be seein' you later on, I reckon."

"Same here," Toby said. "I know your brother will be glad to see you." Again he paused. "Good luck to you."

Strange man, Joel thought as he walked back to tell Red Shirt that he was going to round up Riley and the ladies and get started on finding Boone's cabin. He figured it a good time to talk to Red Shirt, now that they had reached Silver City, and let him know that he didn't expect anything further from him.

"I help with horses till we find your brother," Red Shirt said when Joel told him that he had completed his side of the bargain.

"That'll be fine, if that's what you wanna do," Joel said. "You brought us to Silver City, just like you said you would. So I just wanted to let you know you earned your horse, and you don't owe me a thing."

He shrugged. "I help with horses."

"Suit yourself," Joel said. "I'll go see if I can round up the rest of our party."

It seemed he was facing the same situation with Red Shirt that he had with Elvira and Ruthie. *Everybody wants to stay with me and Riley,* he thought.

His first stop was the saloon, because he figured it would take a little time to wrench Riley away from the bar. A couple of miners sat on the one step in front of the building advertising itself as the Silver Dollar

Saloon. They barely leaned aside to give him room to enter the building. Inside, he paused at the door to look the room over, his carbine hanging casually in one hand. He failed to see Riley at first, but on a closer look, he spotted his stubby partner seated at a back table. Two men sat with him, and there was a bottle of whiskey in the middle of the table.

"Joel!" Riley yelled when he spotted his young partner in the doorway. "Come on over and have a drink!"

Uh-oh, Joel thought. *Ain't been in here thirty minutes and already drunk.* He walked over to the table.

"Kinda early in the day for heavy drinkin', ain't it, boys?"

"Yeah, mister," one of the men said, "set down and have a drink."

"Thank you just the same," Joel said, "but I expect me and Riley here best be gettin' along. Ain't that right, Riley?"

Riley favored his drinking companions with a wide grin, tossed the rest of his drink down, and got immediately to his feet.

"Well, you heard the boss, fellers. I reckon I've got to go, but I wanna thank you for your hospitality. It's a friendly little town you've got here." He turned to Joel and said, "It's a right friendly little town, Joel, I swear." Turning back to his drinking companions then, he said, "I'd like to stay a little longer and talk some more about that mine, but the man says I gotta go."

Joel wasn't sure just what was going on, but Riley was up to something. And one thing was sure, he wasn't as drunk as he had first thought, for he strode as soberly as usual on those short, bowed legs as he headed for the door. "Come on, Joel," he called back over his shoulder.

"What the hell . . . ?" One of the men at the table jumped to his feet. "You can't just walk outta here! You drank a helluva lot of whiskey."

"That I did," Riley called back. "And I enjoyed every drop of it." He paused just before going out the door. "Did I remember to thank you for it?"

The man on his feet took a long look at the formidable figure in the buckskins who was still standing between him and Riley. Not quite sure what Joel would do if he decided to go after Riley, he hesitated to make the move. He glanced at his partner, who was still seated, and seemed satisfied to stay there. So it would be him alone against a man standing a head taller and a helluva lot more sober. But he couldn't let Riley get away with it without at least complaining.

"That friend of your'n drank up half a bottle of rye whiskey and he ain't paid a damn cent for it. He owes me money."

"I'd just let it go, if I was you, mister," Joel told him. He didn't know what kind of game Riley had been playing, but he knew his former sergeant would stand behind any promises he made. "I'd advise you not to buy Riley any more whiskey. I don't know what was goin' on here, but I'm thinkin' you boys mighta learned a lesson today."

"Is that so?" the man shot back. "Maybe I ain't the one gettin' the lesson. We got a way of handlin' smart alecks around here. Ain't that right, Sid?" Sid simply nodded in reply, having already decided not to test the man with the carbine.

"What does that mean?" Joel responded soberly.

"It means it'd be a good idea for you and your friend to get the hell outta Silver City before you have an accident."

Joel locked his eyes on those of the man threatening

him for a long moment before replying, "Mister, if you've got something in mind, you'd best get about doin' it, 'cause I plan to be in town for a while." He continued to stare into the man's eyes for what seemed like a long time, but the man made no response.

He'll wait till I turn my back if he's going to make a move, Joel thought. Then he couldn't help wondering how Riley could get two strangers so riled up in such a short time.

When his antagonist remained silent, showing no indication of taking it further, Joel said, "All right, then. Good day to you, gentlemen."

When he turned to leave, the man reached for the .44 he wore at his side. Expecting just such a move, Joel swung his rifle around in one quick move, catching the man on the side of his head with the barrel of the carbine with enough force to lay him out cold. The crack of the gun barrel against his cheekbone made a sound almost like that of a rifle shot.

Joel turned his gaze upon Sid, who showed no indication of interfering. To the contrary, his wide-open eyes and worried look were evidence enough that he had no interest in backing up his partner. To make certain Joel understood that, he held up his hands in surrender and announced, "I got no part in this fight."

Joel nodded and backed slowly toward the bar, keeping an eye on both Sid and the bartender, who had made no move to take any action. When he was close to the door, he stopped to ask the bartender, "Does my partner owe you any money?"

"Nope," Jake Tully answered. "Sid and Leon bought the bottle. Your friend didn't buy anything." He smiled then and added, "Includin' what they were sellin'."

"Good," Joel said. "We wouldn't wanna start off on the wrong foot here in your town."

Jake laughed. "I reckon you got off to a good start, tanglin' with two of Boss Beauchamp's boys. Let me welcome you to Silver City, young feller. What's your name?"

"Joel McAllister."

"McAllister?" The bartender reacted much the same as the blacksmith had. "Well, now, that makes it more interestin' by the second."

"What's that supposed to mean?" Joel asked.

"I'll just give you a friendly little piece of advice," Jake said. "Watch your back. There's a lot of decent folks around Silver City, but there's enough of the other kind to make it smart for fellers like you to keep a sharp eye." He was about to say more, but Riley stuck his head in the door at that moment.

"Come on, Joel. What the hell are you doin'? If I'da known you were gonna hang around in the saloon, I'da come back to join you." He looked over at the bartender and said, "See you later, Jake."

"Maybe, maybe not," Jake mumbled to himself.

"What the hell were you doin' with those two in there?" Joel asked when they were outside.

Riley chuckled, satisfied with himself. "Those two boys were nice enough to stand for the drinks while they were tellin' me about this minin' claim that was startin' to pay off big. Only problem was they had too much luck with their other claim and they couldn't work both of 'em. So they were gonna sell that claim to me for a helluva good price." He paused to have another good chuckle. "Why? Was there any problem?"

"No, but you'd best be careful where you do your drinkin' from now on. I don't think you made too many friends in the Silver Dollar."

"I figured as much," Riley said, still enjoying the

thought of all the free whiskey he had downed. "Elvira and Ruthie have gone back to the horses. They came outta the store while you were wastin' time in the saloon."

"Glad to hear it," Joel said. "I think we might as well get on our way." He shot a quick glance toward the door of the saloon to make sure Riley's drinking companions didn't suddenly appear.

"I was gonna ask ol' Sid and Leon back there if they knew where your brother's mine was," Riley said. "But I figured it's just as well they didn't know where we were headed."

"I expect so," Joel replied with a smirk of amusement. "No matter, I know how to get there."

Chapter 7

The trail was easy to find, just as the blacksmith had said. They had followed the creek north, and not far after crossing the main road to the east that connected Silver City to the rest of the world, they came to the little pile of rocks.

"Looks like a grave," Elvira remarked. "I hope that ain't your brother's idea of welcome. Looks more like a warning."

"It's just a pile of rocks," Joel said. His thoughts were on the narrow trail that wound its way up through a band of spruce trees before disappearing from sight, and how difficult it was going to be to drive their small herd of horses up it. "I'm thinkin' I'd best lead, then start the horses up after me. With the rest of you behind 'em, they oughta follow right on up that trail."

No one had a better idea, so he started up the trail, and Riley and Red Shirt drove the horses onto the bottom of the path. As Joel had predicted, the horses strung out in single file and followed dutifully up the mountain.

Once through the band of spruce, the trail climbed a slope sparsely dotted with runty-looking pines and wide areas of grass still wearing the remnants of a recent snow. Joel thought immediately of the potential for raising cattle and horses on the mountain meadows. He wondered if Boone had made any plans along those lines. Just ahead of him now, the trail wound around a huge outcropping of rocks. He looked back below him to make sure everyone was keeping up. Satisfied, he nudged the gray with his heels and started around the rock overhang. That was as far as he got before a rifle slug ricocheted off the rock over his head, and a voice bellowed out above him.

"That's about as far as you need to go! Turn around while you've got a chance, 'cause I ain't gonna tell you again."

Below him, the horses continued to push up around him, while Riley and the others looked around frantically for someplace to take cover. Joel reined his horse back as best he could, trying to keep the rocks between him and his unseen antagonist.

"Hold on, damn it!" he yelled. "Boone, is that you?"

There was a long moment with no response. Then the call came back. "Who wants to know?"

"I do. It's me, Joel, and I didn't come all the way from Texas just to get shot."

"Joel?" the astonished voice replied. "Is that really you? Ride on past that rock ledge and let me see you."

"It's me, all right. Now don't shoot. I'm comin' out." He nudged the gray and rode past the ledge out into an open meadow, looking all around in an effort to spot his brother.

"Well, I'll be damned," Boone drawled as he rose from his position behind a rock that had been wedged between two scrubby pines, "if it ain't my little brother." He threw his head back and laughed as if it was the funniest thing he had ever seen. "I swear, I never thought I'd ever see you again." Then he saw the extra horses pushing up around Joel. "What the hell have you got with you?" He hobbled down to meet his brother, moving as nimbly as a person could expect with one stiff leg.

Even though he had imagined his big brother moving with a limp, Joel did not anticipate the impact it would have on his emotions upon first seeing Boone literally dragging one leg as he hurried down the slope to greet him. Boone, always strong and agile as a mountain lion, now descended the narrow trail in an uneven, jerky motion. He still displayed that wide smile that Joel remembered, however. Joel dismounted and climbed to meet him.

"Helluva way to welcome your brother," he said upon reaching Boone's outstretched hand. He shook his hand, then pulled him close enough for a big bear hug.

"I can't believe you actually made it out here," Boone said joyfully. "I thought you'd end up goin' to Mexico with Shelby." He pushed Joel back to arm's length to take a good look at him. "You don't look none the worse for wear. The army musta suited you."

"I could say the same for you," Joel lied. For in truth, there were lines in the weathered face that had no doubt been deepened by the war, and the hair across his temples had turned to gray. "Looks like you picked up a little snow around your ears," he teased. He didn't mention the leg.

"Wisdom," Boone replied, laughing. "That's what turns your hair white. Maybe it'll happen to you."

The reunion was interrupted then by an impatient voice from below.

"Well, is it safe for the rest of us to come up?" Riley yelled.

"Come on," Joel called back.

"What in hell did you bring with you?" Boone asked then. "How many's back there?"

"When I decided to come out here, I figured there wouldn't be nobody but me, but I picked up a few more on the way." He briefly told Boone how each member of his party had happened along as they watched them move up to join the two brothers. "I picked up these horses, too," Joel went on. "Figured I might wanna try my hand at raisin' horses. These Indian ponies ain't been gelded, so I'm plannin' to put them to work. I'm gonna need to find some mares, though, so the stallions can do their stuff. Whaddaya think?"

"Well, there's plenty of room for them to graze," Boone replied. "Sounds like you and I have a lot to talk about. Damn, I'm glad to see you!" Then he turned to greet Riley, who was the first to reach him. "This the sergeant that served with you?"

"Say howdy to Riley Tarver," Joel said. Boone greeted him warmly.

"Reckon you wasn't expectin' this bunch to show up at your door," Riley said as they shook hands.

"It is a surprise, but I've come to expect surprises whenever Joel is concerned. There's plenty of room for everybody," Boone replied. He greeted each of the others in the same gracious manner, with nothing but a questioning glance at his brother when introduced to the Indian and the two females. When the introductions were done, he said, "Let's go on up to my cabin. You folks are most likely hungry, so we'll get something to eat. You can turn your horses loose up near the cabin. I've got a few head of cattle and an extra horse in a pasture up there. Just follow me."

"I drive horses," Red Shirt said.

"Good idea," Joel replied, fell in beside his brother, and led his horse. "That wasn't what I'd call a real friendly greeting with that rifle when I stuck my head out from behind those rocks. Wanna tell me about that?"

"There's a lot to tell," Boone answered. "Let's let it wait till later when we've got time." He glanced at Elvira and Ruthie walking behind them, then lowered his voice. "What I wanna know is what you're plannin' to do with the women and the Indian."

"I'm damned if I know, to tell you the truth," Joel answered. "Riley and I are the only ones who were supposed to be comin' out here to work with you. The other three just decided to come with me. I told you how I happened on Elvira and the girl. I thought I was goin' to get rid of 'em at Fort Hall, but Elvira had other ideas. You'll see when you get to know her. She pretty much does what she wants." He was quick to qualify his remarks. "Don't get me wrong, though. She's damn handy to have around, does the cookin' and works like a man. I've kinda got comfortable havin' her around. She takes care of Ruthie, and the girl's a willin' worker, too."

"What about the Indian?" Boone asked.

"Red Shirt? He's damn good with horses and knows the country well. I get the feelin' he'd like to stay with us, even though that wasn't the plan when we left the Snake." He shook his head, knowing he had brought a lot of trouble with him. "I know you didn't expect to have this bunch show up at your door. Hell, you didn't even expect Riley. But I'll deal with it, and get the others started somewhere on their own." He paused to think out loud. "Red Shirt won't be a problem. He was a loner when we met him. He'll just go back to livin' in the mountains like he did before, I reckon."

Boone gave the matter some serious thought before he spoke again. "Well," he finally said, "there ain't any hurry about doin' anything about it right now. Let's just let it go till after supper and we'll talk about it some more then."

"All right," Joel said. He knew his brother well enough to tell there was a lot more on his mind. He had a notion that it had a good deal to do with the warning shot fired over his head earlier.

Boone led them about three-quarters of the way up the mountain until coming to a huge outcropping of rock that appeared to reach all the way to the top. The path led around the mountain from that point, but they had only gone a couple of dozen yards when he pointed to an opening between two rock columns. "That's where I'm workin' right now."

"Are you pullin' anything out of this mountain?" Joel asked.

"I'm gettin' a little more than grub money, but I'm sure that mine's got a lot more to give. I just haven't gotten into the heart of it yet, but it's in there. I just need the time to get to it. With you here to help, maybe we'll find out where she's hidin' the real stuff." He pointed toward a ring of pines farther down the side of the mountain. "Tell the Indian to head those horses toward those trees. There's a stream on the other side, and that's where I built my cabin." He then drew a revolver from his holster and fired two quick shots in the air. "Hold on!" he yelled when his shots caused his guests to start. "Just warnin' shots."

Standing at the corner post of the small porch, her eyes straining to stare at the path where it emerged from the pine trees, a .58 Springfield musket in her hand, the somber Shoshoni woman watched and waited. She grunted softly to herself when she heard the two shots in rapid succession and propped the musket against the wall. The first shot from Boone's Henry a short time before had caused her to pick up the musket and go out on the porch. Now she turned to return to her work, only to pause, surprised, when the horses suddenly appeared in the opening between the trees. In a minute or two, the horses were followed by more horses with riders, and then she saw Boone on one of the horses behind another man. Astonished, she stood still and waited for an explanation.

"We've got company for supper, Blue," Boone called out from behind Joel. The Indian woman made no reply, but stood watching the strangers dismount by the corral beside a small barn. Her dark eyes darted back and forth between her husband and the five strangers, lingering momentarily on the Bannock warrior as he slid deftly from the back of the bay horse. "I expect you'll need to cook up that elk haunch hangin' in the smokehouse," Boone told her when he stepped up beside her. Turning to his guests, he said, "This is Blue Beads." She turned to cast a reproachful glance in his direction, prompting him to add, "I guess you'd say she's my wife. She takes care of everything inside the house, and I take care of everything outside. Ain't that right, Blue?"

Elvira was the first to step forward. "We're pleased to meet you, Blue Beads. My name's Elvira. We're sorry to pile in on you all of a sudden, but me and Ruthie here will be glad to help you with the cookin'." She glanced at Boone then and said, "We've got supplies and food with us, too. We expected to take care of ourselves. We can make a separate camp down by the stream so we don't cause you too much bother."

"No such a thing," Boone responded. "We've got plenty of room in the house. You and the little lady can use the storeroom. It's mostly empty, anyway. And the men can sleep in the front room."

"A corner in the barn would do for me," Riley spoke up. "No need to put yourself out. I ain't slept inside a buildin' in so long, I wouldn't know what to do under a roof." He nodded to Red Shirt then. "Me and ol' Red Shirt will do fine in the barn." Red Shirt shrugged.

"We get some pretty cold nights up here," Boone said. "You might wanna stay in the house by the stove. But we'll work all that out later. Come on, and I'll help you with your horses." The men went to the barn to unsaddle the horses and unload the packs. Elvira and Ruthie went inside with Blue Beads.

"Blue Beads, huh?" Joel teased with a wide grin for his brother. "So there's a Mrs. McAllister now, you rutty ol' dog."

"Well, it ain't exactly official," Boone responded, "but I reckon she's my wife. Hell, I needed someone to help me take care of the place."

"Looks to me like you've built yourself quite a place here, and if you've thinkin' about raising some cattle and horses, you're sure gonna need more than you and a woman."

"Well, I figured I could handle it till you got here, and to prove I counted on you, I filed for this claim in both our names, so you're half owner. The territorial government approved our claim for three hundred and twenty acres just as long as I proved up the land. That meant improvin' it and locatin' water. I did all that, so it's officially our land, and nobody else has any claims on it."

"Well, damn, Boone," Joel started. He had not expected to be an owner. "That's mighty considerate of you, and you know I appreciate it, but I feel like I oughta earn it first." He shook his head, amazed. "And you've done all this by yourself?"

"To tell you the truth, I had a couple of fellows helping me, but they got run off," Boone said. "But at least it wasn't until after we got the house and barn built."

"Whaddaya mean, they got run off?" Joel asked.

"Well, that's something I need to talk about with you fellows, and I reckon we might as well do it now." He was watching Joel and Riley opening the packs and supplies. Eyeing the Sharps carbines and ammunition, he commented, "Looks like you're fixin' to start a war somewhere."

Joel smiled. "We just had an opportunity to help ourselves to some firearms. I figured they'd be handy for trade goods."

"You might be glad you brought 'em," Boone said. "You just mighta rode right into a war that's already started." Thinking of Riley and Red Shirt in particular, he said, "You might not want to hang around."

Seeing his brother's obvious concern, Joel said, "I was wonderin' what's goin' on."

"There's a fellow in town who owns one of the biggest mining operations around. His name's Ronald

Beauchamp. His men call him Boss Beauchamp, and I reckon he thinks he oughta be the boss of everything around Silver City. I didn't have a problem with the man until about six months ago. And that's when he decided I was sittin' on a hunk of ground he wanted. He came to me at first and offered to buy me out, but I knew what he knew. There's a seam of gold runnin' half the distance of this mountain. Add to that, it's the best acreage around for raisin' stock—cattle or sheep. He wants to put sheep up on this mountain. What it amounted to, though, he was lookin' to steal it from me. I told him I wasn't interested. Well, he kept after me for more'n a month before he got it through his head that I wasn't goin' to sell. Then a little while after that, I had a streak of bad luck. Somebody shot two of my cows over on the other side of the mountain. Then my two hired hands left me. Seems somebody told 'em it was gonna be bad for their health if they stayed. A couple of months ago, somebody dynamited the entrance to my mine. So they've got me in a bind. I can't work my mine and watch the stock and the house all at the same time."

"Damn, Boone," Joel murmured slowly. "You've really been in a fix. I wish I'da got here sooner."

"I knew you'd be ready to help," Boone said. "I counted on it, but you might not feel like it's worth the risk," he said, turning to Riley. "You not bein' family, I wouldn't expect you to wanna stick your neck out."

Riley didn't have to think about it before answering. "Hell, I like a good scrap, and things have been gettin' kinda dull lately. Besides, I've been lookin' after ol' Joel here for so long that I'd feel guilty if I didn't help."

"Welcome, then," Boone said. "I appreciate it. I can pay you wages in gold dust if you want, or shares of the take if you'd rather. What about the Indian?"

"Him?" Riley replied. "He's his own man. I don't rightly know what he's got on his mind. He might notta been plannin' to stay at all. Whaddaya say, Red Shirt?"

Red Shirt shrugged, and when Riley continued to wait for an answer, he said, "I stay. I fight."

"Hot damn!" Riley exclaimed. "That's the spirit!" He looked back at Boone then. "What about his pay?"

"Same as yours," Boone said.

One hundred percent in on the deal, Riley was eager to get started. "First thing, why don't we go have a little talk with this Boss Beauchamp?"

"Waste of time," Boone told him. "I already went over to his ranch to see him. Of course he told me he didn't know anything about the problems I was havin'. The lyin' ol' son of a bitch said he was right sorry to hear about my trouble. I told him I wasn't gonna be easy on anybody I caught on my range after that. He said he didn't blame me, said he wouldn't either if he was me. I counted six hired hands when I was ridin' out, all lookin' at me like I was a hog on a tether. I don't know for sure how many Beauchamp's got workin' for him, but I'm sure there's more than six, and that ain't countin' how many are workin' in his mine."

"Seems to me like we need to split up so we can watch all three places," Joel suggested. "If we can catch one of 'em snoopin' around the mine, or messin' with the cattle, and identify him as one of Beauchamp's men, then we can carry the fight right to Beauchamp."

"Sounds like a plan to me," Boone responded enthusiastically. "In fact, I've been tryin' to catch one of 'em in the act. Trouble is, when I was watchin' the mine, they got to the cattle. Of course I was watchin' the cattle the night they dynamited the mine. I reckon they musta had somebody watchin' me the whole time to see where I was."

"This all happenin' at night?" Joel asked.

"That's right. They ain't had the guts to do nothin' in the daylight yet."

"Then I reckon we might as well get started tonight," Joel said. "That all right with you, Riley? Red Shirt?" He got affirmative nods from both men. "I guess we're set, then. You just tell us where you want us," he said to Boone.

"Damn, I'm glad to see you!" Boone couldn't help exclaiming. "I've gotta be honest with you, I don't know if I coulda held out by myself. I just couldn't be in two or three different places at once. We're still badly outnumbered, but damn it, now we've got a reasonable chance."

The discussion over, and plans laid, the men returned to the house to inform the women. "You're in for a real supper tonight," Boone told Joel and Riley. Blue will slice some offa that elk haunch I killed a while back. She smoked it and we've been eatin' off it ever since. I remember you were always a big hunter, Joel. You'll like this country around here. There's all the game a man could want runnin' through these mountains."

"Who wants coffee?" Elvira asked, then informed them that there were only four cups when everyone responded. "I reckon we'll have to get our cups outta the packs."

Ruthie volunteered to go out to the barn to fetch three cups. They sat around the kitchen table, drinking coffee, for a good part of the afternoon. Joel and Boone had a lot of catching up to do, with Riley embellishing much of what Joel told his brother regarding his time in the war.

When the supper was ready, they ate the meal that Blue Beads and Elvira had prepared, then headed back down to the barn to saddle up in preparation to watch the three spots that Boone had specified. Riley and Red Shirt rode back up to the mine. The first job was to find cover for their horses so that they would not be seen. So after tying them in a stand of pines high up the mountain, the two men moved down the slope to a large boulder about fifty yards up the slope from the mine entrance. The Bannock warrior was now armed with a new Sharps carbine.

Halfway around the mountain from the mine, the brothers McAllister took a position above a mountain pasture where Joel's horses were grazing with Boone's cows. They agreed that the house was the least likely target for Beauchamp's men, since they would have to pass by the mine or come up the other side where the stock was grazing. Because of this, they were comfortable with the defense of the house in the hands of Blue Beads and Elvira. Boone knew that his Shoshoni wife was deadly with her musket. She had been hunting with him enough times to prove it. And Joel assured him that Elvira was as capable as a man with a weapon in her hand.

"Hell," Boone exclaimed, "the house might be our strongest defense." Joel couldn't disagree.

The first night passed peacefully, with no sign of intruders at any of the lookout posts. It was not until the second night, when they received visitors, that the

initial confrontation between the two camps occurred.
It was the ill fortune of three of Boss Beauchamp's riders to attempt to drive Boone's cattle off the mountain.
It was around midnight when Joel suddenly reached
over and gripped his brother's forearm. When Boone
reacted, Joel pointed toward a flat slab of rock at the
lower end of the meadow that shone shiny white in the
moonlight. Three shadows moved around the rock
and materialized into three men on horseback as they
drew closer.

"They're goin' after the cattle," Boone whispered,
his heart pumping excitedly. "Let 'em get closer up in
the openin', and then we'll give 'em a hot welcome." He
had waited for a chance to retaliate for the frustration
of their earlier attacks, and now that it was here, he
wanted to make it count.

So they waited, with rifles ready, watching the cattle
thieves as they moved up into the meadow, gradually
coming closer. Then, instead of continuing, the rustlers turned to cut out only a part of the herd, about
fifteen head, and started to drive them back down the
slope.

"Uh-oh," Joel exclaimed softly, realizing they would
soon ride out of range. "The one on the right," he said,
picking his target, and opened fire.

Boone didn't hesitate. He sighted on the rider next to
that one and pulled the trigger. The rider on the right
tumbled from the saddle as Joel immediately brought
the carbine around to fire at the remaining target. Boone
continued to throw lead at his initial target, who
remained in the saddle, although he had slumped over
onto his horse's neck.

Taken totally by surprise, the two rustlers remaining

in the saddle fled the meadow, leaving their fallen comrade behind and making no motions toward defending themselves. Joel and Boone scrambled out of their ambush and ran down the meadow trying to get a couple more shots, but the raiders were obviously through for the night. The horse with the empty saddle chased after them. When they got to the lower end of the meadow, they found the body of the man Joel shot. Boone rolled him over on his back to see if he recognized him.

"Know him?" Joel asked, staring down at the whiskered face clearly exposed by the bright moonlight.

"No," Boone answered. "Can't say as I've ever seen him before."

"Too bad," Joel said. "I'd like to be able to tie him to Beauchamp." He paused to think about it for a moment. "Those two that got away, one of 'em was hit pretty bad. He'll most likely go to the doctor. Maybe we can find out who he is. What about the sheriff? Has Silver City got one?"

"You can forget about gettin' help from the sheriff," Boone said. "Beauchamp put him in office. If he does anything, he's likely to come after us. The trouble is nobody in Silver City knows what's goin' on in these mountains outside town. There ain't no law out here. It's just what a man is strong enough to hold on to. I've got a legal claim filed on this land, but there ain't no law around to make sure a man's property is protected."

"Well, at least Beauchamp knows he's gonna keep losin' men if he sends 'em after you again." He paused when he caught sight of something metallic in the moonlight. Walking over in the grass a few yards away, he picked it up. "This jasper had a fine-lookin' rifle," he said, turning a 'sixty model Henry over in his hands. "Wonder why he pulled it. They never fired a shot." He pitched it to Boone, who caught it and looked it over, too.

"I've been thinkin' about gettin' one of these for Blue," he said. "She's pretty damn good with that Springfield she totes, but it's a real bother, especially if you're tryin' to shoot as fast as you can."

"Well, give her that one," Joel said. "That's a nice romantic present for a man to give his wife." He knelt down to unbuckle the dead man's gun belt. "Here, give her this to go with it," he said as he stood up, pulling the belt from around the corpse in the process. When Boone took the belt, Joel grabbed the body by the boots and dragged it over in the rocks. "Might as well leave this where the buzzards can get to it." They both turned then when they heard the sound of horses galloping.

"Everybody all right?" Riley called out as he and Red Shirt rode up to join them. "We heard the shootin'."

"Everybody but him," Joel replied, pointing toward the corpse. "I'm afraid you missed the party. Don't worry, though. I'm sure there'll be some more when those other two get back to Beauchamp's ranch. Nothin' stirrin' over your way?"

"Nope," Riley replied, "quiet as can be."

"I suppose we should get back to the house and let the womenfolk know ain't none of us got shot," Boone said. "I doubt we'll see anybody else tonight. That's the way it's been, just a little deviltry about every two or three nights, hopin' I'll get sick enough of it to move out. After tonight, though, things might get a little bit hotter. Maybe we can get a few hours' sleep tonight while we've got a chance."

"Maybe I stay little bit longer," Red Shirt said, and shrugged.

"Suit yourself," Riley said, "but I think Boone's right. I don't think those boys will be back tonight."

Already noticing a trend, Boone asked Joel, "Does he always shrug his shoulders before he says something?"

"Almost," Joel replied.

Chapter 8

Boss Beauchamp did not like to be interrupted when eating his breakfast, so he was more than a little annoyed when his foreman showed up at the back door of the sprawling ranch house at the foot of Blackjack Mountain. Mike Strong knew better than to disturb his employer during a meal, but he thought that Boss would want to be told about the problem he was faced with right away. Leon Smith was lying in the bunkhouse with two bullet holes in his back, and he needed to see the doctor soon, because he didn't look as though he was going to make it.

That wasn't the worst of it. Shorty Doyle didn't come back from that little party he and Leon and Sid Hadley were supposed to pull off last night. Boss was short of patience when his orders were not followed, and Strong knew he was going to hit the ceiling when he found out about Shorty. Sid should have known Boss would raise hell with him for leaving Shorty's body on McAllister's property, but he didn't think about anybody's hide but his own. And now it was Strong's job to tell Beauchamp about the fouled-up raid on McAllister's cattle. He could hear him cursing Lena as he pushed his chair back from the dining room table. Strong unconsciously took a couple of steps back from the kitchen steps in anticipation of his employer's arrival.

"Mike," Beauchamp roared, "what is so all-fired important that it can't wait till I've had a decent amount of time to drink my coffee?"

"There's a little problem with some of the men," Strong started, but got no further before Beauchamp interrupted.

"I believe that's what I hired you for, isn't it—to take care of any problems with the men?"

"Yes, sir," Strong replied meekly. "And I reckon I do a pretty good job for you. But this is somethin' I think you'd wanna know right off, and that's the only reason I disturbed your breakfast."

"All right," Beauchamp said. "Make it quick. I need to be at my office at the mine. I've got idiots working there that might blow up the place if I'm not there to tell them what to do."

"Yes, sir," Strong said. He went on then to relate the mishap that was supposed to be another step in the plan to force Boone McAllister to give up and move out. Beauchamp listened without interrupting, although it was apparent by the tightening of his expression that he was approaching a state of unbridled fury. Still he said nothing until Strong finished up with "I figured it best to check with you before I sent for the doctor to come look at Leon."

"It's a good thing you did, you damn fool," Beauchamp roared. "I don't want the doctor to know Leon's getting shot has anything to do with me. I can't have him coming out to my ranch to tend to somebody who got shot on McAllister's place."

It irritated him even more to have to explain something so simple to his foreman. He paid his men good money to do what he asked without question and have enough sense to keep their mouths shut about it.

"Yes, sir," Strong said. "Whaddaya want me to do about Leon?"

"The same thing you do when a horse goes lame," Beauchamp replied coldly. Realizing then that he might have been a little too blunt, he softened his order a bit. "Let Fuzzy take a look at him and see if he thinks Leon's going to pull through it. Then we'll see. It might be the humane thing to put him out of his misery if he's headed that way anyway. The damn doctor couldn't do much more than that."

"Yes, sir, I'll go tell Fuzzy."

"Then bring Sid back here," Beauchamp ordered. "I want to talk to him."

After Strong went to the cookhouse to find Fuzzy Chapman, he walked with him to the bunkhouse, where Leon still lay in the same blood-soaked quilt that had been placed on him the night before.

"Boss says to see what you can do to fix him up," he told the cook.

"I'll take another look at him," Fuzzy said, "but he don't look much better'n he did last night."

"See what you think," Strong told him. "Let me know when I get back." He took a moment to stare at the pitiful man, lying helplessly on his bunk, clutching the quilt in pain. "It's a damn wonder he made it back at all," was Strong's final comment before turning away.

Breakfast was long since finished, but two of the hands were still sitting at the table at the end of the building, drinking coffee. One of them was Sid Hadley, still wearing a large swollen cut on his right cheekbone, the result of a barroom confrontation at the Silver Dollar Saloon.

"Come on, Sid," Strong said. "Boss wants to see you."

At once wary, Sid replied, "What's he want with me? Ain't nothin' I could do 'bout Leon gettin' shot."

"I reckon Boss will tell you," Strong responded impatiently. "Now get up outta that chair before I decide to kick your ass all the way over to the house."

Lena Three Toe opened the kitchen door and stood back to let the two men inside. "Mr. Beauchamp's in the dining room, waiting for you."

As Hadley passed by her, she reached out and slapped him on the back of his head. "Take your hat off when you come in this house," she snapped.

"Yes'm," Sid replied meekly, and removed it at once, even as he cursed her under his breath. There was no love lost between Beauchamp's hired guns and his prickly tempered housekeeper. Boss set himself up as a king in his house and Lena conducted herself as the queen. To the people in town, she was perceived as Beauchamp's Indian cook and housekeeper, but the men he hired to do his evil work knew that she performed other functions that Boss preferred to keep to himself.

With an ambitious eye for the future, he concentrated his attention at the present on the building of a financial empire, without regard for anyone who stood in his way. And that certainly included the likes of

Boone McAllister, who somehow had acquired the papers for the mountain that stood between Beauchamp and the city proper of Silver City. When he was finished, Boss Beauchamp intended to have Silver City named the capital of Idaho Territory, with himself as governor. He intended to buy it, if possible, steal it if that wasn't successful, or kill for it if that was necessary.

Lena followed the two men into the dining room, where Beauchamp was seated, drinking coffee.

"You want some more coffee?" she asked.

When he nodded, she left to fetch the pot. In a minute, she was back to fill his cup. Then she returned to the kitchen. There was no offer of coffee for the two hired hands, who stood quietly waiting for Beauchamp to speak. He made them stand and fidget for a long moment before he acknowledged their presence. When he did, it was in the form of a piercing stare that Sid Hadley could almost feel scorching his skin.

When he finally spoke, it was as disconcerting as Sid had expected. Directed squarely at him, Beauchamp uttered a question, his voice approaching a growl.

"You left one of my men on McAllister property?"

Sid was afraid to answer, but knew he had little choice. "Well, yessir," he stumbled. "That there's the way it turned out, but there wasn't nothin' I could do about that. They was waitin' for us. We didn't have a chance. They was all around that pasture. There musta been a dozen of 'em, and we didn't have no choice but to get outta there. I thought Leon and Shorty were comin' right behind me. I didn't know both of 'em got shot. If I'da known Shorty was knocked off his horse, why, I'da gone right back to get him."

He stood there nervously shifting back and forth

from one foot to the other, waiting for Beauchamp's reaction.

"You make me sick," Beauchamp snarled. "You ran like a yellow-livered coward. What do you think people will say if they find out Shorty worked for me?"

"Oh no, sir, Mr. Beauchamp, don't nobody know Shorty worked for you. There wouldn't be no way of knowin' who he worked for," Sid pleaded. "But there was just too many of 'em for us to handle."

"How do you know how many there were?" Beauchamp demanded.

It was of critical importance to him to know if McAllister had, in fact, hired on some extra hands. If he had, he might find himself in a full range war, something he wished to avoid.

"Well, sir, it was dark, so I couldn't count the exact number, but the shots was comin' from everywhere. But I know for a fact that he hired on some men. I was in town when some of 'em came through the other day." He unconsciously reached up to gingerly touch the cut on his cheekbone. "They was lookin' for McAllister's place. A couple of 'em came in the Silver Dollar where me and Leon was havin' a drink before we rode back to the ranch. We got into it a little bit till one of 'em snuck behind me and cracked me with his rifle barrel. And I'll tell you the truth, he was a hired gun, if I ever saw one." He paused to take a breath, but continued when Beauchamp appeared to be taking him seriously. "And I'll tell you another thing. When we rode into that pasture last night, there was a helluva lot more horses grazin' there than there was the last time we was up there."

Beauchamp was beginning to feel real concern by then. "Are you telling me you actually saw more horses, or are you just trying to cover your ass for running away?"

"No, sir," Sid insisted as earnestly as he could manage. "I'm tellin' you that McAllister never had more than three horses that I ever saw up there. And last night there was at least fifteen or sixteen in that bunch with the cows."

"That damn gimp-legged son of a bitch," Beauchamp snarled. "Where'd he get the money to hire on a bunch of gunmen?"

He paused to think about Boone McAllister's tiny one-man operation. He felt sure he would scare him off when he hired two men to work for him, and Strong, with two of the men, paid them a visit. Now he found out that instead of running, McAllister hired on a crew.

"He must be pulling some real pay dirt out of that mine of his."

It was confirmation of what he had already suspected, and made him even more desperate to get his hands on that property.

Maybe I'm going to need more men, he thought.

He decided that the important thing to do next was to find out exactly how many men McAllister had. With Shorty dead, and Leon probably so, Beauchamp was down to thirteen men who had been hired specifically for their guns.

"All right," he finally ordered, "get out of here. I've got to go into town. Strong, have one of the men saddle my horse." He cast another seething look at Sid. "Maybe he can do it without fouling up. And, Strong, see what Fuzzy says about Leon. You know what to do."

The two men split up, Sid on his way to the barn and Strong headed back to the bunkhouse. When he arrived, Fuzzy was still bending over Leon, trying to clean him up a little. When he saw Strong walk in, he straightened up and signaled the foreman with a slow shake of his head. Strong understood.

"Done about all I can do for him," Fuzzy said. "I was just tryin' to make him a little more comfortable."

"All right, Fuzzy," Strong said. "I reckon you'd best get back to your work." He waited until the cook walked out the door before going over beside Leon's bunk to look at him. "How ya doin', partner?" Strong asked compassionately.

Leon's eyes blinked painfully as he looked up at Strong. "I been better," he rasped between lips crusted with blood that Fuzzy had been unsuccessful in cleaning up. "I need to see the doctor," he pleaded, his voice barely above a whisper.

"Right you are," Strong said. "And that's exactly what we're fixin' to do, so you just rest easy now. You'll feel better when the doctor sees you." Leon closed his eyes and relaxed a little. He was too weak from the loss of blood to put up much resistance when Strong suddenly grabbed him by the throat and clamped down on his windpipe. Leon put up as much effort to survive as he could, but Strong was a big man, and his hands were like two large vises as he increased the pressure on the helpless man's throat. He held on to the doomed man long after Leon's weak but desperate flailing of his arms and legs ceased and death came to claim him.

When he was sure Leon was gone for good, Strong walked outside, where he spotted two of the men near the barn.

"Jim," he called out, "you and Sledge get yourself a couple of shovels. Poor ol' Leon didn't make it, so I reckon you'd best carry him over beyond the hill and dig him a grave."

When Sid came out of the barn then, leading Beauchamp's horse, Strong walked over to intercept him.

"I heard what you told 'em," Sid said. "So ol' Leon went under. Nothin' much a body can do about it when his number's up, I reckon."

Strong took the reins from him and said, "That's a fact. Go get yourself a pick and help them bury him." Then he led the horse up to the kitchen door and knocked. When Lena opened the door, he said, "Tell Mr. Beauchamp that Leon Smith passed away, and I'll tie his horse at the hitchin' post out front."

Jake Tully looked up from behind the bar where he was rinsing some shot glasses in a bucket of water, surprised to see Ronald Beauchamp at this early hour of the day. Boss Beauchamp visited the Silver Dollar occasionally, but usually to have a drink later in the day, after he left his office at Beauchamp No. 2.

"Well, good mornin', Mr. Beauchamp," he greeted him. "Don't normally see you in here this time of day. What can I get you?"

Jake didn't count himself as one of Beauchamp's admirers, but he was smart enough to know he had to respect the man's power.

"Tully," Beauchamp acknowledged. "I don't need a drink right now. I just want a little information." He didn't waste any time getting to the point. "I understand a couple of my men got into a little disagreement in here a few days ago, and I just wanted to check with you to see if there was any damage done to your saloon that maybe I should take care of."

That'll be the day, Jake thought. He was sure he already knew what Beauchamp really wanted to know. He had talked to Toby Bryan, the blacksmith, and they were sure there was going to be trouble with another McAllister in town.

"Well, now," he replied, "that's mighty generous of you to offer, but there was no damage to anything. There was a pretty bad-lookin' bump on the side of Sid Hadley's face, but no harm done to the saloon."

"Well, I don't want my men causing any trouble in town," Beauchamp continued. "Just a little barroom fight between my men and some of the miners around town, I reckon."

Now you're getting down to it, Jake thought, *so I'll tell you what you really want to know.* "No, sir, your boys—really was only Hadley—got into it with a couple of strangers, just come to town. The feller that laid Sid out cold said his name was McAllister, and said he was Boone McAllister's brother. I don't know who his friend is."

Beauchamp didn't reply for a second or two, his face expressionless, and his eyes locked unblinking on Jake's. "There was just the two of them? Nobody else with them?"

"That I can't say," Jake replied, although he knew. "It was only the two of 'em that came in here."

Beauchamp paused again to think about it. "Well, like I said, I just wanted to make sure my boys didn't do any damage in here." He turned abruptly and made for the door.

"Good day to ya," Jake called after him, a sly smile on his face. *There'll be hell to pay for somebody*, he thought.

It was not a secret that there was bad blood between Beauchamp and McAllister, and it would be only a matter of time before somebody ended up getting shot. Jake, like other honest businessmen in town, had no notion of the war going on between Beauchamp and McAllister.

Sheriff Jim Crowder quickly put his coffee cup on the shelf behind his desk when he glanced out the window and saw Boss Beauchamp striding across the street toward his office. Hurriedly getting to his feet, he moved to open the door.

"Good mornin', Mr. Beauchamp," he said.

"It's afternoon," Beauchamp replied curtly. "What do you know about McAllister's brother coming through town?"

"Yes, sir," Crowder said, "I heard he was in town the other day."

"Why didn't you let me know?" Beauchamp demanded. "How many men did he have with him?"

"I didn't have any idea you'd wanna know. It was just him and another feller, an Injun, a woman, and a young girl. That's what Toby Bryan told me. I didn't even see 'em. He said they drove a small herd of horses with 'em—left 'em to graze behind Toby's forge while they went in the saloon. You know I'da sent somebody to tell you if I'd thought you wanted to know."

Beauchamp's mind was spinning, at first with disgust for the report Sid Hadley had given him of a dozen or more gun hands, but then it struck him that the opportunity to drive McAllister out for good might not be slipping away after all.

"Three men—one of them an Indian—and two females, eh?" Hadley had him thinking he was going to hire on more gun hands to combat the crew McAllister had brought in.

"That's what Toby said," Crowder replied.

Three men were not enough to concern Beauchamp since he still had an advantage in numbers, and his men were all hardened gunmen. But what if these new arrivals were only the first to show up? What if McAllister was planning to bring in more men, preparing for an all-out war? He rapidly came to the conclusion that, if he was going to drive McAllister off that mountain, it needed to be done before McAllister had a chance to further strengthen his hand. Beauchamp's mind began working on a plan to get rid of his nemesis for good and all.

"You know," he told Crowder, "something's going to have to be done about McAllister stealing cattle off my range. I've stood it for as long as I intend to, and I might have to do something about it. I've gone out of my way to try to be neighborly with him, but he just doesn't want any part of it. So the next time I catch him rustling my cattle, I'm going to have to take matters into my own hands."

"You want me to ride out there and talk to McAllister about this?" Crowder asked.

"I don't know if it would do any good," Beauchamp replied. "A man like that doesn't have much respect for the law. It might be best to just let me handle it. Maybe McAllister and I can have a little talk and settle our differences."

"Yes, sir," Crowder said, relieved to have an out. "You're probably right about that. He oughta have enough sense to know he can't go up against your boys."

"We don't have any room for troublemakers like Boone McAllister in our town, and I'm willing to stand up against his kind, for the good of Silver City. I'll see what I can do to settle this thing peacefully, but I'll fight if I'm forced to."

"Yes, sir," Crowder replied. "No man could fault you for that. Maybe I should ride out to his place with you, though."

"It's your job to keep the peace here in town. Best let me handle the rustling problem."

"Right," Crowder said with relief. "You know best. I'll keep an eye on his crew if they show up in town again."

Beauchamp left the sheriff's office satisfied that he was free to get rid of Boone McAllister, the thorn in the side of his plans, for good and all. He felt secure in the thought that Jim Crowder would testify that he was within his rights to protect his cattle from being rustled. There was no one else to prove his accusations false.

He almost laughed when he thought about the opposition he was preparing to face, if he was quick to act: two white men, one Indian, and two females, maybe three if McAllister's Shoshoni woman was to be counted. There was no longer a question of frightening the obstinate squatter to pack up and leave. Now it was war, and he intended to wipe them all off the face of the earth.

No reason to wait another day, he thought. Then he cautioned himself not to act too soon. It wouldn't hurt his cause to let the sheriff think he was trying to settle the problem peacefully.

Two days, he decided. *You've got two days, McAllister.*

Unaware that all hell was about to come down upon them, the brothers McAllister made their plans to protect themselves. They had decided there was no way they could definitely say that the dead man lying at the foot of the north meadow was on Beauchamp's payroll, or that he had acted on Beauchamp's orders. Consequently, they decided that they could expect a continuation of the harassing raids on the cattle and the mine.

Joel was in favor of carrying the battle to Beauchamp, but Boone argued that he wanted to build a solid future in Silver City. And while it was legal in the eyes of the law to defend one's property, the army and the U.S. Marshals Service might come down hard on both sides of a range war. Finally he persuaded Joel that it was best to continue to maintain a defensive position and hope to demonstrate to Beauchamp that the McAllisters were here to stay.

"If he keeps losing a man or two every time he sends one of his little raiding parties over here, he's gonna have to give up eventually."

"What if he gets tired of sending two or three men to pick away at us?" Joel asked. "What if he decides to storm over here one night with all his men, hopin' to rub us all out at once?"

"I don't think even Beauchamp has that much brass," Boone said. "Hell, he's tryin' to take control of the whole town. How would it look to everybody if he murdered us all?"

"Maybe you're right," Joel said. "You were always smarter than me. At least, you always thought you were." He chuckled at his attempt at humor. "I'm thinkin' I might ride into town, tomorrow or the next day, and see if the sheriff knows what's goin' on out here."

"Suit yourself, but remember I told you Beauchamp

is the one who put that dumb bastard in the sheriff's office in the first place."

Lena Three Toe led Mike Strong into the parlor where Boss Beauchamp was waiting.

"You wanted to see me, Mr. Beauchamp?" Strong asked.

Beauchamp nodded toward a chair. "Sit down, Mike. I want to have a little talk."

"Yes, sir," he responded, and dutifully seated himself on a straight-back chair opposite his boss. He was not totally at ease with the situation, because Boss never invited any of the men to sit down with him, so he wondered what trouble he had gotten himself into.

"I think it's time I found out if you and your men are worth the money I pay you. Up till now you'll have to admit that you haven't had to do a helluva lot to earn it."

"No, sir," Strong replied, thinking that he was about to get a cut in pay.

"Well," Beauchamp went on, "I'm going to give you and every one of your boys a chance to earn a bonus of a hundred dollars if you successfully do the job I've got in mind."

Strong's expression of concern was immediately replaced with one of enthusiasm. "We're ready to do whatever job you've got in mind," he assured his boss.

He had no concerns regarding the nature of the job, assuming it had to do with killing someone. For that was the primary reason he and every one of his men were on the payroll. They were all wanted men in different states or territories, and not a man hesitated when it came to murder.

Beauchamp then told Strong what he had in mind

to do. It did not surprise him that his foreman was
immediately receptive to it. Beauchamp had given his
plan a lot of thought since his visit with the sheriff. His
initial plan to simply massacre everyone on the McAllister spread, under the guise of a range war over cattle, had caused some concerns to arise. The report of a
range war might possibly cause the army to send a
troop in to investigate. He wanted to prevent that at all
costs. Then Strong made a comment that gave him
another idea.

"Too bad ol' McAllister don't have an Injun raid like
that one that killed that family over on War Eagle
Mountain last year," he said with a smug grin on his
face.

"By God," Beauchamp exclaimed, "that might be
the very thing to happen—an Indian massacre to wipe
out the whole damn bunch of them." He paused to
recall the incident on War Eagle Mountain and think
about it for a moment. "All for nothing, too. There
wasn't enough gold on that claim to bother with."

"That'd sure 'nough be bad luck for poor ol' Boone
McAllister, wouldn't it?" Strong commented with a
chuckle, warming to the idea. "Hell, we've even got an
Injun—ol' Slow Sam. Leastways, he's half Injun." The
man he referred to was wanted in Oklahoma Territory
for the murder of a family of five. His name was Sam
Slow Pony, but the men called him Slow Sam. "We could
even dress up like Injuns," Strong said, completely carried away by the novel idea of the murderous raid.

"There won't be any need to, if you do the job right,"
Beauchamp said. "There won't be any witnesses to tell
anyone who did it. You get the men together and get
them ready to ride." He hesitated a moment, wondering
if McAllister had any more men coming. "Tomorrow

night," he decided. "That should give you any time you need to make your plans." Strong got up to leave. "And, Mike, I'm holding you responsible to get the job done. There can't be one person left alive on that mountain."

"You don't have to worry about that," Strong assured him. "We'll have the army out lookin' for the Injun war party that done in them poor folks."

Chapter 9

There was a definite threat of snow in the clouds that hovered over the stark wooden structures of Silver City, giving the dull gray buildings an even more forlorn appearance as the gray Indian pony loped along the one road through town. To Joel McAllister, the town looked less hospitable than it did when he had seen it before. He reminded himself that the people of Silver City had no knowledge of the murderous war waging between Ronald Beauchamp and the McAllisters. He didn't expect much cooperation from the sheriff, but as he had told Boone, he thought it was in their best interest to let the law know their side of the story. This was just in case it became necessary for the law to become involved in the dispute.

Riley had bemoaned the fact that he was missing an opportunity to visit the saloon again, but he understood the necessity of staying behind to help guard the ranch. Joel assured him that he planned a short visit, so there wasn't going to be any time wasted on drink-

ing whiskey. This in spite of the contention Riley made
that time spent drinking whiskey was never wasted
time.

Toby Bryan looked up from his work and gave Joel
a nod as he rode past the blacksmith's shop, reminding
him that he had to bring the horses in to be shod. Joel
returned Toby's nod with the touch of his finger to his
hat brim.

Across from the Silver Dollar, a small building proclaimed itself to be the sheriff's office. Joel wheeled the
gray in by the hitching rail and dismounted. As on most
occasions, Jim Crowder was seated at his desk, drinking
coffee. He glanced up when Joel walked in the door,
thinking he was probably one of the many prospectors
with a claim somewhere who had come to complain
about a claim jumper or some other bothersome problem. On second thought, on seeing that Joel was dressed
in buckskins, he had the notion that he was one of the
men Beauchamp had warned him about.

"Mornin', Sheriff," Joel said. "My name's Joel McAllister. I thought I'd best come in and tell you about
some cattle rustlin' goin' on at my brother's place."

"Oh, now," Crowder replied, already with a hint of
skepticism, "is that a fact? McAllister cattle?"

It seemed an odd question, but Joel answered,
"Yeah, McAllister cattle, and it ain't the first time it's
happened. This time, though, we were able to catch
them in the act. There were three rustlers. We drove
them off, except one, and he's still lyin' out behind a
pile of rocks where we left him for the buzzards. I'm
pretty sure one of the two that got away was hit once,
maybe twice, but he stayed in the saddle. We thought
you just might wanna know about it, since a man got
killed."

Crowder reacted at once. "You shot a man? Who was it?"

"I don't know for sure," Joel replied. "He didn't have anything on him to identify him, but I suspect if you took him over to Blackjack Mountain, some of Beauchamp's men could tell you who he was. You might even find the other one that got shot." He paused to watch Crowder's obviously confused reaction. "Matter of fact, if you're inclined to do that, you might still beat the buzzards to the body, and you could take him over to Beauchamp's."

"Well, I ain't inclined to do that," Crowder retorted. Then he remembered Boss Beauchamp's complaint that his cattle were being stolen and he suspected McAllister was the culprit. "These fellers you shot, were they on Mr. Beauchamp's property?"

Joel was rapidly coming to appreciate Boone's assessment of the bungling sheriff. "No. Like I just said, they were rustlin' our cattle. We don't keep our cattle on Beauchamp's property."

"Is that a fact?" Crowder replied. "How come I'm gettin' reports that somebody's been rustlin' Beauchamp's cattle?"

"I don't know," Joel answered. "Who reported it?"

"Different folks," Crowder came back. "Never you mind. The fact of the matter is we didn't start havin' no trouble like that around here until your brother staked a claim on that mountain."

"What's that supposed to mean?" Joel asked.

"It means that maybe you and your brother might be the ones I'd better be watchin', instead of you comin' in here tellin' me somebody's stealin' your cows. That feller you killed, how the hell do I know you didn't just murder some drifter that came on your land by mistake?"

Joel's patience was already wearing thin, and he could already see that Boone had been right when he said it was a waste of time reporting to the sheriff. "'Cause I wouldn't be stupid enough to come in and tell you I murdered a man. Maybe you oughta come out and take a look at him. If he's one of Beauchamp's men, there's a good chance you might recognize him. While you're at it, why don't you check the doctor's office, if you've got a doctor in this town? Might be he's treated a man for gunshot wounds."

Crowder was only getting more and more confounded. He knew what Beauchamp had told him, and he didn't want to hear anything that would make him doubt it. He had made no mention of losing a man, and Crowder was pretty sure Doc Murphy hadn't treated any gunshot patients recently. Doc would have told him if that had been the case. McAllister was a troublemaker. That much he had been convinced of, and the sheriff owed Beauchamp too much to question his word. Now he wasn't sure if he should take some kind of action while one of the troublemakers was standing in his office.

"I'm thinkin' it might be a good idea to lock you up till I find out the straight of things," he finally said.

Joel's expression turned stone cold. "That would be a mistake to even try," he said evenly. "Of all the things possible to happen here today, that ain't one of 'em. I reckon I found out you wouldn't do anything about the cattle rustlin'. That was my mistake, but it's the only one I'm plannin' to make, so I'm fixin' to walk outta here now and leave you to go back to drinkin' your coffee."

Crowder started to get up from his chair but thought better of it when the move caused Joel to swing his carbine up to grasp it with both hands, cocking it as he did.

"You're ridin' on rocky ground, mister," Crowder warned. "I'm gonna be keepin' my eye on you and all the rest of that bunch on that mountain."

"You do that, Sheriff. You might find out what's goin' on outside your little town."

He backed carefully to the door until he felt the doorknob. Then, never taking his eyes off Crowder, he opened the door and wasted no time climbing into the saddle. Backing the gray, while keeping his eye on the open door, he continued past the general store before wheeling his horse and galloping back to the north end of town. He halfway expected a rifle shot to ring out after him, but the sheriff was still too undecided to act.

When Joel got back to the ranch house, the men had already been fed and were gone, and the dishes were washed and put away. Only Ruthie was in the kitchen when he walked in.

"Elvira said you'd be getting back pretty soon," she said. "We saved a plate for you. It's warming in the oven. Sit down and I'll get it for you."

"I 'preciate it, Ruthie," he responded, then walked over to the coffeepot sitting on the corner of the stove, shook it back and forth to see if there was anything in it, and picked up a cup and filled it. "Where are the women?"

"Out behind the barn," Ruthie said. "Aunt Elvira is showing Blue Beads how to shoot that Henry your brother gave her." To confirm it, a shot rang out from that direction, followed after a long pause by another. Joel started at once, but Ruthie laughed and assured him that it was Blue Beads. "She wants to be sure she knows how to shoot the rifle if she has to, and she keeps wanting to put the cartridges down the barrel like she did with that musket."

The comment caused Joel to chuckle, as he pictured Elvira giving shooting lessons to the Shoshoni woman. "I'm surprised Elvira has the patience to teach anybody," he said. "But seems like she knows something about everything—more'n a lot of men." He went to work on the plate of food then.

"Riley said to tell you that he went with your brother to the mine, so you should go on over to the north side and help Red Shirt with the stock," Ruthie told him.

"Right," Joel replied. "I'll be leavin' as soon as I finish this fine supper you and the women fixed."

Ruthie blushed. "I didn't fix much of it. Aunt Elvira and Blue Beads did most of it."

"Well, it's mighty good," he said. "You all did a good job."

He watched the young girl as she poured herself a cup from the pot and sat down at the other end of the table. He hadn't allowed himself much time to think about the child's welfare, so he thought to ask how she was doing. She never mentioned her late family, at least not around him, but he knew that she had taken to Elvira, and he supposed the gregarious woman was taking care of the girl's needs.

"You and Elvira ever talk about what you wanna do," he asked, "I mean, whether you're gonna try to make it on out to Oregon in the summer?"

"Sometimes we talk about different things we might

be able to do," she replied, then paused to make a face after she took a sip of the coffee. "Ugh," she grunted. "This coffee is strong enough to take the hair off a porcupine." He laughed. No doubt her words came directly from Elvira. She continued. "I think Aunt Elvira would just as soon stay right here with you and Riley and Blue Beads, but I'm not sure that's what everybody wants."

He took a long sip of the strong coffee. The girl was right, it did have a helluva bite. While he sipped, he thought about the commitment he was about to make. *Hell, it's the right thing to do,* he thought, and proceeded.

"Well, let me tell you this, young lady. You and Elvira are welcome to stay with me for as long as you want—for the rest of your life if you want."

Her face broke out with a wide smile. "I know that's what Aunt Elvira wants."

"What about you?"

"Me, too," she said with a delighted giggle. On an impulse then, she jumped up and scurried over to give him a huge hug. "We're like your family, then," she said.

"I reckon so," he admitted. When he had time alone to think about it, he would almost become choked up when recalling the young girl's delight. He wasn't sure what Boone and Riley might think of his generous offer to take on the woman and girl. Maybe he should have asked them first, but he figured they weren't likely to want to set the two of them off on their own.

"I guess I'd better get my horse and head out for the north side of the mountain before it gets any later. I wanna see Boone before I head up to the pasture. If I show up there after dark, Red Shirt might think I'm a rustler and shoot me."

* * *

Boone took another look at the clouds that were almost sitting on the tops of the mountains. They looked even more like snow clouds, and he felt sure they couldn't hold their heavy load for much longer. The afternoon light was already fading by the time he reached the mine. Having watched his brother's approach up the trail, Boone came out from the large boulder he and Riley had taken cover behind.

"How'd it go with the sheriff?" he asked when Joel rode up to them.

"Pretty much like you said it would," Joel answered. "I tried to get him to come out and take a look at that rustler we shot to see if he recognized him. He wasn't interested. In fact, he acted like he wanted to arrest me. Beauchamp told him we were rustlin' *his* cattle."

"I figured that would be the way of it," Boone said. "The son of a bitch has got the whole town by the testicles. Even folks like Toby Bryan and Jake Tully believe what he tells 'em. They know better, but they're too damn scared of him not to believe him. That goes for the bank, the hotel, and Marvin Thompson, who owns the general store." He paused to look up at the sky when the first snowflakes suddenly began to fall softly on the brim of his hat. "Looks like we might get more than a couple of flurries outta this one," he said.

"Looks like it," Joel agreed. "I expect I'd best get on over to Red Shirt before we get enough snow to leave tracks." He looked at Riley then and joked, "How come you're teamin' up with Boone tonight? Wouldn't Red Shirt let you get a word in edgewise?" He grinned at Boone then and said what they all knew to be true. "Riley talks all the time, but he needs somebody to answer once in a while. Red Shirt doesn't do anything but shrug his shoulders. Ain't that right, Riley?"

"Huh," Riley grunted. "I just figured it wasn't fair to deprive Boone of some of the knowledge I've been collectin' all my life—things he ain't likely to learn from young fellers like you."

"I'm glad we came out from behind that rock," Boone said. "The horse shit's likely to get too deep to stand in if you two keep talkin'."

"All right," Joel said with a chuckle. "I'll get along over to my post. Red Shirt's probably gettin' lonely over there by himself."

He nudged the gray with a touch of his heels and was off, leaving them to take up their position behind the boulder again.

As he had speculated, a steady snowfall continued on into the night, causing Joel and Red Shirt to drape a large deer hide over the pine branches that served as their lookout post.

"I'd be surprised if we get any visitors tonight," Joel commented as the snow began to accumulate to form a blanket.

It was a dry snow and the horses and cattle were still content to graze in the meadow, showing no signs of seeking shelter in the stand of pine trees at the lower end of the meadow. Along about midnight, the snow stopped, leaving a blanket about four inches thick to cloak the mountainside. An hour later, they heard the first shots.

"Oh, hell!" Joel uttered, immediately alarmed because the initial shots soon became a volley, and he knew Riley and Boone were under attack from more than the usual two or three men.

"Many men," Red Shirt confirmed. It was apparent to them both that Beauchamp had decided on all-out war, and had sent his entire gang to seek vengeance for the killing of one of his men.

Frantic to come to the aid of Boone and Riley, Joel and Red Shirt scrambled out from under their deer-hide shelter and ran back up into the band of spruce trees where their horses were tied. Suddenly they were met by three simultaneous muzzle flashes that erupted in the darkness of the trees. Joel instinctively dived to the ground. Red Shirt was not so fortunate, as he was knocked off his feet by a shot that hit him high in his chest.

After the volley, the three men waiting in ambush ran out to confirm their kills, thinking they had hit both targets. The first two fell when Joel fired at almost point-blank range, and Red Shirt, straining from the pain of his wound, managed to get off a shot. The unexpected return fire was enough to cause the remaining assailant to try to run back to cover, but it also gave Joel time to eject the spent cartridge and put a round in the middle of the man's back.

Lying still in the snow-covered needles, Joel listened for signs of life from their attackers. The only sounds he could hear were the continuing reports of gunfire from the direction of the mine. When he felt certain the three were dead, he whispered to Red Shirt, "Are you shot?" He wasn't sure if his friend had been hit or not.

"I'm shot," Red Shirt replied, breathing hard. "I don't know how bad. Hurt like hell."

"Let me make damn sure they're dead. Then I'll see if I can help you," Joel said, and got to his feet.

When no shots came to greet him, he went quickly

to confirm the deaths. He found one already dead, and the other two evidently mortally wounded. One of them looked somehow familiar to him, and it occurred to him that it was the man he had left lying on the floor of the Silver Dollar Saloon. The nasty cut on the side of his face confirmed it. Seeing no reason not to, he quickly dispatched them to hell along with their partner in ambush.

Hurrying back to Red Shirt then, he tried to determine how badly he was hurt. It was hard to tell. The Bannock warrior was obviously in great pain, but there was some hope for him since the bullet had struck him high in the chest. Although he was breathing very hard, there was no sign of blood in his mouth, so Joel hoped that meant his lung had not been hit.

The question before him now was what to do about the apparent attack still going on at the mine. From the sound of the shooting, Boone and Riley were badly outnumbered. He had to help them, but he was reluctant to leave Red Shirt. Guessing as much, Red Shirt said, "Go to help brother."

"I can't leave you like this," Joel protested.

"I wait for you. You help brother." When Joel still hesitated, the warrior insisted. "I make it all right. Go."

Joel didn't hesitate further. "I've gotta go help them and the women," he said, "but I'll be back to get you."

He went back to their lookout post and got the deer hide they had used for shelter. Spreading it over the wounded Indian, he tucked it in about him to help keep him warm. As an added precaution, he scattered some snow over the hide. "I'll be back for you," he assured him once more. He hurried back up into the trees then, past the three bodies, to find his and Red Shirt's horses tied where they had left them. In a few seconds, he was on his way around the mountain, aware that he no longer heard any gunshots coming from the direction of the mine.

He was not halfway there when he realized the gunfire now seemed farther away, and in a horrible instant, he knew that what he was now hearing was the ranch house and the women under attack. His brain was spinning insanely as he pictured the scene at the house, and he kicked the gray frantically, demanding extra speed. Not sure of anything in his panic, he thought he could distinguish the sound of the Sharps carbine that Elvira now used.

I'm coming, he said to himself. *Hold on. I'm coming.*

When he reached the mine, there was no one in sight under the dark sky, so he charged straight up toward the boulder where he had last seen Boone and Riley. Seeing the bodies lying behind the rock, he jumped from the saddle, his weapon at the ready, but there was no one but the dead, a grim picture of the battle that had occurred there. Almost choking on a sob, he rolled his brother's body over. Like Riley's next to him, Boone's body was riddled with bullet holes, and also like Riley, he had been scalped.

Joel cried out in anguish too painful to contain. His brother was covered with blood, his cold, nonseeing eyes staring up at him. Lost for a moment in his grief, he was suddenly jerked back to the present by more gunshots ringing out at the house.

The women, he thought. Maybe it was not too late to save them. He had to caution himself to make sure there was no longer any threat at this position, so he took a few moments to search the trees just above the boulder where their horses had been tied. He found evidence of Boone's and Riley's fight to defend themselves in the form of two bodies lying near the tree line. That was as much time as he would spend before climbing on his horse and galloping over the snow-covered path to his brother's house.

When he approached the gap in the trees where the trail cut through to the house, he saw the smoke at the same time he became aware that he no longer heard the shooting. Moments later, he found himself flying through the air to land heavily on the ground, rolling over and over before he could stop. Thinking at first that he had been shot, he then realized that his horse had tumbled, throwing him from the saddle. Farther down the hill, he was relieved to see the gray getting to its feet and shaking off the snow. His next thought was to find his rifle, so he scrambled to his feet and looked quickly around him until he spotted it lying several yards above him in the snow. Not sure how many his enemies were, he picked up his carbine and hurried down the slope to his horse. Taking the tired horse's reins, he left the trail that cut through the gap and led the gray into the band of pines above the house.

His intention was to approach the house from behind, so as to have the opportunity to see where the raiders were before they saw him. By the time he reached the edge of the trees behind the barn, however, he could see flames from the house reaching far up into the cold night air, and he knew he was too late. It was a deep, sickening feeling that churned in his stomach. Leaving his horse there in the trees, he made his way down behind the barn and climbed through the rails of the empty corral. From the front corner post, he paused to look over the yard. There was no one in sight near the house or barn. They had done their evil business and gone—and he was too late.

He ran across the brightly lit yard, which was pock-marked with hundreds of hoofprints in the snow, evidence of the murdering mob of gunmen circling the house, shooting at the windows, terrorizing the three women left to defend it. Looking for an entry into the burning house, he found the kitchen door was the only way, so he plunged through the flames lapping at the doorjambs into the smoke-filled room. With little time to spare before the roof gave way, he moved frantically from room to room. He found them in the living room, each of the three shot more than a dozen times, their bodies lying side by side. Ruthie's body had been partially stripped of her clothes, and all three had been scalped. Unable to control it, he howled out his grief, to ring out over the sound of the crackling flames and the burning timbers, penetrating the uncaring night like the howl of a wolf.

He stood motionless, drowned in his despair, until his lungs began to choke in the smoke-filled room, and he thought again of Red Shirt lying helplessly waiting higher up on the mountain. His emotions turned from despair to rage as he pictured the wanton massacre of the women and the girl. In a hurry now to go to the aid of the wounded Indian, he plunged back through the burning door into the cold night air.

Beauchamp intended to disguise his murderous attack as an Indian raid. The scalping was testimony to that, but the three men he and Red Shirt had killed, and the two killed by Boone and Riley, were not Indians, so there was no doubt in his mind where to place the blame. How, he wondered, was Beauchamp going to explain the five dead men who were members of his ranch crew? Five bodies were all Joel could account for. There might have been more of his men killed. It was unlikely that Elvira had not fought like the she-lion he had come to know.

The thought of the tough, fearless woman caused him to grimace as he recalled his last image of her, lying beside the mutilated body of the young girl. He thought that he would never be able to forgive himself for not being there to protect them, no matter how many ways he tried to justify the circumstances. Neither he nor Boone nor Riley had anticipated the depth of evil Beauchamp was capable of, thinking he would not target the women. Shaking his head in an effort to dispel the image of the slaughtered women and the girl, he reminded himself that Red Shirt waited helplessly for his return.

Nothing more I can do for the dead, he thought. *I've got to tend to the living.* He headed back across the barnyard to the trees where he had left his horse.

Mike Strong led the remaining members of his raiding party along the trail that curved back around the mountain to the entrance of Boone McAllister's mine. They had done the job they had set out to do, but at a cost in lives he had not anticipated. Two of his men were killed in the attack on McAllister and the man with him at the mine. And Jim Corbett's body was riding across his saddle, as he'd been shot by one of the women at the house.

Strong was on his way now to retrieve the two bodies at the mine with only six of his original crew riding behind him. Of considerable concern to him now was the fate of the three men he had sent to kill anyone they found guarding the stock in the north meadow. He had heard shots from that part of the mountain, but his three men had not caught up with him yet. He considered the possibility that they had ridden to the mine and were waiting for him there.

Maybe I should have sent a couple more of the men with them, he thought. He was anxious to get off McAllister's property, but he knew there could be none of Boss Beauchamp's men left anywhere on that mountain, since it was designed to look like an Indian attack.

When the outlaws rode up to the boulder above the mine entrance, there was no one there, only the two bodies he had left there before.

"Damn!" Strong spat. "Where the hell is Hadley and the other two?" Not expecting an answer, he issued his orders. "Fetch those two horses." He pointed toward the trees where they had left them. "And load their bodies. We're wastin' too much time. I wanna get the hell off this mountain."

They hustled to obey his orders. There was nothing left to do now but ride over to the meadow to see what had happened to the missing three men, so they started out again, their dead lying across their saddles, following behind them.

After climbing straight up the south side of the mountain, Joel crossed over the top, leading his horse down the steep slope toward the stand of trees above the stock pasture. Halfway through the trees, he came to a sudden stop. Below him, he saw the raiders who had brought this murderous hell down upon his brother and his friends. His initial reaction was to attack, but he managed to hold his temper in check while he attempted to think before acting recklessly.

Where is Red Shirt? Beauchamp's men were loading the three men he and the Bannock warrior had killed onto their horses, but there was no sign of the Indian.

He tied his horse to a tree limb and moved carefully down to a position behind a stunted pine near the edge of the meadow where he could see more clearly. So far, no one seemed to take notice of his movements, busy as they were in loading the three bodies of their companions onto their horses. Joel cocked his rifle and brought his sights to bear on the man directing the actions of the others, but he hesitated to pull the trigger while his eyes followed the slope up into the trees where he had carried his wounded partner. It struck him then that the party of raiders had taken no notice of the figure lying motionless under the snow-covered deer hide just inside the tree line. Dead or alive? There was no way he could tell.

The burning desire to open fire on the murdering rabble was almost overpowering, but he could not risk exposing his wounded friend. For if he opened fire, the natural instinct of the outlaws would be to scurry for cover in the trees, and that would lead them right to Red Shirt. Aching to retaliate for the evil they had inflicted upon his brother and his adopted family, Joel watched helplessly as the raiders loaded the bodies and prepared to ride. All he could do was keep his rifle aimed at the leader of the pack, waiting in case one of the men discovered the Bannock warrior lying no more than sixty feet from where they were working.

It seemed an eternity to the man with the carbine aimed and cocked, but in reality, it was only a matter of minutes before the bodies of the would-be assassins were loaded on the horses and the intruders were in the saddle. Finally they turned and rode back down the mountain. Joel got up from his position on the ground and stood watching them until they disappeared in the trees below the meadow.

It struck him hard then, the magnitude of the evil that had changed his life so suddenly, and so drastically. Nothing experienced in the savage battles he had survived in the war just ended could match the wanton and senseless murders of these innocent people. He was not conscious of thinking it, but his life was changed from that moment forward. Lost from his world were all traces of joy and celebration, to be replaced by one relentless crusade to exact the vengeance demanded by the innocent dead.

Finally he brought his tormented mind back to the business at hand and went back for his horse, then hurried down through the trees to the tangle of bushes where he had left Red Shirt. Even though he had carried the Bannock there himself, still he had to look twice before he spotted the deer hide. There was nothing to indicate a living being under the snow-covered hide, no movement, and no signs that there had been. It appeared that once again he was too late in returning. He started to pull the hide aside to make certain, but something cautioned him to be careful.

"Red Shirt," he said, "it's me, Joel." Then he reached down and pulled the hide back to be confronted with the muzzle of a Sharps carbine aimed at his chest.

"Joel," Red Shirt said with obvious effort. "I wait. I know you come."

It was with a great feeling of relief when Joel found his friend still among the living. His one thought now was to get the wounded warrior someplace where he could find help. There was a doctor in Silver City, but Joel felt it was a risk to take him there. Based upon the reception he had received from the sheriff, and the general feeling that Beauchamp owned the whole town, it didn't seem like a safe place for him or Red

Shirt. The second option was to try to tend to Red Shirt's wound himself. He had seen many men in the war with bullet wounds, but he was not confident in his skills as a doctor.

Thinking he had little choice, he said, "I reckon I can try to see if I can dig that bullet outta you." Red Shirt nodded his understanding. "First, I think I'd better move you to a better place where I can build a fire to keep you from freezin' to death before I get it out. Are you up to bein' moved?" Again, Red Shirt nodded. "All right," Joel said. "I'll try to be as easy as I can on you."

He left his patient for a little longer while he moved up the slope, looking for a better place. About thirty-five yards higher up in the band of trees that extended halfway around the mountain, he found a tiny clearing that would be suitable. Shelter with room for a fire was important, but he also was wary of the possible return of the raiders, even though it had seemed apparent to him that they were in a hurry to retreat from the mountain.

It was with a great deal of effort that Joel managed to carry Red Shirt up to the campsite he had selected. Although the Indian made few sounds of suffering, Joel could see the pain he was feeling by the determined grimace in his expression. If he could have, he would have used his horse to carry the injured man up the slope, but it would have been difficult to lead the horse through the thick forest without Red Shirt getting bumped off on the ground. Joel was strong, but Red Shirt was a sizable man, so it would have taken no small measure of strength to lift him up onto the horse anyway. So once he got him up piggyback, he decided to forget the horse, and just climb on up the slope with him.

When finally he had made Red Shirt as comfortable as he could, and had a fire built, he set about taking care of the wound. Upon close examination, he was dismayed to find it an ugly wound where the bullet had entered his chest. It looked as though the angle of the shot sent the slug deep in the muscle of his shoulder, where it was not readily seen. With total trust in his doctor, Red Shirt made no protests of pain—in fact, no sound at all—as Joel probed deeper and deeper with his knife. At last, he felt the tick of the knife point against the rifle slug, which led to a lengthy, torturous procedure of loosening the bullet until it was finally free enough to be extracted. Only then did the tormented warrior comment.

"Gott damn," he muttered when Joel held the slug up for him to see.

"I'm afraid I made a mess of that wound," Joel told him. "I'll try to clean it up as best I can."

In the absence of a stream nearby, it was necessary to melt snow in a coffee cup for water to clean the wound. He took a close look at his patient then and decided that he didn't look too well. He needed a better place to recover. Joel couldn't think of a place where that might be, but he also knew they couldn't stay there. It was not a suitable campsite for any lengthy stay, and they needed to be close to a stream. To add to their problems, they had only one horse. Beauchamp's men had evidently driven the stock down the mountain when they left, for there wasn't one horse in the meadow.

The raiders had gone for now. That much was true, but Joel also knew they would be sent back when

Beauchamp found out that he and Red Shirt had some-how escaped the massacre. It was his assumption that they would most likely return before daylight in an attempt to silence the only two witnesses to the cow-ardly attack. With that in mind, he told Red Shirt what he was going to do.

"We can't stay here. We've got to find a place to give you a chance to recover, somewhere I can defend if they come after us. So I'm afraid you're gonna be in for a rough ride, but I've got to put you on my horse. I don't see hide nor hair of your horse. I reckon they musta drove him off with the rest of our horses."

"You right," Red Shirt replied painfully. "Can't stay here."

Chapter 10

Following the trail left in the snow by the raiders, his mind numb from the sudden catastrophic night of terror, Joel led the gray, with Red Shirt slumped over the horse's neck. Down through the random patches of spruce and pine, toward the valley below, he walked carefully through the outcroppings of jagged rocks, now covered with a cloak of snow.

He thought about the bodies of his brother and Riley, lying, unburied, on the cold open ground, exposed to the elements and discovery by scavengers of the wild. It agonized him to think of leaving them, and he knew he would probably blame himself forever for not being able to help them. But he promised himself that he would avenge their deaths, no matter how long it took him. Running away now was not what he wanted to do, but he knew that he had no choice if he stood a chance of taking every life that had a hand in this senseless bloodbath.

Common sense told him that he could not defend

Red Shirt and himself against another attack by Beauchamp's hired assassins, given the present circumstances. There was a very good chance that they might
come back to look for Red Shirt and him. He knew, in
that event, he would account for two or three of the
assassins before they gunned him down. And that was
not good enough. His promise to Boone and the others
was to make each participant pay.

His mind was so absorbed in his feelings of regret
that he was suddenly startled by a snort and a whinny
close behind him. Clutching his rifle, he whirled
around to discover Red Shirt's bay pony following
along behind his horse.

"Thank you, Lord," he muttered in appreciation.

Somehow the Bannock's horse had managed to
avoid Beauchamp's men when they were rounding up
the rest of the stock. Joel immediately stopped and
went back to take the reins of the bay. His intention was
to climb aboard the horse and lead the gray, but the bay
was having none of it. Each time Joel tried to get his
foot in the stirrup, the horse would sidestep away.

After a few unsuccessful attempts to mount the cantankerous horse, it jerked its head away, causing Joel to
lose his hold on the reins. Fighting an urge to shoot the
stubborn horse, Joel stood exasperated while he and
the horse gazed at each other from a distance of several yards. Then an idea occurred to him. It was not
likely, and would mean a hell of a lot of trouble, but
Joel was desperate to try anything at this point.

"You're gonna have to bear with me, Red Shirt," he
said. "I'm gonna pull you onto my shoulder. Then I'm
gonna try to put you on your horse. I know it'll hurt
like hell, but it might be the only way we're ever gonna

get started again." Red Shirt made no response beyond a painful grunt.

The strange actions of the man must have fascinated the stubborn bay horse. It fixed a suspicious eye on him, but made no move to bolt when Joel staggered toward it with Red Shirt on his shoulder. The bay took a couple of steps to the side as Joel approached, but settled down and snorted a couple of times, possibly recognizing Red Shirt's scent. It held steady then while the Indian managed to get a leg over and settle down in the saddle.

With a long sigh of relief, Joel stepped back and asked, "Are you all right?"

"All right," he said. "Horse don't like nobody but Red Shirt."

"Reckon not," Joel said.

Then, back in the saddle on his gray, he took Red Shirt's reins and led him down through the rocks. When they reached the valley floor, the trail the raiders had taken pointed toward Blackjack Mountain, as Joel anticipated.

He turned north, following the watercourse the white men called Reynolds Creek. His intention was to follow the shallow stream along the valley to put as much distance as possible between them and Blackjack Mountain before daylight. The rugged terrain offered little in the way of a safe camp site, with high, rocky bluffs on either side of the narrow valley. But he knew he could not continue to ride much longer without giving Red Shirt a rest. With no food other than some deer jerky wrapped in a cloth in his saddlebag, he began to worry about finding some kind of game to kill.

Walking the horses up the middle of the creek, scanning the sides for a campsite, he happened to look back in time to see Red Shirt leaning to one side, precariously close to dropping from the saddle.

Well, I guess this is where we camp, Joel thought, and quickly pulled his horse around to catch Red Shirt by the shoulder and straighten him up in the saddle. He looked quickly from side to side then before selecting a gully framed by berry bushes.

"Hang on tight for just a few minutes," he told Red Shirt, "and we'll ride up to the back of that gully and make camp."

After getting Red Shirt off the horse, he spread the deer hide they had used for a shelter and let him sit on it while he cleared the snow from a small area of the gully. Once the Indian was settled on the hide, he left him to unsaddle the horses, in order to use the saddle blankets and the saddles to make a bed.

"It ain't as good as the bedrolls we had back at the house, but I reckon it's the best we've got, so it'll have to do. And I think I can find enough branches from these bushes to make us a little fire."

He checked his pockets then to make sure he still had his flint and steel, and gave a silent word of thanks when he found them.

Once he got Red Shirt as comfortable as he could under the circumstances, with a warm fire burning, he tried to get him to eat some of the jerky from his saddlebag, but Red Shirt did not feel like eating, so Joel let him rest. Tired himself, after the night just past, Joel determined he had better stay awake while his Indian partner slept. When the morning sun finally reached a height that permitted it to send its warming rays down into the narrow valley, however, it found both men sleeping.

Something nudged his brain in its sleep, causing him to reluctantly return to consciousness. With a flicker of his weary eyelids, he opened his eyes to find himself gazing into a round black eye that he realized too late was the muzzle of a rifle.

Although startled, he remained still as his gaze dropped to focus on a pair of Indian moccasins. He raised his eyes again to see the deerskin leggings and shirt of a young Indian man as he stared down at him in curious wonder. Showing no aggression in his tone, the young man spoke, asking a question in his native tongue as he gestured toward Red Shirt, who was now also awake. The question was directed at Joel, but Red Shirt answered in the same dialect. The Indian nodded in understanding.

"What did he say?" Joel asked softly, lest the Indian take offense.

Red Shirt grimaced in pain when he spoke. "He is Shoshoni. He ask if you did this to me. I tell him no. You are my friend—try to help me. I tell him bad men shoot me. I am *Agai-deka* Bannock, friend of Shoshoni."

The young Shoshoni spoke again, and Red Shirt translated. "He say his name is Cold Wind. He take us to village. They help me there."

"Tell him we are grateful for his help," Joel said, still feeling more than a little perturbed at himself for having been caught sleeping.

If not for just plain stupid luck, he and Red Shirt would both be dead. He could blame it on the past few nights of little sleep, because of the necessity to stand guard against Beauchamp's men, and the night just passed with no sleep at all except these one or two hours just before dawn. But he knew he could not be so careless again and expect to live to tell about it.

He got to his feet then while Red Shirt explained to Cold Wind the circumstances that had brought them to this makeshift camp. The Shoshoni warrior nodded his understanding frequently, occasionally turning to look at Joel, and nodding again.

"I'll saddle the horses," Joel said. "Did he say how far his village is?"

"Beyond bend in creek," Red Shirt replied, now supporting himself on one elbow. He pointed to the bend some one hundred yards ahead. "Then through pass. Not far."

Joel saddled the horses while the two Indians continued to talk. When he was ready, he helped Red Shirt get on his feet. The Bannock warrior tried to hide his pain, but it was obvious that his wound was serious. Their Good Samaritan helped support him, and between the two of them, they got Red Shirt in the saddle again.

Cold Wind jumped on the back of the paint pony he had left standing beside the other two horses, made a motion with his hand for Joel to follow, and then led them down the wide stream toward the bend.

The Shoshoni warrior led them through a narrow pass between two mountains that took them to another mountain. This mountain, however, was in sharp contrast to those Joel and Red Shirt had seen while following Reynolds Creek the night before. More like the hills that surrounded Silver City, it was sparingly covered with stunted pine trees and broad meadows.

Following a trail around to the north side of the mountain, they came upon a village of sixty tipis beside a busy stream that came down from the peak above. Joel was amazed. It was like the little valley and the stream had been placed by a giant hand among the more inhospitable peaks around it. A sizable herd of horses grazed in the snow-covered grassy meadow on the other side of the stream.

The trio of riders was spotted by some children playing near the edge of the stream, and upon seeing the two strangers riding behind Cold Wind, the kids ran to alert the village. Soon a small crowd of children and adults gathered to meet the visitors, only realizing that one of them was hurt after they had ridden into the center of the village.

Sliding deftly from his pony, Cold Wind sent one of the young boys to get the medicine man. Joel dismounted and went at once to help Red Shirt off his horse. Half a dozen willing hands were immediately around him to help. They walked him over beside a large campfire in the middle of the village, and lowered him gently down upon the deer hide that Joel spread there.

When Red Shirt was settled, Joel stepped back and looked about him at the people pressing close around him. *Like wolves crowding around a buffalo calf,* he couldn't help thinking. But he could sense a feeling of open curiosity, not one of hostility. *A good thing,* he thought, *because I ain't in much of a position to do anything about it, if they decide to turn hostile.*

The crowd behind him parted then to permit an elderly man through. Joel knew at once that he was either the chief or the medicine man. He was surprised when the distinguished-looking man spoke to him in English, better even than Red Shirt's rudimentary attempts.

"Welcome," he said, after looking at the wounded man on the deer hide. "My name is Walking Eagle.

Your friend looks badly hurt. Crooked Arrow will look at his wound."

"Thank you," Joel said "I appreciate your help, and I know Red Shirt does."

The chief looked at him and smiled, nodding slowly. Then he looked more closely at Red Shirt's wound and spoke to him in the Shoshoni language. When Crooked Arrow, the medicine man, parted the spectators again, he examined the wound carefully. Afterward, he told four of the young men to carry Red Shirt to his tipi, leaving Joel to stand undecided as to what he should do. The feeling lasted for only a few seconds before Walking Eagle took charge of his guest.

"Come," he said to Joel. "You must be hungry. Cold Wind said that he found you while you slept, so you must need food."

"Yes, sir," Joel replied. "I surely would appreciate some breakfast. Red Shirt and I lost about all the supplies we had after we were attacked. At least we had our weapons and cartridges with us. I didn't have much choice but to get him outta there after he got shot. Figured I'd hunt for something to feed us this mornin'."

"Your friend's wound looks bad. Crooked Arrow will tend to it," Walking Eagle said as he led him to a large tipi in the center of the circle of lodges. Two women walked along behind them, and when they reached the tipi, Walking Eagle gave them instructions that sent them hurrying to comply.

Inside the tipi, a small fire in the center of the lodge sent a thin column of smoke up to escape through a smoke hole at the top. Joel looked around him at the snug structure of buffalo hides, and the perimeter of the wide floor where a series of large hide bags were packed with the belongings of the chief and his family. He had never been inside a tipi before. The thing that caught Joel's eye, however, was a small coffeepot at the edge of the fire. He felt he would kill for a cup of coffee on this of all mornings, and he had been convinced that he would never get one in an Indian village.

"Come, sit," Walking Eagle said, motioning toward some blankets at the rear of the tipi. "While my women fix you some food, we can talk about these men who killed your people." He paused then to ask, "What are you called?"

"My name's Joel McAllister and I can tell you right off that I'm mighty glad you speak American so well, because I don't know your tongue at all."

Walking Eagle smiled and repeated the name. "I was a boy when the Hudson Bay Company built a fort near the place where the Snake and the Boise rivers meet. My father was a scout for them. I learned your language then. The Hudson Bay Company left the fort many years ago, but the army opened a new fort near there and called it Fort Boise. It was to protect your white settlers passing through these mountains on their way to the Oregon country. There are soldiers there still, and they are at peace with the Shoshoni, and Colonel Wilcox there is my friend."

He paused to give an order in his tongue to one of the women when she came into the tipi to get something from a parfleche near the back wall. She nodded vigorously and reached down to pick up the coffeepot. She must have read the look on Joel's face, for she smiled at him before disappearing again through the flap of the tipi. He figured the women were cooking his breakfast on the big fire outside.

"These men who attacked you," Walking Eagle said, getting back to the conversation he was most interested in, "how many were they?"

"I can't rightly say, because I never got a chance to see them all together." He went on to explain how he and his people split up to defend three different positions. "Red Shirt and I killed the three men who jumped us at the meadow, and we could hear the gunshots comin' from the mine and the house, so we knew there were more than a couple more. By the time I was able to get to the rest of my people, everybody had been killed. When I went back to get Red Shirt, I counted six men pickin' up the three we shot. But I couldn't see how many were drivin' our horses and cows off."

Walking Eagle thought about it for a few moments before commenting again. "You say these were white men, but they scalped the victims?"

"That they did," Joel answered. "They pretty much wanted it to look like Indians did it. I figure that's why they scalped 'em, and that's why they were so set on not leavin' any of their dead behind."

"I think you're right," Walking Eagle said. "It calls to mind a raid on a small family that had a claim on War Eagle Mountain. It was a little over a year ago. Everyone in the family was scalped, so they thought it was the work of a war party. Soldiers from Fort Boise went to Silver City to look for the Indians, but there was no sign of them anywhere. The white people in Silver City were sure it was a war party. Some said a Blackfoot party slipped into those hills that night. Some said it was Utes. Some said that maybe it was a war party from my village. But Colonel Wilcox knew better. We do not make war on the whites. It was the spring of the year, and we had already left this valley to hunt buffalo. The soldiers know that we have been wintering here in this valley, where the cold winter winds are not so fierce, for many years. I hope that the soldiers don't come to my village to see if my warriors raided your camp."

"If they do, you can say there are two witnesses who can tell them the killers were white men, and I know who they are," Joel said. His comment seemed to reassure the chief.

Talk was interrupted then when one of the women, the older one, entered the tipi carrying a plate of roasted venison.

"Food," she said in English, and smiled when she placed it before Joel.

"This is my wife, Yellow Moon," Walking Eagle said.

"Ma'am," Joel said with a nod.

"Please, eat," Walking Eagle encouraged.

In a moment more, the younger woman entered, holding the coffeepot and a metal cup. She smiled shyly at Joel as she raked a little pile of coals from the fire, arranging them in a circle. Then she filled the cup with coffee, placed it before Joel, and set the pot in the little circle of coals.

"My daughter, White Fawn," Walking Eagle said proudly.

Joel had suspected as much. He smiled at her and nodded politely. Eager to taste the coffee, he reached down for the cup, releasing it instantly when it proved to be too hot to pick up. His sudden reaction caused White Fawn to giggle delightedly.

"Burn," she commented, then handed him a cloth she had used to hold the handle of the pot. "Wait," she advised.

"Wait," he repeated, feeling like an idiot for not thinking before picking up a metal cup of hot coffee.

He went to work on the plate of venison then while Walking Eagle and his daughter looked on approvingly. He hadn't realized how really hungry he was until he attacked his food. By the time his coffee was cool enough to drink, he had only a few small chunks of meat left. He could have finished those as well, but he had been told that if a guest finished everything on the plate, his host assumed that he had not been satisfied and wanted more. Joel knew he could not put away another plate of food, so he put it down and patted his stomach to indicate it was full.

"Thank you," he said, and finished his coffee, whereupon White Fawn immediately refilled it.

"I learned how much the white man loves coffee when I was at Fort Boise," Walking Eagle said. "I like it, too. I get the beans at the fort. There is a trading post there."

"Well, I appreciate it," Joel assured him. "I doubt there's a white man alive who loves coffee more'n I do."

Looking very pleased, White Fawn smiled at him, then carried his plate out of the tipi. When she had gone, he thanked Walking Eagle once more for the food and said, "I'd like to go see how Red Shirt is gettin' along now."

"I'll take you to him," Walking Eagle said, and got to his feet.

Joel followed him out of the tipi and walked beside him toward Crooked Arrow's lodge. There was still a small gathering of curious spectators outside, waiting to get a look at the white man who brought the wounded Bannock to their camp. They parted to make a path for the chief and Joel. As they walked past the large fire in the center of the circle, Joel saw Yellow Moon and White Fawn standing beside it. Yellow Moon nodded solemnly while her daughter smiled at him, then shyly looked away.

They found Red Shirt asleep on a woven mat by the fire in Crooked Arrow's tipi. The medicine man explained that he had placed a poultice on Red Shirt's wound that would draw some of the poison out of it, and given him some broth made of special herbs that let him sleep. With Walking Eagle acting as translator, Joel was told that Red Shirt's wound was very serious, and that he might die if the poison was not removed.

"It is very deep," Crooked Arrow went on to tell Walking Eagle. "The herbs will bring the swelling down. It is good that you got the bullet out, but I think he will be weak for a long time before he can be on his feet. The flesh is very angry and must be given time to drive the poison out."

The diagnosis was worse than Joel had hoped for, and he wondered if he should have taken Red Shirt on to Fort Boise to find a doctor. If he had done so, he wondered now whether his friend would have survived the trip. Walking Eagle must have read his thoughts, for he told him that Crooked Arrow was a wise man, and that he had healed the battle wounds of his warriors for many years.

"It would be best to leave Red Shirt here where my people can take care of him. You are welcome to stay with us for as long as you want. Then you can see how he is healing."

"I can't stay here," Joel said. "I've got something I have to do."

As he said it, a picture of Elvira, Ruthie, and Blue Beads came to his mind as he had last seen them—scalped, their bullet-riddled bodies covered in blood. The image caused a feeling of sickness in his stomach, and each day that passed would make it worse. He knew that he could not turn back the tide of revenge that threatened to drown him until he rid the earth of such evil.

It was not difficult for Walking Eagle to guess what was eating away at the young man's soul. He was a warrior. He understood the fury that made Joel's heart pound.

"You must do what your heart tells you to do," he said. "I wish you success against your enemies. We will take care of your friend, and welcome your return."

"Thank you," Joel said. "There are a few things I need to get before I return to Silver City. Is there a trading post near your village?"

He wanted to buy extra cartridges as well as the basic utensils he would need to survive and had lost in the raid. He was fortunate that he still had money from the weapons and things he and Riley had sold on their way out to Silver City. That, his horse and saddle, and his weapons were all that he had. Anything he had planned to accumulate in the future was to have come from his and Boone's efforts. His plans to raise cattle and horses were the most difficult to give up, but until his blood quest was done, there was only one thing that dominated his mind—total vengeance.

Walking Eagle told him there was a trading post on the Snake River, due east of the village, not too far, but because of the mountains in between, it was a much longer trip.

"The trail is easy to follow," he said. "You can see

where my people have gone that way. The man's name at the trading post is Beecher. He will treat you fairly."

"Much obliged," Joel said. "Since it's still early, I reckon I'll leave right now."

The chief walked with him to his horse, where they found Cold Wind waiting to ask if Red Shirt was going to be all right. With no way to tell him, Joel relied on Walking Eagle to give him the Bannock's status, whereupon Cold Wind nodded solemnly and smiled at Joel. Standing within earshot, Yellow Moon and her daughter heard the chief ask Cold Wind to show Joel the trail to the trading post. Since there were many trails heading out from the village, it was necessary to start on the right one. When Cold Wind went to get his horse, which he had tied beside his tipi, White Fawn ran back to her mother's tipi. Back within a few minutes, Cold Wind started to ride, but reined his horse back when he saw White Fawn running to catch them. Hurrying to reach Joel's horse, she held a cloth bundle up to him, a shy smile adorning her young face.

"Get hungry, need food," she said. Then stepped quickly away as soon as he took it from her.

Surprised, he nonetheless managed to mutter, "Thank you, ma'am," and watched her as she stepped back to stand beside her mother. "This'll come in handy," he added. Turning to Walking Eagle then, he said, "When Red Shirt wakes up, tell him I'll be back. It might be a while, but I'll be back."

Walking Eagle had been right, there were many trails that led back and forth from the Shoshoni village. Communicating with nothing more than hand signals, Cold Wind set him on the right trail as evidenced by the many hoofprints, both recent and old, that had all but beaten out the thin covering of snow. The Shoshoni warrior sat on his horse at the head of the trail and watched him until he disappeared around the foot of the mountain. Satisfied that Joel would stay on the right path, he returned to the village.

As he had been told, he found the trail to the trading post long with many turns before finding its way through the mountains that seemed crowded shoulder to shoulder with narrow valleys. These led him through juniper-covered slopes and sheer-walled canyons. Arriving at the trading post, he found a low, flat log structure, built right into the riverbank on one side, little more than a dugout. There was no other customer about as Joel rode the gray up to the hitching post and stepped down from the saddle. As a matter of habit, he pulled the Spencer carbine from his saddle scabbard and went in the door.

"Howdy," Horace Beecher greeted him from his rocking chair next to a round iron stove near the center of the store, which was a room with one short counter at one end and the walls on three sides lined with barrels and shelves and sacks of grain, flour, several kinds of beans, including coffee, and several big tin tubs of lard. "Don't recall seein' you before," Beecher said as he placed a pocketknife and a piece of pine he had been carving on the floor beside his chair and got to his feet. "Little doll," he said, explaining his carving. "I make 'em for the Injun young'ns that come in here."

"Howdy," Joel returned his greeting. "I need a few things."

"Well, I've got most of whatever anybody needs," Beecher replied.

"I need a fryin' pan," Joel started, then listed his

basic needs, ending up with a question. "You by any chance have a coffeepot?"

"Only one I've got is a little one," Beecher said, "but if you're fixin' to be stayin' around here for a while, I can get you a big one in the spring."

"Little one's fine. I don't need a big one—too hard to carry on a horse."

"I swear, mister, you were about out of everything, weren't you?"

"Pretty much," Joel replied. "What about cartridges?"

"Forty-fours?"

"No, fifty-fours." He held his carbine up.

"Ain't sold many of them lately," Beecher said. "But I got some—three boxes, as a matter of fact."

"I'll take all three," Joel said. He was planning to go to war, and he didn't want to run out of cartridges.

Looking at the assortment of supplies and ammunition, Beecher began to worry a little. The stranger was a fair-sized man, and he was holding the carbine as if it was a natural part of him. There had been no mention of money, paper or otherwise.

"That's a right big order," he said. "I hope you ain't plannin' on robbin' me."

His comment puzzled Joel. "Why would you think that?" he asked. "I was hopin' you don't try to rob me. You ain't told me the price for all this yet."

His response caused Beecher to chuckle in relief. "I didn't mean no offense. But your wearin' animal hides and all, I thought you were most likely a trapper, but I didn't see no packhorse totin' pelts to trade. And I've been held up before."

"Well, I'm sorry to disappoint you," Joel said, "but I was plannin' to pay for my goods, if they ain't too much. How much do I owe you?"

"Let me figure this up real quick," Beecher replied, more enthusiastic now to complete the transaction since it seemed that it wasn't a holdup. He immediately began to itemize Joel's purchases, jotting each one down on a scrap of paper with the stub of a pencil. Finally, after checking his figures a second time, he looked up and said, "I make it out to be sixty-three dollars. You know them cartridges ain't cheap." He stepped back from the counter a couple of steps to wait for Joel's reaction. When there was none to speak of, he asked, "How you figurin' on payin'?"

"Dust," Joel replied, reached under his shirttail to untie a small skin sack, and placed it on the counter. "There's a good bit more than sixty-three dollars' worth in that."

Grateful for the sizable order, and especially the method of payment, Beecher pulled his scale over from the end of the counter and said, "I'll round it off to an even sixty dollars just to show you I appreciate your business. I doubt if I'da ever sold that little ol' coffeepot to anybody."

"Much obliged," Joel said.

Beecher helped him carry his purchases out to load on his horse, and stood watching while Joel took a few minutes to figure out how best to balance them on the gray. "You need a packhorse," he observed aloud.

"I had one," Joel replied stoically, "but it's gone now."

Beecher continued to study the quiet young man for a few moments, wondering what might lie in his past to cause him to be so solemn.

"If you don't mind me askin', are you just pushin' on through to Oregon or California, or are you plannin' to stay around this part of the country for a while? None of my business, I was just wonderin'."

Joel paused to look at him for a moment before answering. "I don't know. I ain't goin' to California and that's a fact, but I ain't hangin' around here, either." It wasn't true that he didn't know. But he didn't consider telling Beecher that he intended to return to Silver City to kill a dozen men, or however many there were, and the man who had hired them. "I might show up here again. I've got a friend over in that Shoshoni village."

"Ol' Walkin' Eagle?" Beecher responded. "Well, come on back when you need something. Glad to do business with you, especially dealin' in gold dust."

Joel nodded in reply. His possibles all packed on his horse as best he could manage, he climbed into the saddle and turned the gray back toward the mountains. Beecher stood watching him for as long as he was in sight.

He sure wasn't much of a talker, he thought. *A loner like that in this country, he's got a story behind him, I'll bet. I wonder how he came by that sack of gold dust, because he wasn't carrying any mining tools. Not even a pan.*

Chapter II

"Hell, Mr. Beauchamp, I wouldn't worry none about McAllister's brother and that Injun. The way I figure it, I expect they're still hightailin' it as far away from Silver City as they can get. It's been five days since that little party up on the mountain. If they were gonna do anything about it, they woulda done it by now. I figure Sartain and the two boys with him musta got a couple of shots in 'em in that little set-to at that meadow before they got killed. Them two might be dead by now. I wouldn't be surprised if we don't run across their bodies back in the hills one day."

Beauchamp cast a cold eye on his foreman. Strong might be right. Maybe Joel McAllister and the Indian were wounded in the confrontation with Sartain and the two with him. Maybe they were long gone from Silver City, or even dead, but Beauchamp didn't like to deal with "maybes." The raid on McAllister's claim had not gone according to plan, not only with the two who got away, but also with the cost in Beauchamp's men.

"Six men dead," he chastised Strong, "six men, and one of them shot by one of the females at the house. If you had pulled the raid off like you should have, you shouldn't have lost a single man."

Beauchamp was satisfied that the attack had resulted in getting rid of Boone McAllister and his bunch, but he was not pleased with the messy way Strong and the men had accomplished it. At least it had saved him six hundred dollars in bonus money he had promised to each man.

"They put up a bigger fight than I figured they would," Strong said, looking for an excuse for his failure. "They were ready and waitin', but we got 'em all, just like you ordered."

"Yeah," Beauchamp replied sarcastically, "except the brother and the Indian. And you set fire to the house. Why in hell did you burn the house down? I could have used that house."

"They shot Blanchard. All three of them women had guns, Sharps carbines. We brought 'em back with us—looked like they was pretty new, and plenty of cartridges to go with 'em. They weren't hittin' nothin', but one of 'em got Blanchard when he rode right up next to the house. The three of 'em couldn't watch all four sides of the house, and Slow Sam slipped in a window then on the side they weren't watchin'. He got two of 'em with his knife and shot the other'n. I reckon it was the Injun in him that made him kick the stove over and set the place on fire. It went up pretty fast. By the time we finished scalping the women, it was blazin' pretty good, so there wasn't nothin' to do but get the hell outta there."

"Who's up there watching the place now?" Beauchamp asked.

"Slow Sam, Pete Gentry, and Billy Garland," Strong said.

Beauchamp snorted his impatience. "Well, maybe Gentry's got enough sense to talk to anybody who comes snooping around up there. Sam and Billy haven't got the sense of a billy goat. Gentry knows what to tell them?"

"Yes, sir. He knows to tell anybody askin' questions about the place that it's already been filed on, and they're watchin' it for the new owner."

Beauchamp nodded thoughtfully. As long as no one from the territorial government came in to question the legality of his claim, there shouldn't be any trouble from anyone in Silver City. As far as the merchants in town would know, Ronald Beauchamp was gracious enough to volunteer his men to look after McAllister's claim until it was determined there was no heir or family to claim ownership.

Jim Crowder, in his capacity as sheriff, had ridden out to the mountain to take a look at the results of the massacre. It didn't take much to convince him that it was the work of a maverick band of hostile Indians. Beauchamp had assured him that there was no further danger from the Indians since they were no doubt long gone, and if the army was contacted, they would surely come to the same conclusion. He reminded him that his responsibility was the town and not what took place in the mountains around it.

"Don't concern yourself with the folks that the Indians killed," Beauchamp had told Crowder. "I'll have my men bury the bodies of poor Boone McAllister's family."

The whole affair could have come off better, but Beauchamp felt confident that the results were what counted, and he could enjoy the satisfaction of having destroyed Boone McAllister.

I'll sit tight for a couple more days before I take over the mine, he thought. In the meantime, Mike Strong's boys could guard the place and discourage any of the many prospectors that had flocked to Silver City after the first real strikes. It was doubtful any of them knew McAllister was pulling top-grade ore out of that mountain.

"To hell with this. I'm freezin' my ass off," Pete Gentry complained. "I'm goin' back down there to that barn. If we gotta stay up here on this damn mountain, we might as well go someplace where we can build us a fire to keep warm."

Mike Strong had told the three of them that Beauchamp wanted them to watch the mine, but there was nothing handy there to build a fire with—at least nothing smaller than the heavy timbers framing the entrance. There was a good-sized space inside the mine, where they could have found some relief from the wind, but there was no way to reach it since Strong and a couple of the men had dynamited the entrance.

"That suits me," Billy Garland said. "At least we can get outta the wind inside the barn. And we can just take turns ridin' back up here to check on the mine."

"You two talk like women," the half-breed, Slow Sam, scoffed. "This ain't cold. Wait till winter really sets in."

"Well, good," Gentry came back, "since you don't mind the cold, you can stay up here, and me and Billy will go down to the barn."

"Ha," Slow Sam spat, "I think we'll take turns settin' on this damn mine. I ain't gonna stay here all the time while you two are takin' it easy by the fire."

"All right, then," Gentry said, "that's what we'll do. You take it first, and me or Billy'll spell you."

"Too bad we burned the house down, ain't it?" Billy laughed. "We coulda set us a pot of coffee on the stove."

"Yeah, if ol' Slow Sam there hadn't kicked it over," Gentry said.

"Go to hell," Sam retorted.

"Most likely will," Gentry replied with a chuckle. "Come on, Billy, let's go to the barn."

They left Sam sitting on a pile of dirt, cross-legged, Indian-style, both men knowing the half-breed was doing it for show, and would hurry over to the entrance of the mine to get out of the wind as soon as they were out of sight.

Joel McAllister stood amid the burned timbers of what had once been his brother's house, his mind sickened by the charred remains of the three bodies and the hell they must have suffered before death came to take them.

I can at least bury what's left of them, he thought. *What manner of man could do this to a woman?*

He made his way back out of the destroyed cabin and led his horse down to the barn to look for a shovel. He found one right where he expected to in the back corner with several other tools. The tools were all that was left since the raiders had taken the supplies he had piled there, including weapons and ammunition that he had acquired. There was a pick left there, so he took it and the shovel and started for the door.

Just about to step outside, he stopped at the door when he thought he heard something in the distance. He dropped the tools he was carrying, grabbed the gray's reins, and led it inside the barn, then ran back to the door to see if he had really heard someone. Coming through the gap in the trees, on the trail from the mine, two riders were approaching while carrying on a loud conversation. It was too late to get out of the barn without being seen. There were two windows, but no door.

Damn it, Boone, why didn't you put a back door on your barn?

He put the horse in one of the two stalls in the back, pulled his carbine from the saddle sling, and looked around for a place to take cover. There wasn't much available. The best he could do was to kneel behind the wall of the stall across from the one his horse now occupied. Getting as much of his body as possible behind the stall doorpost, he waited.

In a matter of minutes, the two riders pulled up before the open barn door, the one rider still jawing away.

"It woulda been nice if ol' Slow Sam hadn't burned the house down," Billy went on. "We coulda watched this place in style, sat around drinkin' coffee while Slow Sam freezes his ass off up at the mine." His mind wandered to other things then as he continued to talk. "You know, I'da liked it a helluva lot better if somebody had got to that young gal before that damn breed messed her up. I'da liked to had a go-round with that little filly. She looked pretty damn good even after Sam sliced her up."

"Did you know she wasn't but thirteen years old?"

Startled, both men were caught off guard by the solemn voice from the back of the barn. Faster than Gentry by far, Billy immediately reached for the .44 he wore at his side. The shot that knocked him from the saddle was already on the way before his pistol cleared the holster. Standing with one foot in the stirrup, the

other leg about to swing over to dismount, Gentry
tried to defend himself. He managed to get off a shot
in the short time it took Joel to crank another cartridge
in the chamber, but it was wild with his horse startled
by the sharp crack of the Spencer. The bullet embedded itself in the stall post Joel knelt behind. There was
no time for a second shot before Joel calmly smashed
his chest with his next shot.

Joel came out of the stall to make sure they were
both finished. They appeared to be, but just to make
sure he wasn't going to be shot in the back by a wounded
man, he put a bullet into the brain of each one.

"That's two of the bastards, Ruthie," he announced
solemnly. Now the question to be answered, and without delay, was whether the two were alone or there
were others, maybe at the mine. If there were others,
they would likely have heard the shots, and Joel did
not want to get cornered in the barn again. So he led
his horse to the door, tied the reins to the latch, and
then walked out in the open and peered out across the
clearing toward the gap in the trees. There was no one
in sight, so he took advantage of the time he felt certain
he could count on before anyone was able to reach the
gap and caught the two horses the killers had ridden.
They made no effort to escape him, standing still while
he searched the saddlebags for anything he might find
useful. Of particular interest were the Henry lever-
action rifles both men carried, and the full gun belts of
.44 cartridges.

Already carrying more on the gray than he would
have desired, because of his recent visit to Horace
Beecher's trading post, he decided to take one of the
horses for a packhorse. A quick decision went in favor

of the sorrel that Gentry had ridden. A thought flashed through his mind then, and he recalled he had seen a rig for a packsaddle hanging on a peg in Boone's tiny tack room. After taking another quick look toward the gap in the trees, and seeing no one, he went back and retrieved the packsaddle. There was no time to try to fit it on the sorrel now, so he left the saddle on the horse and figured he'd hang everything he took on it for the time being.

Hurrying as fast as he could, he tied the sorrel's reins to the back of his saddle and was prepared to leave when another thought caused him to pause. He hadn't thought about searching the two bodies, so he took a few moments more to do that. He was astounded to find that both men were carrying a large amount of cash—blood money, no doubt.

This is what they were paid to murder my brother and my friends, he thought.

He put it in his saddlebag, stepped up into the saddle, and guided the gray around the corral to ride up into the trees behind the barn. When he was well hidden in the belt of pine trees that circled half of the mountain, he dismounted and tied the horses to a low limb. Satisfied that they were out of sight from anyone riding up to the barn, he made his way back down to the edge of the trees to see if anyone came to investigate the shots that had been fired.

"What the hell?" Slow Sam muttered when he heard the shots coming from the direction of the house.

He emerged from the scant cover of the mine opening in an effort to hear better. He wasn't sure, but he thought he had heard five shots. Only one of them sounded like a .44. The other four were from a heavier-caliber weapon, and he was sure they were not from the Henrys both Billy and Gentry carried.

"That don't sound good," he said, and waited to listen for additional shots, but there were none. "That don't sound good at all."

He hesitated for a few minutes, deciding whether he wanted to ride down there to investigate. He might find himself riding into an ambush, possibly outnumbered. His next thought was that he was glad he had stayed where he was, and that it was Billy and Gentry who had blundered into the ambush. He decided he should ride back to Blackjack Mountain and tell Strong what had happened, but the problem with that was he wasn't really sure what had just happened.

If one of them doesn't come back pretty soon to tell me, he thought, *then I reckon I'd better go have a look.*

He continued to stand there in front of the entrance to the mine, peering down the trail toward the gap in the pines and listening. After what he could only guess to be about ten or fifteen minutes, with still no sound of more gunshots, he reluctantly climbed onto his horse and headed down the trail to the house.

When he reached the point where the trail passed through the gap in the trees, he pulled up and dismounted, not willing to ride into the open meadow where the house and barn stood. Leading his horse, he walked to the edge of the trees to get a better look at what he might be riding into. At first, he saw nothing to indicate anything was wrong, but after a minute or two, he saw Billy's horse walk out of the barn. It struck him as strange that Billy would let the horse run loose.

They got to be in the barn, he thought. But why didn't Billy come out to keep his horse from wandering off?

"I got a bad feelin' about this," he muttered to himself, and decided that he wasn't going to ride down there to present a target to whoever was doing the shooting. And he was convinced that his two companions had been the unfortunate victims of the four shots he had heard. "Damn!" he cursed softly, hesitant to get any closer, but knowing he would catch hell from Strong if he wasn't able to tell him what had happened to Gentry and Billy.

Suppose nothing has happened to them, he thought. *Then I'd play the fool back at the ranch.* With that in mind, he made himself move in a little closer to try to get a better look.

He picked a pine larger than the others that was separated a few yards from the rest of the trees. After peering intently at the open barn door, he moved quickly to take cover behind the tree. There was still no sign of either of his two companions, and nothing in the barnyard except Billy's horse, still wandering idly around. The reluctant half-breed was at the limit of the risk he was willing to take, and he couldn't decide what to do.

Finally he decided, and yelled out, "Hey, Gentry! You in the barn?" There was no answer. He waited. Maybe they were in the barn and didn't hear him. He edged a little farther around the tree. "Hey, Gentry, Billy, you in there?" he yelled again. This time he received an answer when a large piece of pine bark was ripped off right above his head, followed immediately by the report of the rifle.

He didn't wait to see where the shot had come from. Running for his life, he jumped into the saddle and kicked his horse into a full gallop. It was an ambush, just as he had feared. He didn't know how many, and at the moment, he didn't care. But he was convinced that Gentry and Billy were dead, and he wasn't going to be the next one.

Running down through the trees, trying to get a clear shot, Joel found that he was too late to stop the man racing away toward the mine.

"Damn it," he cursed for missing with his one shot, not willing to excuse it even though he had not had much of a target. He knew now there had been only the three men watching the place. His regret was that Beauchamp would know that he had come back. "Well, he was gonna find out anyway," he said aloud, knowing that he had only started seeking revenge. He figured he had a little time before any more of Beauchamp's gunmen showed up to look for him, so he went back to the barn to complete the job he had started to do when he suddenly had company.

There was so little left of the three charred bodies that a big hole was not required, so he dug only one grave and put them all in it. Using a piece of canvas he found in the barn, he carried each body to the grave as gently as he could. When all three were resting in the bottom of the hole, he covered them with the canvas, pausing to apologize to them for not being there to help them when their murderers struck. He had not had time to know Boone's wife, Blue Beads, but he felt the pain his brother would have suffered. Elvira and Ruthie had been his adoptive family, and the grief he felt for them was almost unbearable. Billy's horse approached to within a few yards to watch the man suffering with his conscience and berating himself for his failure to protect. Finally Joel asked God to treat them kindly, then started shoveling the dirt back into the grave. Before leaving, he promised them that their killers would all pay for what they had done.

The question before him now was what his next move should be. He had not expected Beauchamp's men to be on Boone's property when he rode in that morning. His plan had been to scout out Beauchamp's place, waiting for an opportunity to catch his prey in singles or doubles, away from the rest of the gang. After the confrontation just passed, it was likely Beauchamp would send his men to search for him, so he was convinced he was now the hunted and not the hunter.

Either way, he thought, *they'll pay.*

The next thing he decided to do was to find a suitable camp, a place where he could leave his extra horse. With that in mind, he went back into the tack room to get a coil of rope hanging there. At some time or another, there was always a need for a length of rope. There was one more job he had to do before looking for a camp, so he tied his newly acquired packhorse there at the barn, took the pick and shovel, and went back to the mine to bury Boone and Riley. When he finished that soulful task, he returned to the barn.

Knowing that Beauchamp's men would be scouring this entire mountain, he decided that he could not stay there, so he started off down the back side of the mountain, leading his packhorse. Billy's horse watched them leave until they had gone about fifty yards; then it tossed its head a couple of times and loped after them. This was not something Joel desired, considering his current circumstances. Hiding one extra horse was going to be challenge enough. He didn't want the bother of another horse. But the horse continued to follow some several dozen yards behind him, no matter that he tried to chase it back. He finally gave up trying, and resigned himself to the fact that he was going to have to find a place to keep both extra horses.

The mountains to the east of the one Boone had settled on looked to be much more rugged and offered a better chance to find the spot he was looking for, so this seemed the best place to go. He spent most of the day searching, but he finally found a place just made to order, where a busy stream made its way down from the mountaintop through steep rock walls to form a small waterfall at the back of a high, narrow canyon. There was only one way into it on horse or foot, and only wide enough for horses to enter single file, so he felt confident that it would be difficult for anyone to surprise him there. He led his horses into the small clearing at the bottom of the falls and proceeded to make his camp.

Boss Beauchamp was furious. He had planned to ride into town in the afternoon to spend the night in the hotel, and much of the next morning in his office at Beauchamp No. 2. His late dinner was interrupted by the arrival of Slow Sam on a thoroughly lathered horse, yelling something as he skidded to a stop in front of the barn. Knowing the half-breed was supposed to be up at McAllister's claim, he assumed he could anticipate bad news of some kind, and he was getting sick and tired of hearing about things that had gone wrong.

"Lena!" he roared, and pulled the napkin from his neck and threw it on the table. "Lena!" he roared again when she didn't appear in the doorway immediately. He pushed his chair back and stood up.

"What are you yelling about?" the somber Ute woman asked.

"Put my dinner in the oven to keep warm. I'm going outside to see what those damn fools have fouled up now."

He didn't wait for her response, but picked up his heavy coat from the hall tree and stormed out to the front porch.

"What is it, Mike?" Beauchamp called out to his foreman, who was talking to the obviously agitated half-breed.

Strong glanced up when hailed by Beauchamp, and held his hand up to signal that he had heard him. With Slow Sam in tow, he went immediately to stand at the bottom of the front porch steps.

"Yes, sir," he said. "I was just gettin' ready to come report to you." He turned to point at Sam. "He says he thinks Billy Garland and Pete Gentry are dead."

"Dead?" Beauchamp exploded. "He thinks? What does he mean, he thinks they're dead? Doesn't he know?" He was so angry he began to sputter. "Who killed them?" he demanded.

"Tell him, Sam," Strong said.

Slow Sam told them what had happened to send him racing down the mountain. "I don't know how many there was waitin' for Billy and Pete. They wanted to go down to that homestead and get in the barn to keep warm." He glanced at Strong. "I stayed up there at that mine, like you told us to do, Mike, keepin' my eye out. Well, I heard the shots, and I hightailed it down there as fast as I could go. I didn't see hide nor hair of either one of 'em, so I figured they was dead. Then somebody started shootin' at me. Damn near got me, too." He cocked his head to show them a couple of small scratches where pieces of the bark had hit him. "There was just too many of 'em, and they was all hid too good. Wasn't nothin' I could do. Wouldn't've done no good if I rode down there in the open and got shot, too. So I figured the best thing for me to do was to get on back here so you'd know what was going on up there."

Without interrupting, Beauchamp listened to Sam's accounting of what had happened on the mountain, but he was not convinced that there was a gang of men up there. Seething with anger, he nevertheless remained calm.

"He's back," he said, looking at Strong accusingly. "That son of a bitch McAllister, the brother, he's back—maybe him and the Indian, too. There's no gang of gunmen up there." He shifted his gaze to lock onto Sam. "You say you got shot at. How many times?"

"Well, I was too busy to count the shots," Slow Sam claimed.

"Most likely one or two before you ran," Beauchamp said sarcastically. "There's only two men up there—the two you let get away. And now they've come back to try to sit on that claim again, and, damn it, I want this thing cleaned up. I'm tired of hearing about failures. It's gone on too damn long. Mike, take the men we've got left and go up there and run that son of a bitch to ground. Finish it."

There were cattle and horses scattered over both spreads, McAllister's and his, and he had planned to have his crew rounding them all up by this time.

"Yes, sir," Strong said, "but you know I'm down to five men now, if Billy and Gentry are dead."

"Damn it," Beauchamp exclaimed, "you're only going after one man, maybe two. Hell, take Fuzzy with you, if the six of you can't handle it." Getting angrier by the minute, he added, "Maybe I should send Lena up there with you. That would give me one I might be able to count on."

Properly chastised, Strong and Sam backed away a step.

"Yes, sir," Strong said. "We'll sure as hell get 'em this time. I'll go get the boys ready to ride, and we'll stay up there till we find McAllister."

"Just do what I pay you to do," Beauchamp replied in frustration. He remained there on the porch for a moment, trying to settle his anger down. The hills were being littered with the bodies of men he had hired to do his killing, and he wanted to end this war before the people of Silver City found out what was really going on.

Still irate, he charged back in the front door, in time to collide with Lena, who was coming from the front window where she had been listening to the discussion outside. It was enough to provoke his anger even more.

"Damn you, you nosy bitch!" he roared, and shoved her out of his way. "You're worse than a damn dog, getting underfoot!"

"I not your dog," Lena spat back.

He slapped her for her insolence. "You are if I say you are. Now get my supper out of the oven before I give you the beating you deserve."

Her face red and stinging, she did as she was told, having no choice but to do so.

Chapter 12

•

They didn't wait long, Joel thought as he lay at the base of a pine tree, watching the trail Beauchamp's men had always used when making their raids on Boone's property. There were six of them, riding two abreast up the steep path. It was obvious they intended to flush him out of the barn, if he was still there, using the advantage of numbers.

He planned to methodically reduce their number advantage, and this was the reason he had positioned himself over the trail halfway up to the mine, before they were in sight of it. He had no intention of shooting it out with six men. He preferred to take his time and reduce the odds, thinking he had a better chance of completing the mission he had set for himself.

He cocked the Spencer and steadied it upon a small mound of dirt, snow, and pine needles that he had raked up by the base of the tree, and waited. It would be better, he thought, to let them get a little farther up the trail, close enough to make sure he hit his mark, but not so close as to be upon him right away.

When he decided it was time, he laid the front sight of the carbine on one of the riders at the head of the column, hoping it was the leader of the bunch. Very slowly, he squeezed the trigger until the weapon finally spoke. As quickly as he could, he ejected the spent cartridge and fired again. His initial target fell from the saddle, but his second shot missed when the rider beside him jerked away. He made no attempt to fire a third shot.

That will do for now, he thought, as he pushed his body back away from the base of the tree, satisfied that he had reduced the number of his hunters to five.

When back far enough to get to his feet without being seen from below, he hurried back up the slope to his horse and retreated up toward the top of the mountain. He knew he was leaving a trail in the snow, but he planned on ending it when he reached the stream at the foot of the mountain on the other side. Behind him, there was momentary chaos.

"Behind those rocks!" somebody yelled needlessly, for there was already a frantic rush by all of them to seek cover behind an overhanging rock shelf, with the exception of Bris Snyder, who was lying in the trail. He had been the unfortunate one riding beside Mike Strong at the head of the column.

"Where is he?" Strong shouted. "Anybody see where those shots came from?"

"I did!" Zach Turner answered excitedly. "Up yonder, in them pines, near that big one on the right edge." As soon as he said it, two of the men started shooting at the tree Turner had pointed out.

"You see him?" Strong demanded.

"No, but we might as well make it hot for him," one of them replied.

"Quit wastin' cartridges," Strong told him. "He's pretty much got us pinned down here. We've got to circle around these rocks and come at him from above."

"What about Bris?" Tom Larkin asked. "Is he dead? Can anybody see him?"

"He don't look like he's movin'."

"We oughta make sure he ain't dead."

"I ain't goin' out there to find out, and get my ass shot," Slow Sam said. No one volunteered to risk it.

"Hell," Strong said, "throw a rope out there to him. If he ain't dead, he can grab hold of the rope and we'll pull him in behind the rocks."

That seemed like the perfect solution to them all, so Steve Tatum, who was closest to the path, uncoiled a length of rope, tied a big double knot in the end, and tossed it out toward Bris. His aim wasn't very accurate, leaving the rope several feet from Bris, but he left it there for a minute or two to see if he would try to reach for it. When he didn't, Tatum drew the rope back and tried a couple more times, the final try coming to rest across Bris's shoulders with no response from the body.

"He's dead," Strong pronounced. "Let's get goin'. We've got to get around behind that bastard and smoke him outta there."

"There might be two of 'em up there," someone reminded him. "There were two shots."

"They weren't that close together," Strong said. "I think he's all by his lonesome."

The time spent trying to determine Bris Snyder's status was enough to afford Joel a good head start down the other side of the mountain, where he rode his horse into the shallow stream and followed it at a lope through the narrow valley beyond, remaining in the water all the way through the valley.

Having already selected an exit point the day before when he was looking for a place to make his camp, he guided the gray out of the stream when he came to a rock shelf that extended down into the water. Being careful to walk his horse on the dry areas where the sun had melted the snow on the shelf, he rode the gray across it to a grassy area between the rock and the edge of a stand of pine trees.

Once in the trees, he dismounted and left the horse to stand there while he picked up a dead branch and went back to try to disguise his footprints. Deciding it was the best he could do, he climbed into the saddle and guided the gray through the thick stand of pines, the floor of which was thick with pine needles that would make it hard for a tracker to follow.

Satisfied that he had struck a telling blow in his war against Boss Beauchamp, he proceeded to his camp by the waterfall to await the night. Then he would see if the five remaining gunmen would return to Blackjack Mountain or set up camp on McAllister property.

Two mountains to the west of the narrow canyon that held Joel's camp, Mike Strong knelt at the center point of a half-circle line of attack, two of his men on each side of him. On his signal, with rifles ready, they began to slowly converge on the one pine that towered above the rest. Within twenty yards of the spot from which the sniper's bullet had come, they suddenly stopped when a laurel bush beside the tree moved. Not waiting for a signal, all five opened up with their rifles, spraying the tree and the area around it with a devastating rain of hot lead. When it was over, they stormed down upon the hapless victim of their assault, a thoroughly dead marmot that had been attracted to the little mound of dirt and snow.

"He's gone." Tatum stated the obvious.

"What did you expect?" Slow Sam replied sarcastically. "I coulda told you he wouldn't be here. Hell, it took us about thirty minutes to get around behind this spot."

"All right, you damn half-breed," Strong said. "You're always braggin' about how you can track anybody. There's still a little bit of snow on the ground. Let's see if you're worth what Boss is payin' you."

Sam looked around the tree for only a minute, then said what all of them could see for themselves, "It's just one feller. See by his tracks? He left his horse up there in them trees and walked down here." He followed the obvious footprints, and the other four men came along behind him, all with cautious eyes scanning back and forth, leery of another ambush. Sam found the place he figured the horse had been tied, because the pine needles had been pawed up. It was not so easy after that until they found tracks leading out of the belt of trees, heading toward the top of the mountain.

"Looks like he took off," he said, gazing up at the crown. "Ought not to be too hard to follow his trail, now that he's out in the open."

Sam's assumption proved to be accurate, for they easily followed the tracks over the top of the mountain and down the other side until they reached the stream at the bottom. "I'm good, but damned if I can track him in water," he said.

"Well, he had to go upstream or downstream," Strong said, "'cause it don't look like he crossed. He was headin' east, so he most likely went upstream." So they rode up the stream, looking for a place where he might have come out of the water. There was nothing to indicate he ever did.

"Take a look at that rock shelf there," Strong told Tatum. "That looks like a good place to get out without leavin' tracks."

Tatum guided his horse up on the shelf and walked him across it to the other edge. Taking a quick look beyond the rock, he said, "He didn't come out here. There's still a right good cover of snow on the grass and there ain't a track in it."

They continued on up the stream until they came to a place where it was underground, gushing forth from a large hole in the side of the mountain. After scouting the ground around the opening, they could find no tracks indicating that Joel had left the water there.

"Well, what did the son of a bitch do, fly outta here?" Larkin asked.

"No," Strong said. "He just outsmarted us this time. He musta gone downstream. It's gettin' too late to be stompin' around in these valleys now. The sun'll be gone in about an hour. We'll go on back and set up camp in McAllister's barn for the night. Then we'll comb these damn hills in the mornin' till we route his ass outta wherever he's hidin'."

"That might take some doin'," Zach Turner said. "He could be hidin' out anywhere in these mountains."

"That may be so," Strong argued, "but he's actin' like he's still got some idea that this place is his. At least, he's hangin' pretty close. We'll just camp back there at that barn, so if he shows up again before mornin', we'll be waitin' for him. If he doesn't, we'll start lookin' for his camp."

*   *   *

With a sizable fire built in the open doorway of the barn, so as not to fill their sleeping place with smoke, Strong's men cooked some bacon they had brought with them and boiled some coffee. As a precaution, Strong assigned his four remaining men to a guard watch, each man to stand a two-hour watch. Zach drew the first two hours. When darkness descended upon the mountainside, the horses were unsaddled and led into the corral, and the hunters settled in for the night—all except Zach. With his blanket wrapped around his shoulders, he took a position up across the yard, against a piece of the outside wall of the house. It was the only section left standing after the house was burned down.

It was a short but cold tour of duty, and uneventful, as Zach waited out his two hours under a three-quarter moon that gave him a fairly bright view of the barnyard from his post in the shadow of the log wall. In a good bit less than his two hours, since he had no watch, he decided he had been there long enough, so he headed back to the barn to awaken Slow Sam, who had drawn the next watch. Reluctant to leave his bedroll close to the fire in the doorway, Sam complained that it didn't make sense to stand out in the cold when common sense told him Joel McAllister wasn't fool enough to show up there as long as the five of them were waiting for him.

"Quit your bellyachin' and get your ass out there," Zach told him. "I took my turn, so you can damn sure take yours." He stood over him until Sam eventually crawled out of his bedroll and got to his feet. "I sat down against that piece of wall over at the house," Zach offered. "That'll keep the wind offa ya. There's a pretty bright moon out, so you can see the whole barnyard good enough." Sam grunted begrudgingly, grabbed his rifle and blanket, and walked out.

In the open yard between the barn and the house, Sam paused to check the time. He pulled the pocket watch he had taken from a stagecoach passenger several years before in a holdup in Wyoming, and held it up to catch the moonlight on the face of it. "That son of a bitch," he grumbled, for he was twenty minutes earlier than he should have been. His immediate reaction was to go back to the barn and roust Zach out of his bed, but he changed his mind, since he was already up and awake. "What the hell?" he muttered. "I'll just wake Tatum up twenty minutes early." Still perturbed, however, he remembered Zach's advice and went to settle down against the partial wall of the house.

Only an hour into his guard tour, his eyelids became heavy, and soon he caught himself nodding, so he admonished himself to stay awake. But it was to no avail. In a matter of minutes, his chin dropped down to almost rest upon his chest. A few minutes later, he began to snore.

Behind him, a dark figure rose from the ashes and burned timbers of the destroyed home and moved silently like a shadow to the section of wall where the sleeping man sat hunched against it. Slow Sam jerked his head slightly when the hand clamped over his mouth and pulled his chin up from his chest. His whole body stiffened when the long skinning knife slashed his throat, his legs thrashing violently as he desperately tried to pull away from his executioner. But there was no escaping the powerful hands that trapped him.

When finally the last trace of life drained from his victim, Joel released his hold and let him slump to the ground. He felt no guilt from the savage way he had killed the man. He would have felt even more gratified had he known that, by a twist of fate, he had dispatched the very murderer who had killed the women with a knife. It was a matter of necessity anyway, for with what he planned to do, he could not afford a noisy killing.

Crouching there in the shadow of the wall, he paused to listen. When he was certain that all was quiet in the barn, he made his way quickly across the open yard to the corral, stopping to listen again before continuing. There was still no indication that all was not peaceful among the sleeping outlaws inside the barn. Satisfied, he began to remove the rails that served as the gate to the corral. When they were all out, he went inside, got behind the horses, and gently herded them out of the corral. They needed little encouragement, and were soon quietly walking out into the open barnyard. He walked along behind them, encouraging them on until they were close to the edge of the clearing.

Aware then that he was pushing his luck, for anyone who happened to walk out of the barn would instantly see him out in the open moonlit yard, he turned and ran back to his horse. The gray was waiting patiently where Joel had left it near the edge of the trees behind the barn. He climbed into the saddle and rode around the ruins of the house to the front corner, where he could see the open barn door. He looked toward the horses again and saw that they had stopped to mill around near the edge of the trees on the other side of the clearing. Three quick shots from his carbine encouraged them to trot for a few yards before slowing to a walk again, but were successful in scattering the freed mounts among the trees. He turned then to focus on the door of the barn.

"What the hell?" Tatum shouted, bolting upright out of a sound sleep.

"The horses!" Strong yelled. "Somebody's after the horses!"

Tatum didn't hesitate. Grabbing his Henry, he ran out the door, looking frantically from right to left. His eyes found the man on horseback aiming a rifle at him a split second before the muzzle flash and the solid impact of the bullet when it entered his chest. He ran half a dozen steps farther before crumpling to the ground, dead.

"Hold on!" Strong barked when Larkin started to follow Tatum. "He's sittin' out there, waiting for us to come out."

"Damn it!" Zach swore. "He's got us trapped in here!"

"Just hold on a minute!" Strong ordered. "He might be waitin' for us to run out, but he can't come in without gettin' his ass blown off. There ain't nothin' we can do till daylight. Then he's gonna have to back off, 'cause there ain't no place to hide out there." He looked around him then to see what their situation was. There was a window in the back between the two stalls, and one on the side facing the house. "One of you get on that window in the back," he directed. "The other'n take that window on the side. I'll watch the door. He'll play hell comin' in here after us."

"What about the horses?" Zach asked as he ran to the back of the barn.

"We'll have to worry about runnin' them down after daylight," Strong said. "There ain't nothin' we can do about 'em now."

Outside, still seated on his horse where the corner of

Boone's front porch used to be, Joel continued to watch
the open door of the barn while keeping a sharp eye in
case one of them slipped out of one of the windows.
After a while, when it appeared that they were choosing to hole up instead, he decided that his work was
done for that night. There was very little chance that he
could successfully storm the barn without giving one
of them a clear shot at him.

Although his need to complete his quest for revenge
was still strong, he knew he could not fight all three of
them out in the open. So he contented himself with the
knowledge that his enemies were now reduced to three,
plus the man responsible for all of the killing, Boss
Beauchamp. He would continue to catch them one by
one until he had extracted full payment for Boone's and
Riley's deaths as well as the execution of the women. So
he turned the gray's head away from the house and
loped up through the pine trees toward the back of the
mountain. He was hungry and he needed sleep.

Tomorrow I'll find them again, he thought.

There would be no more sleep that night for Strong
and his two remaining gunmen. First light of day
found them still watching warily for a new attack.
When it was finally light enough to see, they decided it
best to take the precaution of going out the back window, in case McAllister had sat waiting all night for
someone to show his face. Still, there was no one of the
three eager to expose himself outside the barn, until
finally Tom Larkin volunteered.

"To hell with it," he snorted. "I'll go. We can't stay
here in this barn all day. I've got to find my horse." So,
with a boost from Zach, he went out the window,
landed on his shoulder, and immediately rolled over,

ready to fire. When there were no shots fired, he got to his feet and made his way along the back of the barn until he reached the corner. Peering cautiously around the corner, he waited several minutes with no sign of anyone in the yard between the barn and the house. So he walked around the empty corral to the front of the barn. There was still no sign of anyone, so he decided McAllister had gone.

"Hey," he called out, "you two lily-livered gunslingers can come out now. He's gone."

Strong was not so sure. He considered the possibility that Joel was hidden somewhere, and was waiting to lure all three of them out in the open. So he hung back to let Zach go out the door before he did. When there was still no sign of attack, he cautiously followed Zach, relieved when there was no shot fired. Larkin walked over to look at Tatum's body.

"He hit him right square in the chest, right in the heart, I expect," he said. Then a thought occurred to him and he started checking Tatum's pockets, knowing that, like all the men, he was carrying a large cash bonus for the "Indian raid." He found the money in an inside vest pocket and started to put it away, but Strong saw him.

"What the hell do you think you're doin'?" Strong demanded.

"Well, hell, he ain't gonna need it where he's gone to," Larkin replied.

"We'll be splittin' that money three ways," Strong told him.

Overhearing, Zach went over to Slow Sam's corpse by the cabin wall, intending to search his pockets as well. "I reckon this here's the reason we didn't hear no noise when that son of a bitch was scatterin' the horses," he said as he looked at the half-breed's slashed throat. "I wondered what happened to him. I thought he mighta run off."

Before doing anything else, they counted the money found on their late partners and divided it three ways. Only then was there any thought about what they should do about the fact that they were on foot. "They most likely didn't go very far," Larkin said, "if we just knew what direction they run off in."

"He mighta rounded up them horses and drove 'em off somewhere where he's got 'em hid," Zach suggested. He shook his head slowly and said, "It's a helluva long walk back to Blackjack Mountain, especially carryin' a saddle." His comments were sobering to his two partners, who had not considered that possibility to that point.

"We need to take a look along the creek on the other side of those trees," Strong said, assuming the horses would naturally go to water. He was not at all enthusiastic about walking down this mountain and hoofing it seven miles to Beauchamp's ranch at the base of Blackjack Mountain.

All three knew that they were of little use on foot, hunting for McAllister, or running from him, so they threw their saddles on their shoulders and started up through the trees to look along the stream. It was a fruitless search. They saw not one of the five horses, and soon were at a loss as to where to look further.

"We'd best give up on the horses and start walkin' before that bastard comes back and catches us out in the open," Strong finally decided.

So they started on a line as straight toward home as they could figure. It was their misfortune that only one man had seen the direction their horses had been driven from the corral, and he was shot dead before he could tell anyone. In fact, the horses had fled in the opposite direction from the stream where the three men had searched, running up through the trees at the far end of the meadow where Boone McAllister had built his home. They had not gone far into the trees, and wandered back to the barn later in the morning.

The sun was well up when Joel returned to his brother's home and sat his horse inside the tree line while he took time to look the scene over. By all appearances, it seemed that the three men were no longer there, for their horses were milling about the barn and the yard, still unsaddled. And the two bodies of the men he had killed the night before were left where they had fallen. After a wait of approximately fifteen minutes more, he decided that they were really gone, so he nudged the gray and the gelding walked slowly out of the cover of the trees toward the barn.

With his rifle out and ready to fire, he watched the door of the barn carefully, still alert to the possibility that he might be riding into a trap. But there was no one waiting in ambush as he rode right up to the barn door. Taking a brief look inside, he saw three saddles that had been left behind. Since there had been six of them when they had come up the mountain the day before, that told him that the three had left on foot, carrying their saddles. Evidently they had looked for their horses in the wrong direction.

It didn't take much looking around to discover the trail left by the three where they crossed the open yard between the barn and the belt of pines behind. With a cautious eye, he followed the tracks left by the frequent scuffing of their bootheels on the floor of the pine forest. They led him to a fork in the stream that flowed back to Boone's house below. The tracks were not so easily followed at that point, but he was able to surmise by some broken branches of laurel bushes that they had thrown their saddles down at one point while they apparently searched up and down the stream. It took him some time after that before he was able to find where they had left the trees and set out across an open meadow.

They're heading for home now, he thought as he sighted along the line they had started on. He set out after them.

Tom Larkin stumbled, almost falling, on a shale-covered slope. Cursing, he complained, "These damn boots ain't made for walkin'." He was not as stout as Strong or Zach, and his saddle seemed to have acquired a good bit more weight during the several hours he had carried it.

Neither Strong nor Zach had complained about the load on his shoulders, although they were getting tired as well. Neither man wanted to admit to a weakness.

"I reckon we could set 'em down for a little while and give you boys a rest," Strong said. "Maybe when we get to that pile of rocks down yonder."

"I don't need no rest," Zach boasted, although he was glad someone had finally called for a break.

They continued down toward the large outcropping of rocks that Strong had indicated. When within a dozen yards of the rocks, Larkin stumbled again, but this time he went down and a rifle shot was heard immediately after.

"Run!" Zach yelled, not waiting for Strong to follow. Running as fast as he could to gain the protection of the rocks, he felt the impact of a second bullet when it smacked into the saddle he carried on his shoulder. It caused him to run even faster.

Gasping for breath, the two men dived behind a finger of rock that jutted out beyond the boulders. Fearing for their lives, they dropped the saddles and pulled their rifles out of their scabbards.

"Up there!" Strong shouted, and pointed to a large boulder that sat on a flat rock base with another boulder behind it. "We'll have cover from both sides up there."

Zach moved immediately without questioning. He wanted something solid between himself and the determined avenger, and the boulder looked to be the best place to be at this moment. He was only a step ahead of Strong as they scrambled up over the smaller rocks to squeeze in between the two larger boulders. Back-to-back, they were confident they could handle an attack from either side.

"Let the bastard come on now!" Zach bellowed, once he felt the security of the rock protecting him. He rose a little in an effort to spot the shooter. "Come on down here now, you son of a bitch!" he shouted out. He was immediately answered by a bullet that glanced off the boulder a foot from his head, causing him to drop down on his knee before the next shot came. "Damn!" he muttered, knowing the next one might have his name on it. His sense of bravado having been corralled, he pressed Strong. "We're in a helluva bind in these damn rocks. What are we gonna do? That bastard's got us pinned down here."

The question was already troubling Strong's mind, and he couldn't see an answer that was satisfactory. "Nothing we can do right now," he said. "He can stay up there above us all day if he wants to. Our only chance is to sneak outta here after dark." It was an option, not a good one, but better than the other remaining one—charge out in the open to take him on in a shoot-out.

"It's a helluva long time till dark," Zach complained, "and I ain't got much water left in my canteen as it is."

"You'd best scrape up some of that snow between these rocks, then. But I'll tell you, dyin' of thirst ain't your main problem right now."

He dropped to his knees and crawled a few feet to the side in an effort to see where the shooter was. A small space between the curved bottom of the boulder and the flat shelf it rested on afforded him a tiny window to look through. After a few minutes of scanning back and forth across the slope above them, he suddenly snapped his gaze back to a low clump of laurel a few yards below the crest of a ridge.

"I got him!" he exclaimed excitedly. "He's up there behind some scrubby little bushes. Move over to the other side of this rock and you can see what I'm talkin' about." Zach moved at once, and when he reached a space where he had a view of the ridge above them, Strong gave him directions. "See them two little bent-over pines on the right side of where that ridge slopes up on the right? Now come on over to your left to that little clump of bushes. He's behind the biggest one right in the middle."

Zach followed Strong's directions and located the bush. "I see where you're talkin' about," he said. "But I don't see nobody. How do you know he's behind that bush?"

"I just saw it movin' about a minute ago. He's behind it, all right. He's just settin' up there waitin' for one of us to stick our heads out. And that ain't no protection a'tall, so if we fill that bush up with lead, we stand a damn good chance of gettin' him."

"Might just be another marmot," Zach said, remembering the last time they had massacred a bush. "But, hell, I don't see any better place he could be up there." He shifted his position to a point where he could aim his rifle through the small opening between the rocks and waited for Strong's signal.

Seeing that Zach was in place, Strong slid his Henry into the gap under the large boulder. "All right," he said, "let's give it to him." Both men opened fire, cranking out spent cartridges as fast as they could.

Strong's hunch proved to be a good one, for Joel was caught by surprise, suddenly finding himself amid a hailstorm of rifle slugs shredding the leaves of the laurel and kicking up dirt beside him. The risk he had taken turned out to be a bad one, and the only reason he was alive to regret it was the fact that he had moved over to a smaller bush. Even then, the bullets were landing all around him. He had no choice other than to make a run for it, and it didn't take him long to decide. His carbine in hand, he scrambled out from behind the bushes and sprinted toward the top of the ridge, almost making it over before a rifle slug slammed him in the back, knocking him down. When he hit the ground, he was close enough to the top to continue rolling over and over until he had the protection of the ridge.

Cursing himself for being so stupid for thinking that he would be able to shoot either of them before they could see where the shots were coming from, he lay still for a brief moment, trying to decide how bad he was hurt. If they had seen him get hit, and he was sure that they must have, they would probably be coming after him to make sure. They would have to come up the slope to find out, leaving themselves vulnerable in the open expanse between the rocks and the top of the ridge. Because of the possibility of that, he had to make himself crawl back to the top and wait for them.

Confronted with the same uncertainty that Joel struggled with, Strong and Zach were concerned with the risk of leaving their rocky fortress to confirm a kill. "He's hit, damn it," Zach insisted. "I think it was my shot that got him."

"Maybe," Strong countered. "It's hard to say whose shot got him, but he caught one, all right. If you think it was yours, then you can walk on up that hill to see if he's dead."

"Shit," Zach replied. "I know damn well he got hit, but I don't know if he's dead. Maybe you wanna go up there and see."

With neither man willing to take the risk, they waited and watched for some sign until, tired of waiting, Strong said, "We need to know if that son of a bitch is dead or not, so we can tell Boss. Besides, he's got a horse up there that would sure come in mighty handy right now."

They continued to wait.

Above them, behind the crown of the ridge, Joel was trying to get into position to defend against any advance by the two outlaws. He labored to get to his feet, staggering from the stabbing pain in his left arm each time he tried to use it. The bullet felt like a live coal deep in his back, and he found it was too painful to support the light carbine with that arm while he pulled the trigger with his other hand. He could also feel a steady trickle of blood down his back, and he had no way to stop it.

Finally he accepted the fact that he was in no condition to defend himself, so he reluctantly withdrew, promising Boone, Riley, Elvira, and Ruthie that it was not over yet. With a great deal of effort, he climbed into the saddle and turned the gray back the way he had come.

The wait became almost unbearable as the day wore on, finally coming to the point where Strong was ready to take a chance, rather than wait for nightfall.

"Damn it," he exclaimed, "I'm goin' up that ridge. I think he's dead, or we'da heard something outta him. You can stay hid here if you want, but if you do, I'm ridin' that horse home by myself, and you can walk on in."

He stood up then, put his hat on the barrel of his rifle, and held it up over the top of the boulder. There was no response from above them, so he waved it back and forth a few times.

When there was still no shot coming their way, Zach volunteered, "Hell, I'll go up that slope with you."

At Strong's suggestion, they went up the slope about twenty yards apart, walking slowly while holding their rifles up to their shoulders and aiming at the top of the hill. There was no gunfire to greet them. When they reached the top, they halted until each man was ready, then rushed over the narrow crown of the ridge, ready to shoot. There was no one there. "Gone!" Zach stated the obvious.

"He was hit, though," Strong said, pointing to a little pool of blood and a bloody trail leading to a place where a horse had stood. "Bad enough so he couldn't fight, but not too bad to keep him from ridin' a horse."

"Damn," Zach said in disappointment. "The bastard's still alive."

"Maybe not for long. He's losin' blood," Strong said. "He might just be lookin' for a place to die."

"I wish to hell he'da died right here so we could use his horse." He looked up at the afternoon sun. "I reckon if we get started walkin', we might make it back to Blackjack before dark."

"We need to get Larkin's share of the bounty money and his guns," Strong said as they turned to walk back down to pick up their saddles.

Chapter 13

He continued to berate himself as he rode slumped in the saddle for being so eager to finish off the two raiders who had come after him. Thinking he had a chance to get them both, he had carelessly left himself exposed to their gunfire. The farther he rode, the more he became convinced that he was going to have to take time to heal before the score could be settled.

His concern was the location of the wound. If it was in his arm or leg, he could doctor it on his own, but the wound was in his back. He couldn't even see it, but he could damn sure feel it, and he knew he was going to need a doctor or someone to treat it. The only doctor he knew of was Crooked Arrow, the medicine man in the Shoshoni village, and the longer he stayed in the saddle, the more he was convinced that he had to have help. The sooner he could get to that help, the better, but he had the worry of the two extra horses back at his camp, plus his supply of ammunition. So he turned the gray's head toward the camp, figuring that he would make it to the Shoshoni village, or he would not. Either way, he had to free the horses first.

Determined to do what he had to do, Joel made the long ride back to his camp in the narrow canyon. As soon as he rode into the small clearing at the back of the steep canyon wall, he painfully climbed down from the saddle and knelt by the pool at the bottom of the waterfall to splash the cold water on his face. The shock of the ice-cold water helped to clear his senses, so that he could force himself to untie the rope hitching rail he had fashioned across the stream. Then, afraid he was going to lose his strength if he stopped to rest, he tied the reins of the horses to a lead rope, and that he tied to his saddle. He left the saddles where they were, planning to come back for them when he was able.

As he secured the packsaddle on one of the horses, he felt a fresh trickle of blood running down his back, but he didn't stop until he had loaded ammunition, supplies, and two Henry rifles he had picked up. Finally ready to ride, he felt exhausted, but he strained to pull himself up into the saddle once more, afraid that if he lay down to rest, he might never get up again. He pressed the gray with his heels and left his secluded camp by the waterfall, hoping to reach the Shoshoni village of Chief Walking Eagle.

Young Black Fox paused on his way to the thick grove of trees downstream from the Indian village when he spotted three horses approaching the village in the fading light of dusk. The two horses in front appeared to be loaded with packs, but as they came closer, he realized that the lead horse was carrying not a pack, but a rider slumped over its neck. The discovery was enough to make him forget the urgency to visit the trees downstream, and he ran back toward the circle of tipis to alert the village.

Responding to Black Fox's cry, most of the villagers came from their tipis to see who was approaching their village. One of the curious in the crowd was Red Shirt, the Bannock, still wearing a bandage, but otherwise strong and healthy. The lead horse looked like the one that Joel rode, but he wasn't sure. So like the others, he watched in silence as the lead horse walked slowly up in the semicircle of puzzled spectators and stopped. The body lying across the gray gelding's neck did not move until someone reached out to touch his elbow. It was enough to cause the unconscious man to slide from the horse's neck and land in a heap on the ground. It was then that Red Shirt realized it was indeed Joel McAllister.

"Joel!" he exclaimed, and hurried to his side. Seeing the bloody shirt, he feared that his friend was dead. He quickly rolled him on his side so that he could press his ear to Joel's chest to listen for a heartbeat. When he heard the slow, steady beating of the white warrior's heart, he called out for someone to tell Crooked Arrow.

"I am here," Crooked Arrow said, having already joined the gathering of onlookers. "Let me see him." He knelt on the other side of Joel and, upon seeing the bullet hole in the back of his shirt, he said, "Some of you carry him to my lodge. Maybe I can help him fight this wound. It has already spilled much of his blood."

Red Shirt and three other men lifted Joel and carried him to Crooked Arrow's tipi, where the medicine man directed them to lower him down on a bed of doeskin and blankets. He removed the bloody shirt and looked at the ugly black hole in Joel's back for a few minutes. Then he came outside with a large pan.

"I need some fresh water to clean the wound."

Standing with the others close to the entrance flap of the tipi, White Fawn immediately volunteered and took the pan before Owl Woman, Crooked Arrow's wife, could reach for it. She was away to the stream at once. Her eagerness to help the wounded white warrior did not escape her father's notice. She had been especially attentive to the young man when he was there before. Crooked Arrow had thought it merely curiosity then. Now he wondered if it might be more than that. Their young daughter had been somewhat of a puzzle for Yellow Moon and Walking Eagle. She was of an age when most of the other girls had already taken a husband, but White Fawn had shown no interest in any of the young men of the village. Fighting Horse, one of the most feared warriors of the village, was prepared to give Walking Eagle six ponies for her hand. Most young girls would have been proud to be the wife of Fighting Horse, but White Fawn begged her father to refuse. A doting father, Walking Eagle didn't have the heart to insist.

I must talk to Yellow Moon about this problem, he thought.

In a few minutes, White Fawn returned with the pan of water and took it inside the tipi. "I can help you clean his wound," she volunteered, surprising Owl Woman, who had assumed she would have that responsibility. Indifferent, however, she shrugged, gave White Fawn a cloth she was holding, and stepped out of the way, but not before giving her husband a knowing glance. White Fawn went quickly to her task, cleaning the dried blood from Joel's back, carefully rinsing the fresh blood that continued to ooze from the wound.

The cold water served to bring Joel out of his fit of unconsciousness for a brief moment and he opened his eyes, not knowing where he was. The first thing that registered with his muddled brain was the image of an angel's face hovering close over him. Still groggy, he did not question it, and thought that he might even be dead, but he felt that someone was watching over him. So he closed his eyes again and slid back into sleep.

"Good," Crooked Arrow said, "I'll dig the bullet out now."

White Fawn stepped back out of the way, but she remained inside the tipi while Crooked Arrow probed for the rifle slug embedded deep inside the muscles of Joel's back. The bullet did not come out easily, but Crooked Arrow eventually managed to dislodge it. When it was out, he cleaned the wound again and applied a poultice containing a mixture of healing herbs. Then Owl Woman stepped in and bound the wound with a length of cloth. Crooked Arrow turned to discover White Fawn still standing there, on her face a question of concern.

"He is strong," Crooked Arrow told her. "But he must rest and let it heal."

Outside the tipi, only two of the people who had first gathered still remained, Red Shirt and Walking Eagle. White Fawn stepped outside and smiled when she saw them waiting. Speaking to Red Shirt, she said, "Your friend will be all right. Crooked Arrow took the bullet out of his back, but he must rest." She could see the deep concern on his face relax a bit and he nodded solemnly.

Walking Eagle spoke to her then. "You must go to our lodge. Yellow Moon wants to talk to you." White Fawn smiled. She had a fair idea what her mother wanted to talk about.

Crooked Arrow came out to join them as White Fawn walked away. He looked at Walking Eagle and smiled. "I think you might have a problem on your hands."

"I know this," Walking Eagle replied. "She seems taken by the young white warrior. Maybe her mother can talk to her."

Unaware of the problem they spoke of until that moment, Red Shirt was taken by surprise. "Joel is a good man," he stated for his friend's part. "He is an honorable man."

Walking Eagle looked at him and smiled. "I believe that he truly is, but I don't know his heart. I am thinking about my daughter's heart, and I am afraid it might be broken if he has no interest in her. That is all."

Changing the subject then, he asked if Joel was well enough to move. Crooked Arrow told him that he expected Joel would be best served to stay where he was for the night, and then he should most likely be awake and alert.

"Good," Walking Eagle said, and turned to Red Shirt. "We will take him to your lodge in the morning," he said, referring to the small tipi that had been erected for Red Shirt's convalescence.

"I will take care of him," Red Shirt said, and unconsciously worked his wounded shoulder back and forth, testing its condition.

He was much relieved to know that Joel was going to be all right, realizing the gratitude and high regard he had for his white friend. Many days had passed, and many things had happened since Joel caught him trying to steal one of his horses. He valued his friendship highly.

Crooked Arrow was right. Joel was strong, and was alert the next morning, insisting upon walking to Red Shirt's tipi, instead of being carried. The effort caused his wound to start bleeding again, resulting in a minor scolding from White Fawn, who had come to witness the transfer of the patient.

While her attention to the white man was not looked upon with approval by many in the village, she was not judged too harshly primarily because her strong-minded behavior was well-known. When she was content that Joel was comfortably settled in the tipi, and had eaten something, she returned to her regular chores, leaving her patient in Red Shirt's care.

"Good you gonna be all right," Red Shirt told Joel when he woke from a short period of sleep after eating. "I afraid you not come back no more."

"I didn't get the job done," Joel said, grimacing as he tried to get in a comfortable position on the blanket. He went on to tell his friend all that had happened since he had left him in the village to recover. "I came close to gettin' the last two of those bastards that came to clean us out, but I got careless. As soon as I'm on my feet again, I'll finish what I started."

"We finish," Red Shirt corrected.

Joel smiled. "That's right, partner, *we finish*."

Thinking about it for only the first time since he made it to the village, he asked Red Shirt about the horses. He had only to look around him to see what had happened to the packhorse load he had brought with him. It had all been moved into the tipi.

"Horses with Shoshoni herd," Red Shirt said.

Already planning his strategy for his next attack on Beauchamp, he informed his friend that he was thinking about switching over to one of the Henry rifles he had picked up from the dead.

"I don't think they're quite as powerful as the Spencer, but they're a helluva lot easier to handle when you want rapid fire. It's easier to find forty-four cartridges than fifty-fours, and we can use the forty-fours in our pistols. It's up to you whether or not you wanna do the same. If you do, I'm thinkin' we oughta make Walkin' Eagle and Crooked Arrow a present of our Spencers as kind of a payment for takin' care of us."

"Hmm. . . . maybe so," Red Shirt replied, thinking it a good present for each man.

Joel went on. "I brought plenty of cartridges for the Henrys. I'd wanna do a little practice shootin' before I have to use it in a fight."

"You not ready yet," Red Shirt cautioned, afraid his friend was not giving his wound proper respect. "Have to let wound heal." Then a joke occurred to him. "You can't go till White Fawn say so. She keep close eye on you."

"White Fawn?" Joel asked, not aware of the girl's special attention to him. He had assumed that she helped Crooked Arrow as a matter of routine.

"Yeah," Red Shirt said with a chuckle. "She keep close eye on you."

Giving it some thought then, Joel pictured the face that brought him something to eat that morning and realized it was the face of the angel he had seen upon first awakening the night before.

"Why do you say that?" he asked.

Red Shirt laughed heartily. "White Fawn think white warrior big medicine. I think she looking for husband."

"I doubt that," Joel replied, finding it difficult to believe the girl would have any such notions toward him.

He had more important things to think about, he told himself. For as long as Beauchamp and his two men were alive, Riley, Boone, and the women could not rest in peace. So healing quickly and returning to finish the job were all he could concentrate on. He was to find, however, that other thoughts were difficult to prohibit, especially in the silent hours of the night, and sometimes he would have to admonish himself for losing sight of his goal.

It was late at night when Strong and Zach had stumbled into the barnyard at Blackjack Ranch, staggering under the burden of their saddles. Lamps in the main house had long since been blown out, so no one had been aware of the two gunmen's return—no one, that is, except for Fuzzy, who was still up in the bunkhouse. With none of the hands to cook breakfast for, there was no need to get up early, so he allowed himself the pleasure of sitting up later in the evening. Since they were on foot, he had not heard them walking up to the door to startle him when the door suddenly opened.

"What the hell . . . ?" he had started when they walked in the door. "I didn't hear no horses comin' in."

"'Cause we ain't got no horses," Zach had replied.

Fuzzy had looked at the door behind them, expecting others to file in behind them. "Where's the rest of the boys?"

"They got delayed," Strong had replied. "You got anything to eat?"

"There's some biscuits left over," Fuzzy had offered. "I was gonna have 'em for my breakfast, but you can eat them, and I'll make you some coffee." He had paused to take a long look at the two weary travelers. "Ain't you gonna tell me what's goin' on?"

When Strong and Zach had finished telling him that they were the only two survivors left in Beauchamp's war to take over McAllister's claim, Fuzzy could not believe what he was hearing.

"You're talkin' about one man, ain't you?" he exclaimed. "One man done for everybody but you two? Mister, Boss ain't gonna be happy to hear about this."

"I ain't too happy about it myself," Strong replied.

"But you say you think you shot him before he got away?" Fuzzy asked.

"I *know* I shot him," Strong insisted. "He was able to get away, but I don't know how far he got. We didn't have no horses to ride after him. He might be dead— just run off someplace to die."

"I know my feet are killin' me," Zach complained, having already shucked his boots. "And my back feels like I carried my horse all the way home."

"You might be hurtin' a helluva lot more when you tell Boss about this, come mornin'," Fuzzy remarked. "He's gonna be fit to be tied. Reckon you oughta go up to the house and tell him tonight?"

"Hell no," Strong responded. "You know he don't like nobody disturbin' him after he's turned in. Besides, I think I could use a night's sleep before he hears about it."

"Yeah," Zach agreed. "He might still be ridin' ol' Lena about now, and I know he won't take kindly to interruptin' that."

They finished their coffee and biscuits and turned in to await the meeting in the morning when they would surely face Beauchamp's wrath.

Beauchamp's reaction upon hearing the results of his gang of hired guns against one man was even worse than Strong had anticipated. Beauchamp was livid, his face twisted in black anger when he thought about what their blunder had cost him. They had been wise enough to wait until Lena had served his breakfast before knocking on the back door. Surprised to find that they were back, since he had not heard them come in, he was stunned when told that the rest of the men had all been killed. The fury that threatened to consume him would not permit him to speak for long, agonizing moments while his brain processed the unbelievable report he was hearing. He had hired his own private posse of assassins to crush anyone who stood in his way to build his empire, outlaws all, of no conscience whether they were ordered to steal, rustle, or kill—and their number had been reduced to these two miserable failures standing in his kitchen that morning. Hats in hand, they stood like truant schoolboys, waiting to be punished.

"I'm pretty sure I shot him," Strong reminded him, hoping that would lessen the degree of their failure.

With his temper under control to some extent again, Beauchamp shot back. "You're *pretty sure*, are you?" he asked sarcastically. "Well, here's what I want you to do. I want you to go back up there and find him. Bring his body back here so I can see it. Understand?" He waited for their nods. "You left here with five men, and you come back on foot. There's six horses roaming around loose on that mountain that belong to me. I want them back."

"Yes, sir," Strong replied. "Me and Zach'll find him. I know he's wounded if he ain't dead, so he's gotta be hidin' out up there somewhere. We'll get him, and round up them horses."

"Get out of here, then," Beauchamp ordered, and stood glaring at the backs of their heads as they scurried out the door. Aware of Lena standing behind him, he turned and demanded, "What?"

She held the coffeepot in front of her and replied, "You want more coffee?"

"Did I ask for more coffee?" he came back sarcastically.

Not one to suffer his contempt, she spat back, "No, and I don't give a damn if you want more or not. I ain't the one who let McAllister shoot up that bunch of outhouse scum you hired."

In no mood for her sass, he gave her a sharp backhand across her face, causing her to drop the coffeepot she had been holding. "Clean that up," he ordered, and left the room.

One of these days . . . , she thought as she felt the trickle of blood at the corner of her mouth. She truly hated the man she worked for, cooking and cleaning, and servicing his personal needs as she had done the night before. She often thought of leaving Blackjack, had actually done it one time, only to have him send Strong and Slow Sam after her. She still remembered that beating. It was sufficient to discourage her from trying it again, although she thought about it constantly.

* * *

Beauchamp had hoped to complete the takeover of McAllister's property without anyone of Silver City's legitimate population knowing it was done, or how it was done. Maybe these latest developments called for a different plan of conquest, forcing him to involve the sheriff and a citizen posse to pursue Joel McAllister for murdering his ranch hands. Maybe he could convince them that he had murdered his own brother as well, and the women, too. The plan had some merit. He would give Strong and Zach a few days to dispose of his problem before taking that step.

There were other worries for Beauchamp, caused by the incompetence of his crew of gunmen. He didn't have enough men to run his growing cattle ranch on Blackjack Mountain. Other than Strong and Zach, he was left with Fuzzy and Lena. He was going to have to hire more men to replace those he had lost.

A positive thought occurred to him at that point. There had always been the worry that the irreparable band of outlaws he had hired to do his evil bidding would not be able to keep silent about their lawless activities. If the business with McAllister was finished, he no longer had a need for hired gunmen. He needed cowhands to take care of his cattle, and they were a lot easier to find.

It was a critical time in his plans to rule this part of Idaho Territory. Silver City was growing into a sizable town with reputable businessmen moving in to service the needs of the miners. Still wild and virtually untamed as yet, it might not be in a year or two. And when that came to pass, Ronald Beauchamp must be perceived as an upstanding pillar of the town.

He still allowed for the necessity to eliminate Strong and Zach, who would be the last two who could testify to his past methods of doing business, with the exceptions of Fuzzy and Lena. Both of them could be controlled by threats, or salaries they could not afford to lose. But foremost on his mind was the one problem to be solved: McAllister had to be eliminated.

Chapter 14

Joel brought the Henry up to his shoulder and drew a bead on a patch of cloth he had pinned to the trunk of a tree by a small stream some seventy-five yards distant. He pulled the trigger and the sound of the shot reverberated across the narrow canyon. Cranking the lever, he fired again, and then one more time before dropping the rifle to his side again. He turned then to watch Red Shirt perform the same exercise, aiming at a similar patch on the tree beside his.

"I like the feel of the rifle," Joel said. "I just wanna see if I can hit anything with it."

"Wound not hurt?" Red Shirt asked as they walked toward the canyon wall to check their targets.

"No," Joel replied. "It hurts a little bit, but not enough to slow me down."

Red Shirt had been concerned that his friend might not be giving the wound in his back time to heal. He did not feel it his place to argue the fact with Joel. This was not the case with White Fawn, however, who did not hesitate to scold her stubborn patient about his impatience.

They walked up to the two trees they had targeted to measure their results. The patches of cloth measured roughly six inches square, and they found that both patches had survived the shooting without injury. Joel located three bullet holes within two inches of the bottom edge, indicating the rifle shot just a shade low, but accurate enough to satisfy him. The three shots were close together, telling him that he was steady enough, even with the wound. Red Shirt's results were not very different from Joel's; the only difference was his shots were to the right of the target, but close enough to be considered kill shots. They marked the bullet holes by smearing mud on each one, then walked farther back into the canyon to test the accuracy at a greater distance. At the end of the day, they both decided they preferred to use the Henrys, even though the Spencers might have an edge on the longer shots.

Satisfied that he was ready to return to the fight with Beauchamp and his men, Joel told Red Shirt that he was leaving in the morning. "I know we've been through a lot of hell together," he told his friend. "But this ain't something you have to have a part in. I just don't wanna let Beauchamp get away with the killin' he's had his men do, and I'll be damned if I'll let him move in on my brother's claim. I won't blame you one bit if you'd rather stay with Walking Eagle's village. I feel fit enough to do what I've gotta do by myself."

Red Shirt seemed astonished that Joel would even make such a statement. His response was his usual shrug and "I go with you."

"Well, you're damn sure welcome," Joel said, glad to have his help. "We'll start back in the mornin'."

When they returned to the village, they went to Yellow Moon's tipi to speak with Walking Eagle. When the chief came out to talk to them, Joel held the Spencer carbine out before him.

"I wish to give you the gift of this weapon," he said. "It is a fine rifle and shoots true." Pleasantly surprised, for it was a fine gift, Walking Eagle accepted it graciously. Obviously pleased, he turned the carbine over and over, admiring it from every angle. "I have many cartridges for the weapon," Joel continued, "and I'll leave them for you, and there are more in the camp I made by the waterfall. When I return, I'll bring those."

When they left the chief's lodge, they went to Crooked Arrow's tipi so Red Shirt could present the medicine man with his Spencer. Crooked Arrow was as pleased as Walking Eagle had been, and offered his thanks as well.

When Walking Eagle learned that Joel and Red Shirt were leaving the next morning to seek out the men who had attacked them, he called for a dance to ask Man Above to give them courage and strength. Joel was honored, of course, but he was also uncertain about his participation. He welcomed the food that would be offered, but he had heard that war dances were usually held when Indian tribes were going to go to fight an enemy, and that often these dances lasted into the wee hours of the morning. He preferred not to stay up all night when he was still not feeling one hundred percent fit. Red Shirt assured him that they would be able to excuse themselves from the celebration without offending anyone.

"In that case, let's get the dance on," Joel said. "I'll take all the help I can get from God, or Old Man, or Man Above."

So the dance was begun, and Red Shirt performed

his version along with the young Shoshoni warriors around the giant fire in the village center. Watching the ceremonial dancing, Joel was almost convinced that some of the young men would have volunteered to go on the warpath with him and the Bannock warrior. After a couple of hours, they retired from the dance, their absence hardly noticed, and returned to the small tipi they shared. One pair of eyes watched their departure, however: the dark doelike eyes of White Fawn.

After returning from a visit to the trees downstream where all the male members of the village went to answer nature's calls, Joel felt some discomfort in his wound, a hot, stinging sensation, and he decided to go to the stream to bathe it with cold water. With no desire to stand long in the cold night air without his shirt, he tried to move as quickly as possible. Even though he shivered with the cold, the water felt good on the healing wound. Eager to get back into his warm shirt, he did not notice the figure standing in the path in the moonlight until he was startled by her voice.

"Let me look at the wound," White Fawn said.

"White Fawn! What are you doin' here?"

"I saw you leave the dance, and I wanted to make sure your wound is all right," she said. "Let me see it." She stepped forward and put a hand on his shirt, to keep him from slipping it over his head.

"All right, but make it quick. I'm freezin' to death," he said.

"Ha," she chided, "brave warrior. Women bathe in water and not complain of cold."

"Women crazy." He returned the tease, but stood patiently while her fingers lightly touched the skin around the wound. It caused him to shiver more.

"You didn't do a very good job," she scolded. "One side of the wound is not even wet."

"Well, it's kinda hard for me to reach it down there on my back," he said in his defense.

"Water won't help it heal any faster, but won't hurt it." She held his shirt up for him so he could put it on and watched him pull it down around his waist. "So you go to find these white men who try to kill you. If you find them and kill them, what will you do then?"

"Why, I reckon I'll build a cabin where my brother's used to be and start over again to do what I came out here to do."

"Red Shirt told me there was a woman and a young girl who came with you from Tellus."

"Texas," he corrected.

"Texas," she repeated. "The young girl, you brought her to be your wife?"

"Ruthie?" He had to chuckle. "Lord no. Ruthie wasn't much more than a child. She was younger than you. She was just someone who had lost her family when their wagon was attacked by some hostile Indians, Comanche or Cheyenne, I suppose. They didn't know which."

"I am not a child," White Fawn told him. "Not like Ruthie." Her tone was indignant.

"Why, no, ma'am, I'm sure you're not," he quickly replied, sensing that any implication as such was an insult.

"The gun," she said, "that was a fine gift you gave my father. A gift like that would have been a fine gift for a young man to give to the father of a girl he wanted for a wife."

"Oh?" he replied. "I suppose it would be at that. I don't know about such things. I just wanted to give

your father a gift for takin' care of Red Shirt and me—
and of course for the attention you've given me." Suddenly he wasn't noticing the cold anymore, confused
by the strange conversation he was having with the
young Shoshoni girl.

"I am at the age when most Shoshoni girls take a
husband. Fighting Horse wanted to give my father six
ponies for my hand. A girl would be proud to be the
wife of Fighting Horse, but I did not want to marry him."

"Why not?" Joel asked, still wondering why she was
telling him. It seemed a strange time to discuss her
marriage opportunities, and awkward for her to confess them to him.

"Because I told my father that I wanted to wait until
I found a man that I truly wanted to be with. My father
is a kind, understanding man, and so he did not complain that I didn't want to marry Fighting Horse. I
think I am ready to tell my father that I have found a
man that I want to marry."

"Well, I guess that's good," Joel said. "I think that's
got to be good news for the lucky young man."

She gazed directly into his eyes and replied, "He
does not know yet."

"Well, I reckon you oughta tell him," Joel said.

"No, I think not," she said softly. "If it is right for us,
it will come to him, and then he will come to Walking
Eagle with gifts." She turned then and started walking
briskly back along the path, ending the awkward conversation.

Joel watched her depart. Left with a confused mind,
he wondered what had just happened to make White
Fawn inclined to tell him so much of her personal feelings. He had to admit that the encounter had caused a
strange feeling inside him that he could not readily

explain. He was still standing there when Red Shirt came up the path behind him.

"Was that White Fawn you were talking to?" Red Shirt asked.

"Yeah. She wanted to make sure I was takin' care of my wound, I reckon."

In the darkness, Joel could not see the smile on the Bannock warrior's face. "I think maybe she look for husband," he said.

"She said she's already found one," Joel replied. He hesitated a few moments more, still wondering about his conversation with her. Then he shook it from his mind. "Well, I'm ready to hit the hay. We've gotta ride in the mornin'."

"Look yonder," Zach Turner said, and pointed toward a grassy pocket at the bottom of a steep slope leading down to a stream that flowed out of a narrow pass between that mountain and the one next to it. "I knew they'd all wind up in a bunch somewhere. This might be easier than we figured."

Mike Strong's eye followed the direction Zach pointed in and he saw the horses peacefully grazing on the grass close to the stream. "We'd best take a good look around before we go ridin' down there to get 'em. That bastard mighta set 'em up for an ambush."

"I believe I'da picked a better spot than that to ambush somebody," Zach said. "They're out in the clear. Ain't no trees to amount to anything that a man could hide behind, no rocks or nothin' for a hundred yards or more till you get back to that pass."

"Maybe you're right," Strong admitted. "There ain't no place to hide."

His cautious manner was the result of his experience

in dealing with Joel McAllister, where he had been surprised too many times, and at great cost. Beauchamp's orders were to find McAllister and kill him, and to round up the six horses running loose. It appeared that the less dangerous half of that task could be accomplished with little trouble, since the horses had all gathered together.

The other half was what concerned him the most. He and Zach had searched for Joel at the burned-out cabin, and the entrance to the mine, in case he had decided to take cover in the small space left after it had been dynamited. They had found no trace of the man, so they started scouting the mountain, hoping to find his body somewhere. Strong was certain Joel had been wounded, and he must have found a hole to hide in while he tried to recover, or might have died.

"All right," he decided, "let's take it slow."

They nudged their horses down the side of the ridge. There was no need to guide them, for they naturally went toward the other horses by the stream. Strong was rolling his options over in his mind as he descended the slope. Should he and Zach drive the recovered horses back to Blackjack, now that they had them rounded up? He didn't like the thought of facing his irate boss unless he also had a body to show him. But if they managed to flush McAllister out of hiding, there might be a running gunfight, and they wouldn't be able to drive the horses. Then they would have to find them again. His thoughts were then interrupted by a comment from Zach, who had ridden out ahead of him.

"Damned if that ain't mighty peculiar," he said when they were within a short distance of the horses. "All of 'em got their reins tied to a rope."

"Oh, shit!" Strong blurted, jerked his horse's head

around sharply, and galloped recklessly across the face of the slope, even as he heard the rifle shots behind him.

Zach, whose thought processes were naturally slower, was staring, eyes wide-open, and mouth as well, when the rifle slug knocked him from the saddle, his body bouncing and rolling down the slope after his horse. His assassins rose from the holes they had dug in the open meadow, casting off the juniper bushes that had disguised them to take a couple more shots at the fleeing Strong.

"Make sure he's dead!" Joel shouted to Red Shirt, and ran to untie one of the horses, hoping he picked a fast one.

With his rifle in hand, he raced off after the surviving member of the gang that had massacred his family. The one thought in his mind was not to let the last one get away again. It would be nothing less than a grave sin if even one of the ruthless gang of trigger-men were allowed to escape.

The horse he happened to choose was a good one. Strong and willing, the buckskin responded to his encouragement, and he gradually closed the gap between them as they galloped across the foot of the mountain, recklessly disregarding the potential for a spill on the steep slope. He ignored the shots Strong fired wildly with his pistol, holding the buckskin to a steady pace until the slope began to steepen even more, causing him to have to ease up on him. In fear for his life, however, Strong kicked his horse mercilessly when the animal's natural inclination was to slow down. It was certain to happen. The horse finally slid, breaking its left front leg, and spilling its rider to go tumbling down the slope, almost to the bottom.

Holding the buckskin back, Joel watched the fallen

rider as he came to a stop against a rock and frantically scrambled to collect himself. Cautious now, as he approached him, Joel dismounted and cocked the Henry. He aimed the weapon at the panic-stricken man, who was desperately looking about him for the pistol he had dropped from his hand when he had been thrown from the saddle. Joel spotted the weapon some ten or twelve yards up the slope as he continued to walk toward the cornered outlaw.

"Wait!" Strong finally shrieked. "Don't shoot! I surrender! Beauchamp's the man you want. I was just doin' what he ordered!" He spotted his pistol then and started edging toward it while trying to talk his way out of the execution bound to be coming. Joel did not reply but kept walking slowly toward him. Strong pleaded as he got a little closer to the weapon on the ground, "Ain't you even gonna give me a chance?"

Joel stopped then. "A chance? Yeah, I reckon that would be fair, wouldn't it? I'll tell you what, I'll give you the same chance you gave that thirteen-year-old girl when you burned my brother's cabin to the ground. Is that enough for you?"

Seeing there was no chance for mercy from the cold-eyed executioner gazing solemnly at him, Strong spat out his defiance. "You son of a bitch, I'll see you in hell."

With that, he lunged for the pistol, falling several feet short when Joel fired. The first shot knocked him over on his back, and he was looking up at his fate when the fatal shot entered his brain.

Joel stood over the corpse for a few moments as a sudden feeling of fatigue swept over his body, a feeling that it was all over, but he knew it wasn't finished until something was done about Boss Beauchamp, the primary source of the destruction of Boone McAllister's dream.

The question was what to do about him. He needed killing no less than any one of the men he had sent to murder innocent people. But Beauchamp was looked upon in Silver City as an upstanding businessman, owner of Beauchamp No. 2 mine, a cattle rancher—and worse, owner of the town's sheriff. Joel would have to think on the matter before acting. He had hopes of carrying on with what Boone had started, and becoming a citizen of the town.

How can that be possible, he thought, *if I walk up and shoot one of the town's leading citizens?*

He walked a few steps up the slope where Strong's horse lay, its eyes wide with pain. "Sorry, partner," Joel said softly. "There ain't nothin' I can do for a broke leg." He aimed the Henry at the back of the suffering horse's head and put it out of its misery. Taking his buckskin's reins, he stroked the horse's neck in appreciation for serving him well. "Let's take it easy goin' back," he told it. "I don't wanna break your leg." He had gone no more than a mile when he met Red Shirt, riding his bay and leading the others, including Joel's gray gelding.

Seeing Joel coming back with no extra horse behind him, Red Shirt feared Strong had managed to escape. But then he noticed an extra rifle riding behind the saddle scabbard and the gun belt hanging on the saddle horn. He smiled in greeting his friend. "I think you get him," he said.

"I got him," Joel replied. "Now let's put these horses somewhere safe."

He needed time to think, and his wound was giving him some discomfort. Red Shirt had been right when he said it had not healed enough. He decided to take the horses to Walking Eagle's village, before he made his final move against Beauchamp, a move that he was not clear on yet. Beauchamp was his mortal enemy, and he had never even seen the man. If he walked into his office at the No. 2 mine and shot him down, he would most likely be hanged without a trial by the citizens of Silver City. And that would be the end of the dream Boone had, as well as his own, and probably Red Shirt's, too. For he was becoming rapidly convinced that Red Shirt had decided that he was content to stay with him, whatever the path he chose. The thought brought a smile to his face. Though it seemed unlikely at their first meeting, he had turned into a good friend.

Chapter 15

By the time they crossed the stream that led to Joel's camp by the waterfall, it was late in the afternoon, so they decided it would be better to camp there for the night. The Shoshoni village was still some distance away, and it would be too difficult to drive the newly acquired horses through the narrow canyons at night. It was just as well, for Joel had promised to pick up the cartridges for the Spencer he had left there and give them to Walking Eagle and Crooked Arrow. The little pocket around the waterfall was a bit crowded after they drove the six horses, plus the two they rode, through the narrow pass.

Red Shirt was the last in. He looked around him at the steep walls, then dismounted. "Good camp," he said. "Too many horses now. Two, three days, eat all the grass."

Joel laughed. "I expect they would, but we're not comin' back to this camp. I'm goin' back to my brother's ranch, and I'm gonna build another house. We'll start runnin' some cattle and horses on those meadows, and we'll see if we can strike that strain of gold Boone was so sure was in that mountain." Even as he was telling Red Shirt, he realized that he was believing it for the first time. He had spoken of the possibility before, but now he was certain that it was what he really wanted.

Red Shirt listened, then shrugged. "Plan good, need wife."

"Ha," Joel grunted, "you or me?"

"You need wife."

"Well, maybe," Joel allowed. "I reckon it would help to have a woman around. I'm thinkin' you oughta find you a little Shoshoni gal to cook for you and give you a lot of little babies to bounce on your knee."

The picture that his mind conjured of the stoic Bannock warrior caused him to chuckle. It was the first time he could remember a lighthearted evening spent by a warm campfire with no threat of an attack for some time.

"You need wife," Red Shirt insisted.

"I don't know about that," Joel said. "I might one day, but I ain't got plans no time soon."

As quickly as his lighthearted mood had struck, it suddenly left him when his mind returned to focus on the unfinished business he had to take care of. For he was certain that as long as Beauchamp was alive, he would take whatever means necessary to take the land held by the McAllisters.

As Boone had said, Beauchamp was convinced there was a major strike that mountain was hiding, and now Joel McAllister was sitting on top of it. So it was only a matter of time before Boss Beauchamp hired another assassin to rid him of the obstacle standing between him and the gold.

When they had eaten their supper of jerky and coffee

and turned in for the night, Joel lay awake for a long time, his mind filled with images of Ruthie Ferris, Elvira Moultrie, and Riley Tarver. He didn't know if he could ever forgive himself for their brutal murders. He should have stayed with the women on that night. At least one of the men should have. He was guilty of putting too much trust in the ability of Elvira and Blue Beads, and believing that the house would not be targeted.

Damn, he suddenly told himself, *let it go or you'll never get any sleep.*

He made himself listen to the peaceful sound of the water tumbling gently over the rocks, accompanied by the soft murmuring Red Shirt made in his sleep. Soon he was drifting toward sleep himself. Just before he fell off, a picture of the angelic face he had seen upon awakening from his wound came again to reassure him.

It was late morning when Joel and Red Shirt drove the seven horses across the wide stream to join the horse herd grazing in the valley. Some of the young men of the village came out to greet them, and Red Shirt told them of the fight with the hired gunmen while Joel took the saddle off Zach Turner's horse, then turned it loose with the others. When they walked into the village, they led their two horses over to the tipi, unsaddled them, and tied them to a stake by the tipi. Joel turned then to see Walking Eagle approaching.

"I welcome you back," Walking Eagle said. "Your war party must have been successful. I see you captured more ponies."

"The last two men who massacred my family are dead," Joel told him, "but the man who sent them is still alive."

"Beauchamp?" Walking Eagle asked.

Surprised that he knew the name, Joel said, "Yes, that's his name."

Walking Eagle nodded slowly. "I went to the trading post yesterday and I talked to Beecher. He said he knows of this man, Beauchamp. He says he is big medicine in Silver City, that he might be governor of this territory one day. Any man who kills such a man might bring the soldiers down upon him. That is all I want to say."

You said a mouthful, Joel thought, for he recognized a combination of advice and a warning all rolled up in those few simple words.

"What you say is true," Joel replied. "But this man is too evil to let live. I promise you that should I be the one who kills him, I will not bring the soldiers down on your village. I alone will answer for my deeds. If it works out that I am the one who ends Beauchamp's life, then you will never see me again."

Walking Eagle smiled at the tall young white warrior. "You are a good man, Joel McAllister. Your heart is strong, but you are walking a path that is dangerous and might lead you to a sad place. You have stilled the hands of those who struck your brother and your friends down. Maybe it would be good if you leave your trail of vengeance now. That is all I want to say."

"I hear your words," Joel replied solemnly, "and I will think hard on what you have said, because I respect your counsel."

The Shoshoni chief left him then to think about what he had told him. Walking Eagle was right, Joel had to admit. If he continued with his intention of killing Boss Beauchamp, he would no doubt wind up at the end of a rope, or spend the rest of his days running—and he could say good-bye to his ownership of the homestead Boone had established.

He thought of all of the bodies scattered about the mountain and valley of his brother's land. Maybe he had fulfilled the promise to avenge his family's death. He was certainly sick of the killing. If he called an end to it now, maybe he could live the life that he had told Red Shirt he intended to, rebuild the cabin, use the money he had accumulated to buy seed stock for cattle and horses. It was a pleasant thought, but he quickly told himself that as long as Beauchamp was alive, there would always be the possibility of more bloodshed. Of greater concern, if Beauchamp went on as he planned, to become a major player in the development of the Idaho Territory, it could not bode well for the people who settled here. The man was eaten up with greed, and was absent of morals. He should be stopped, and Joel could see no one to stop him except himself. So be it.

He was not concerned about the men who had been killed by Red Shirt and him. They were all wanted men, hired gunmen. No one of authority would care enough to investigate their deaths, and for the most part, they would probably be glad they were dead. But it would be a different story where Beauchamp was concerned, and for that reason, he intended to do the job alone. He had no desire to place a bounty on Red Shirt's head. His Bannock partner was already settling in with his Shoshoni friends, and Joel thought it the best thing that could have happened for the loner Indian. So he decided to stay in the village for one night only, and then start out on the final leg of his avowed journey. He would not tell Red Shirt of his decision to go alone until morning. He would no doubt protest that he should accompany him, but he would not permit him to go.

After a supper of venison, fresh from a hunt by some of the men of the village, Joel and Red Shirt shared some coffee with two of the hunters. Several of the other people came to sit at the fire and visit, both men and women, to hear details of their fight with the outlaws. Noticeable by her absence, at least to Joel, was White Fawn. He couldn't help wondering why she had not come to ask about his wound, or to scold him for not taking care of it properly. It concerned him, although he could not explain why. Once he saw her come from her mother's tipi, and he thought she was coming to see him, but she turned and followed the path to the stream instead, not even looking toward him.

Strange, he thought, *but she'll probably show up when she sees me getting ready to leave in the morning.*

With the arrival of morning, there was the anticipated protest from Red Shirt when Joel told him that he was going to settle with Beauchamp alone.

"This is for me to do alone," he told him. "I am going to face just one man, and I made a promise to myself that it would be my hand that strikes him down, my hand alone. Only then will I know my medicine is strong."

That statement was enough to gain Red Shirt's reluctant forgiveness, and he finally said that he understood.

Joel saddled the gray and packed food and ammunition in his saddlebags. He wasn't sure how long he would be gone, or if he was actually coming back, so he supplied himself to be gone several days. Ready to ride, he glanced around the circle of tipis, but there was no sign of White Fawn. He shrugged and stepped up on his horse, asking himself why he even cared.

With a nod of his head to Red Shirt, he wheeled the gray around toward the stream and gave him a gentle nudge of his heels. He nodded again to Walking Eagle, who stood gravely watching him as he passed by the chief's lodge. He guessed that the old man figured that he had decided against his advice. Crossing over the stream and setting out on the path that led to the valley where his camp was located, he did not see the Shoshoni maiden watching him depart from the edge of the pines.

Boss Beauchamp arose from his bed in a cross mood, which was his usual mood since the events of the past week. He had slept very little during the night just past, even after he summoned Lena to his bed in hopes of diverting his mind from his troubles. The diversion had been unsuccessful, and he blamed the reluctant Ute woman for his displeasure. The disagreement following resulted in a profane tongue-lashing with a sharp kick to the poor woman's backside as she left his bed. He had reason to be angry. It had been two days since Mike Strong and Zach Turner had gone to settle with Joel McAllister once and for all, and they had not yet returned.

"Lena!" he yelled out for her.

In a minute, she appeared at the bedroom door. "What do you want now?"

"Go down to the bunkhouse and see if Strong and Zach rode in last night."

"I'm fixing your breakfast," she replied. "If they came in, they'll come tell you. I'm busy."

In no mood for her sass, he responded by picking up his boot and throwing it at her. She deftly stepped aside and watched it bounce against the wall, which only served to fuel his anger. Recognizing the indications of a beating in the making, she quickly left the room to return to the kitchen. He continued to dress, then came into the kitchen. Grabbing the broom propped in the corner, he administered a sharp crack across her back as she bent over the oven.

"Now, damn you, you ignorant savage, get down to the bunkhouse like I told you, and send Fuzzy up here." He drew the broom back for another blow, prompting her to hurry for the door.

She found the belabored cook in the barn, where he was busy forking hay down for the milk cow. It had been his lot to inherit the responsibility for all the chores around the ranch since there was no one left of the crew hired to do them. It was more than he could keep up with, but Beauchamp expected him to get them all done.

When Lena told him that Boss wanted to see him, he replied, "What for? I ain't got time to go listen to his bellyachin', if I'm gonna get everything done today."

She didn't answer. He didn't expect her to.

She walked back in the kitchen door to find him sitting in the dining room, waiting for his breakfast. "He's on his way," she told him.

"Finish fixing my breakfast," he said, somewhat calmer. "Bring me a cup of coffee first and be sure you fix it the way I like it."

"Yes, sir," she muttered, and went to do his bidding. She took the pot from the edge of the stove, poured it in his favorite cup, and dropped a heaping teaspoon of sugar in. She went out on the back porch, where a pan of milk was cooling, and dipped a spoonful of cream off the top. Then, for good measure, she worked up a mouthful of saliva and spat in the cup, stirred it up, and said to herself, *And that's the way I like it.*

Answering the knock at the back door, she let Fuzzy

in and directed him to the dining room. "You want a cup of coffee?"

"Why, yessum," he replied, "that would be mighty fine."

He was the only one of the men who worked for Beauchamp that Lena was civil to. He figured it was because he was only a cook, and not a hired gun. He was not to enjoy a cup of coffee, however, because Beauchamp overheard her offer.

"No, he doesn't have time for a cup of coffee," Beauchamp called out.

"No, sir," Fuzzy echoed upon entering the dining room. "I ain't got time for a cup of coffee."

"When did Strong tell you he'd be back?" Beauchamp asked Fuzzy.

"He didn't say exactly," Fuzzy said, surprised that Boss asked, since Strong was more likely to have told him. "But I'm pretty sure he wasn't expectin' to be gone overnight. They didn't take any grub with 'em. They was most likely figurin' on bein' back here for supper that night. I expect they mighta run into some trouble." He stood there shifting from one foot to the other while Beauchamp remained silent, letting what he feared had happened sink in. After a few more moments, Fuzzy asked, "Is that all you wanted?"

"Yes, that's all. You can go now and get back to work. By the way, I still see those two boards that need to be replaced on the side of the barn."

"Yes, sir. I'm tryin' to get to it just as fast as I can," Fuzzy said as he walked through the kitchen, where Lena was cooking Beauchamp's breakfast. She gestured to him with a shake of her head. He answered with a weak smile. He had always had compassion for the poor Ute woman and the abuse she suffered from Beauchamp.

"Don't let these chores get ahead of you," Boss called after him.

"Yes, sir," Fuzzy replied dutifully.

After breakfast and his morning trip to the out-house, Beauchamp donned his heavy coat for his ride into Silver City. It was plain as day that the last two of his hired guns had joined the rest of his crew in hell at the hand of Joel McAllister. He was going to have to find a legal way to get his hands on that property, and he was going to have to go to the law for protection. There was no reason to believe McAllister would hesi-tate to come after him, and with that in mind, he had started carrying a revolver all the time.

Always happy to see him ride off to town, Lena Three Toe stood in the kitchen door to watch him pass eventually out of sight. She was about to turn around to start cleaning up the breakfast dishes when she caught sight of Fuzzy on his horse, loaded with what appeared to be all his meager belongings. He turned the horse and rode off in the opposite direction from town, never looking back.

"Ha," Lena snorted, hardly surprised. "It's gonna be hell to pay when that ol' son of a bitch gets back. I reckon he's gonna want me to do all the chores now."

All the way to town Beauchamp thought long and hard on the best way to handle the problem with McAllister since his planned massacre had backfired, leaving him defenseless against a determined execu-tioner. He finally decided the best way to handle it was to get the sheriff to go after McAllister for murdering his men. Jim Crowder was simpleminded enough to do what Beauchamp told him to do. After all, he owned the man. He wouldn't question the right or wrong of it.

He arrived at his office at Beauchamp No. 2 late that morning to be told by his foreman that the town council had called a meeting to discuss a problem with the sheriff. This news was not well received by the already troubled mine owner. He insisted upon being present at any such meeting the council called.

"Where are they meeting?" he asked.

"In the back of Thompson's store was what they said when they came by here to let you know," his foreman said.

Beauchamp didn't wait. Out the door he went and strode determinedly down the street to Marvin Thompson's general store, anxious to get there before they made some stupid decision that he would have to overturn. He stormed in the door, striding past Thompson's wife without so much as a "good morning," and through the stockroom to the back parlor, where an assembly of eight men sat around a long table.

"Well, good morning, Mr. Beauchamp," Jonah Newberry greeted him from the head of the table. "We sent Clyde Parsons by your office to notify you about the meeting, but you hadn't got in yet."

"What's going on?" Beauchamp demanded.

Marvin Thompson answered him. "We decided to call an emergency meeting after we had some trouble here in town last night and our sheriff refused to handle it."

"What kind of trouble?" Beauchamp asked, already opposed to whatever the council had voted on. "I find Sheriff Crowder to be a capable man."

"If you had been in town last night, you might understand why we've asked Jim to step down as sheriff,"

Jonah Newberry said. "A couple of miners at the Miner's Rest got to drinking too heavily and got in a fight with Jake Tully. It spilled out into the street, and turned into a gunfight, and pretty soon they stopped fighting each other and started shooting up the town. Charley Owens ran to get Sheriff Crowder, but he locked himself up in his office and refused to come out. He said it wasn't his job to get between two crazy drunk men with guns. Well, the whole town was hiding anywhere they could to keep from getting shot. So you see why we decided we needed a sheriff who would enforce the law."

This was not good news to Beauchamp, having decided he would talk Crowder into shooting Joel McAllister on sight. "Wait a minute, gentlemen. Let's not do something here that we might regret later on. We'd best give Jim Crowder another chance. I'll talk to him and see if I can't get to the bottom of this thing last night."

"It's a little too late for that," Marvin Thompson said. "You see, we've already voted, and it was unanimous, so we fired him. Toby just got back a minute or two before you got here with the keys to the office. We voted him the new sheriff till we find a permanent one."

Beauchamp's brow deepened and his nostrils flared red with anger. "You can't do that. You have to vote again, since I wasn't here."

"It was unanimous, Mr. Beauchamp," Newberry said. "It wouldn't do any good to vote again. That would just make it eight to one in favor of firing Crowder."

"Hell, he didn't do nothin' but set in that office and drink coffee," the blacksmith said. "It wasn't just last night. We shoulda fired him a long time ago."

Beauchamp was stymied and he knew it. He had to

keep a respectable facade when dealing with the towns-people, even though he ached to pull the gun out of his inside coat pocket and clear the room. Knowing he was risking the destruction of all the plans he had made, he cautioned himself to calm down and think rationally.

"Well, gentlemen, I guess you have ample cause to make the decision, so I, of course, will vote with the council."

"Then I guess that winds up all the business we had to discuss," Marvin Thompson said, "so I reckon I'm open for a motion to adjourn the meeting."

"Hold on, if you please, Mr. Thompson," Beauchamp said. "I have a pressing problem of extreme impor-tance." Several of the eight who had already risen from their chairs sat back down. Beauchamp continued, now that he had everyone's attention. "I'm afraid my life is in immediate danger. I know the town hasn't been aware of what's been going on out in the mountains right around us, but it seems that Boone McAllister's brother is a hired killer. And he was brought here to murder me and everyone who works for me."

His opening remarks brought grunts of surprise from the men at the table. "My Lord, Mr. Beauchamp!" Toby Bryan exclaimed. "Why didn't you tell Jim Crowder about it?"

"I did," Beauchamp lied. "I told him after three of my men were shot down by Joel McAllister, but Crowder said he had no jurisdiction outside Silver City, so I've been left on my own to deal with this murderer. And, gentlemen, I'm sorry to report that I haven't been successful in dealing with the problem, because he has killed almost all of my people. I have reason to believe the mad dog has even assassinated his own brother." He paused to let that take effect, and was encouraged by their expressions of horror. "We were led to believe it was an Indian raid that killed those people up on that mountain, but there were no witnesses to attest to that. Nobody questioned the fact that Joel McAllister and his Indian friend were the only survivors after that raid. Now he has sent word that he's coming after me and I have to fear for my life every time I ride back and forth between town and my ranch. I fear that he will be waiting for me when I return home tonight."

The room was gripped by complete silence, everyone stunned by the brazenness of the charges. Finally Toby Bryan spoke. "I talked to Joel McAllister when he first came to town. He seemed like a right nice fellow. He sure fooled me."

"Remember what Jake Tully said about him?" Marvin Thompson said. "Jake said he handled himself like he knew what he was doing when he laid that fellow out on the saloon floor. Jake said he was afraid he was gonna start shooting."

"That's right," Beauchamp said, confident that they were all buying into what he was selling. "That man he attacked worked for me, and, gentlemen, that man is now dead, shot down in cold blood by Joel McAllister."

He was gratified by the gasps and concerned reactions that he saw, and realized that he should have taken this approach to solve his problem before.

Toby Bryan stood up and looked around the table to ensure eye contact with every man there. "Well, you gentlemen have voted to give me the responsibility of enforcin' the law in our town. And I want you to know, Mr. Beauchamp, that I take that responsibility seriously when it comes to protecting our most important citizens. So I reckon I'll ride back home with you tonight in case McAllister is waitin' for you. Then we'll see who shoots who."

It couldn't have gone better as far as Beauchamp was concerned. This was even better than persuading Jim Crowder to do his dirty work. He had an idea that the blacksmith would stand firm where Crowder might have decided to run.

"Sheriff," he addressed Toby, "I would be mighty obliged." He looked around at the others and announced, "I think we've made a fine choice to replace Jim Crowder."

"Just let me know when you're ready to go home," Toby told him. "I'll be ready to ride."

Chapter 16

Not sure when she might see Beauchamp return from town, Lena Three Toe went about the usual preparations for his supper. Her mind was occupied with thoughts of Fuzzy's sudden departure that morning, an event that was not totally unexpected by her. She wondered why he had stayed on as long as he had. Maybe this distraction was the reason she did not know she was not alone when she turned to suddenly find him standing in the kitchen doorway, holding a rifle casually in one hand. Startled, she dropped a pan of potatoes she was preparing to peel.

"You're him!" she gasped, and instinctively backed away.

"Where's Beauchamp?" Joel asked.

"He's gone to town," she replied fearfully, and continued to back away until she was stopped by the kitchen table.

He had already assumed as much, since there had appeared to be no one on the place at all when he rode in. Having had no idea if Beauchamp had more men, he had come in from the hill behind the barn. Cautiously checking the barn, then the bunkhouse, the smokehouse, even the outhouse before deciding the place was deserted, he then came to the house.

"You've got no need to be afraid of me, ma'am. My quarrel is with your boss. I've got no quarrel with you."

Something in his eyes and the tone of his voice, softspoken but deadly, convinced her that he was telling her the truth, and her first reaction to that was to wish that Beauchamp was home to face him.

"I reckon you came to settle with him for killing your family," she finally said.

"I reckon," he answered, surprised that she spoke about it so calmly. "You expect him for supper?"

"He'll be here," she said.

Noticing a bruise beside her eye that was just beginning to yellow, he asked, "He do that?" He pointed to her eye.

"Yes," she answered, "when he was in one of his better moods."

"Don't suppose you know when he'll be coming?"

"No, can't say," she replied.

He thought it over for a few moments before deciding. "I reckon it'd be best if I ride on out toward town," he told her, "so's not to have any shootin' goin' on around the house here." There was a thought for her safety, but he also figured that he preferred to confront the man out in the open. He turned to leave, then paused to say, "Sorry about your potatoes."

"No trouble at all," she said, and followed him to the door to watch him ride away. She stood there for a long time, watching until he became too small to see any longer, unable to explain the sense of satisfaction she felt. It had been like being in the presence of an angel of death. It was a feeling that made her heart beat faster with an elation she had not felt since she was a young girl, flush with the expectation that things were going to be better in her life.

He rode for a couple of miles along a well-worn trail to Silver City, contemplating the results of the action he was determined to take. The debt must be settled, even though it was going to cost him dearly because he was forced to resolve it in this fashion. For he was convinced that he would be a hunted man for the rest of his life, wanted for the murder of a respected businessman of the settlement. He would lose the land, and the future, that Boone had staked out for the two of them.

It has to be, he finally told himself. *It does no good to regret.* He tried to put such thoughts aside then and concentrate on the business at hand.

Coming to a ridge off to the side of the trail, he decided to stop, thinking that if he continued, he might wind up in town before he met Beauchamp. The ridge was thick with spruce trees along the base, so he figured it a good spot to wait for his target to show up. He tied the gray to the limb of a tree, pulled his rifle, and walked down near the edge of the trees, where he had a good view of the trail beyond. He sat down to wait.

He sat for almost two hours before someone appeared on the trail in the distance, but it was two riders instead of the lone rider he expected. Leaving the spot where he had waited, he backed up into the trees a little farther, so as not to be seen from the trail. In a few minutes, the two riders came even with his vantage point, and he recognized one of them. It was the blacksmith; he had forgotten his name, but he remembered the face. The other man, with the heavy woolen coat with a fur collar, was Beauchamp. But was he? Joel hesitated, uncertain. He had never seen Ronald Beauchamp before, and he had to be certain. By all reasoning, it had to be Beauchamp, for they were obviously going to Blackjack Mountain. But what if they were the blacksmith and one of the other businessmen of Silver City? He knew he couldn't risk killing the wrong man. To add to his indecision, he didn't like the idea of calling a showdown with Beauchamp if the blacksmith was there to witness it, consequently destroying the slim chance that he might get away with the killing. Realizing there were too many reasons to wait until absolutely sure he was doing the right thing, he reluctantly eased the hammer down on the Henry and watched them pass.

He remained there until the two riders were out of sight before leading his horse out of the spruce trees and starting back toward Blackjack Mountain. Still intent upon finishing the task he had set for himself, he walked the gray leisurely along the trail back to the ranch, planning to watch the house to see if the blacksmith returned to town alone. He resigned himself to the fact that he would shoot Beauchamp at long range if that turned out to be his only opportunity. But he preferred to face the man so Beauchamp would know who shot him and why. With no notion what the night would bring, however, he could only wait to see.

With a feeling of disappointment, Lena looked out the window and saw the two men approaching. She walked to the front door when they pulled up at the rail in front of the house and Beauchamp dismounted.

She didn't recognize the rider still in the saddle, but she noticed the star pinned to his vest when his coat gaped open.

If that ain't something, she thought. *The ol' bastard riding with the law.*

She heard the lawman tell Beauchamp that he was going to scout around the hills surrounding the ranch house to see if there was any sign of anyone hiding out there.

"I appreciate your help, Sheriff," Beauchamp said. "You sure you don't want some coffee or something to eat before you ride back to town?"

"No, sir," Toby replied. "I'll go ahead and take a look around before it starts to get too dark."

"You best be careful, Sheriff," Beauchamp advised. "And you'd better shoot on sight if you do see him."

He stood there for a few moments after Toby loped off to the low line of hills to the east of Blackjack Mountain. When he disappeared Beauchamp turned and peered toward the barn, expecting Fuzzy to come to take care of his horse. When he still did not come, Beauchamp yelled for him, his patience already taxed.

"Fuzzy!" he yelled again with the same results. Then he turned when he heard the door open behind him, and Lena walked out on the porch. "Where is he?" Beauchamp demanded.

"I don't know," Lena answered frankly, and waited for the explosion.

"That lazy son of a bitch!" Beauchamp roared. "I've got a good mind to put a bullet in his worthless hide!" Taking the reins, he stalked down to the barn, leading his horse, to search Fuzzy out. On the way, his eye caught the two rotten boards in the side of the barn.

"He still hasn't replaced those boards like I told him to," he roared loud enough for Lena to hear it back on the porch. It brought a smile to her face that quickly left when she realized that he would probably take out his anger on her. She went back into her kitchen to put the potatoes, which she had peeled and sliced after picking them up from the floor, on the stove to fry. That thought brought back the image that had been framed in her kitchen door earlier, and she found herself wishing he would return.

After storming through the barn and the bunkhouse, yelling for Fuzzy, he finally realized what had actually happened: He had gone for good. That threatened to push his anger out of control. He stalked out of the barn, but stopped at the door when he realized that he should pull the saddle off his horse and turn it out in the corral. He couldn't remember the last time he had taken care of his horse. He thought about sending Lena back down there to do it, but decided she might mess up his supper if he did. Mumbling profanity to himself, he went back and took care of the horse.

As he was walking back to the house, it suddenly struck him how ghostlike the place had become since it was now deserted. He blamed the fix he now found himself in on the incompetence of the men he had hired to work for him. And now, thanks to their incompetence, he was left with a ranch unattended and a gunman that might even now be coming for him.

"Well, he'll find he's not dealing with some brainless hired gun, if he tries to come after me," he muttered. "I'll shoot him as soon as he sets foot on this property." There were any number of men working his mine who would be glad to work on top of the ground for a change, he thought. He would have a working crew inside a week. "Damn that worthless bastard," he exclaimed when he thought of Fuzzy again.

Inside the kitchen, Lena heard him coming back, talking to himself as he stepped up on the kitchen steps. She instinctively went to the other side of the stove to keep it between them, hoping he would concentrate his anger on Fuzzy, now that he was gone, and ignore her. When he walked in the door, the look on his face told her of the rage burning inside him, and she immediately feared he might decide to release it on her.

"I'll have you some supper in just a little while," she said, hoping to defuse his rage, "just as soon as these potatoes are done."

He stared at her as if he was surprised to see her there. His eyes, dark under heavy black eyebrows, seemed to lash out at her, accusingly. "Why didn't you stop him?"

"Hell, how could I stop him?" Lena replied. "He didn't tell me he was going. He just packed up his things and left. There was no way I coulda stopped him."

"You should have shot him," Beauchamp said, meaning it. "He's left you with a lot of chores. You're gonna have to look after the stock until I hire on some help."

"Look after the stock?" she responded in disbelief. "Who's gonna do the cooking and cleaning—you?"

"I expect you'll do it, if you know what's good for you."

"The hell I will," she fired back, having been pushed beyond her patience. "You're crazy if you think I can run this whole ranch and your house, too."

Infuriated by her gall to back-talk him, he stormed around the stove, catching her arm before she was quick enough to escape him.

"You call me crazy? You dumb Indian bitch! I bought

you, just like I bought everything else on this place. If I hitch you up to a wagon, you'll pull it and keep your mouth shut about it."

"I'll bet you don't even know how to hitch up a wagon," she replied, her anger swelling to meet his. It was the wrong thing to say. It only caused him to explode.

"Damn you!" he shouted, and struck her in the face with his fist, holding her arm as she fell to her knees. Then he struck her again. The sight of her blood oozing from her nose and lip seemed to cause him to want to see more, as he took his anger out on her. The only thing that stopped the merciless beating he was set on administering was a loud knock on the kitchen door. He paused, caught in his insane rage, confused for a moment until he realized what the sound had been. Recovering somewhat then, he dropped the helpless woman to the floor, pulled the revolver from his coat pocket, and went to the door. "Who is it?" he asked.

"It's me, Toby Bryan," the answer came back.

Beauchamp forced himself to recover. "Oh, Sheriff," he managed calmly, and opened the door partially.

"I just wanted to tell you that I took a pretty good look around the place, and there ain't no sign of anybody. You want me to stay on till mornin'?"

"No," Beauchamp said, still with the door halfway open. "I think I'll be all right. I want to thank you for helping me, though. I'd invite you in for supper, but my cook has taken ill, so I guess that's all I'll trouble you tonight."

"All right, then, if you're sure. I reckon I'll ride on back to town," Toby told him.

The door closed, but not before he got a glimpse of the woman lying on the floor by the stove. Undecided whether or not he should say anything about it, he hesitated for a few moments, but then chose to call it none of his business. Beauchamp had said she was sick. Maybe she was. He stepped up into the saddle and headed back to town, thinking he had scouted the hills around the place thoroughly. He had not thought it necessary to search the barn, since Beauchamp had been there to take care of his horse. Both men were unaware of the determined executioner who had cautiously made his way into the back of the barn a short time after Beauchamp went to the house.

Beauchamp stood at the closed door, listening for the sound of Toby's horse departing. When he heard it, he put his pistol back in his pocket and turned in time to emit a sickening grunt as the long butcher knife plunged into his gut. Horrified, he reached instinctively for the woman glaring at him in vengeful hatred, her face a bloody mask. She backed out of his reach, watching him intently as he stared down at the knife, driven with such hateful force that it was in almost up to the handle. He reached down to pull it out, only to scream out in pain when he gripped it. His eyes wide with shock, he staggered toward her, reaching out for her. She continued backing away until she reached the corner of the stove and waited. Step by painful step, he advanced until she was almost within his reach. Just then remembering the revolver in his coat pocket, he fumbled to pull it out. Before he could free it from his pocket, she grabbed the iron skillet from the stove and slammed it against the side of his face, knocking him to the floor.

With the butcher knife still protruding from his stomach, he struggled to get to his feet. He managed to make it to his knees before receiving another blow with the hot skillet, this time leaving him unconscious amid a scattering of half-done potatoes. Unwilling to take any chance that he might survive, Lena reached down with her left hand, her right now throbbing with the severe burn from the handle of the skillet, and pulled the knife from his stomach. Then she opened his throat with it. As an afterthought, she used the knife again to scalp him and, in a vengeful euphoria, sang out a Ute war cry.

The sounds coming from the house left Joel uncertain as to what was going on inside. The scream he had heard had come from a man. Of that, he was certain, but the high-pitched howl that followed sounded as if coming from a woman. Without knowing what he might find confronting him, he opened the door, ready to fire. What he found, he was not expecting. The woman, battered and bloody, stared at him, seeming not to see him. She still held the butcher knife in her hand. He looked from her to the body lying still on the floor. There was no need to ask what had happened.

"I guess I did the job you came to do," she said when she finally seemed to return to the present.

"I reckon you did," he replied. "Are you all right?"

Realizing then that she was still holding the knife, she tossed it to land beside Beauchamp's body. "Yes," she answered with a sigh. "I'm a lot all right now."

"Looks like you took a pretty good whippin'. Maybe I can help you clean your face up a little."

"First thing I wanna do is put some lard on my hand," she said. "It burns like hell, but I didn't have time to grab a cloth."

"I'll help you. Just tell me where you keep it," he offered. It was an odd time to think of it, but her remark caused him to recall when a young Shoshoni girl warned him about picking up a hot metal cup of coffee before it cooled.

"Have you got a place to go?" he asked her as he cleaned the blood from her face, after having wrapped her burned hand. "I don't know if it's a good idea for you to stay here, 'cause the law's bound to show up here sooner or later."

"No, I don't have any place to go," she said, "but it doesn't matter. I'll make out on my own."

"I think it would be best if you came with me. I'll take you someplace safe while this all blows over."

"All right," she said, without asking where. Anywhere away from this place of long suffering was all right with her, and she sensed that she would be safe with him.

The glimpse of the Indian woman lying on the floor in Beauchamp's kitchen had continued to work on Toby Bryan's conscience after he returned to town. He intended to take his responsibility as sheriff seriously, even though he was only temporarily in the position. She was only an Indian, but Toby couldn't help feeling guilty about not going inside the kitchen to see what was going on. So the next morning, he went by the post office to let Jonah Newberry know he was going to take a ride out to Blackjack Mountain to see if there was any sign of Joel McAllister. As he approached the barnyard of Ronald Beauchamp's ranch, he saw no evidence of anyone stirring. In the smaller corral behind the barn, the milk cow stood waiting to be milked and a few beef cattle had strayed into the yard. He saw no smoke coming from the chimney at the house. The whole place seemed to still be asleep.

He pulled up to the front porch, dismounted, and knocked on the porch floor, then stood waiting, but there was no response from inside. He stepped up on the porch then and went to the front door. After knocking several times hard enough for anyone inside to hear, he tried the door and found it unbarred, so he went inside. Standing just inside the door, he called out to see if anyone was there. There was no response to his call, so he walked cautiously down the hall to the kitchen, and was stopped cold by the sight of the body lying near the stove.

Beauchamp! The discovery stunned him. McAllister had gotten to him after all. Beauchamp had not been lying when he said his life was in danger.

Feeling a sudden need for fresh air, Toby walked to the back door and opened it. His hand dropped immediately to the handle of the .44 Colt he wore when he saw a rider coming across the barnyard toward the house. He backed away from the door so he wouldn't be seen—just a couple of steps so that he could continue to watch the rider. A little closer and he recognized the man. It wasn't McAllister, it was Fuzzy Chapman, Beauchamp's bunkhouse cook. Toby backed away from the door.

Fuzzy stepped up to the door and knocked on the jamb. When there was no response, he called out, "Lena, you in there? It's me, Fuzzy."

Toby stepped forward then. "Step inside, Fuzzy. Lena ain't here."

Surprised, Fuzzy nevertheless did as he was told. "I was wonderin' whose horse that was out front," he said when he saw Toby. He was about to say more, but he saw the body and drew back in shock. "Where's Lena?"

"She's gone," Toby said. "I thought you were gone, too."

"I was," Fuzzy said. "But I got to thinkin' about how I shouldn'ta run off and left that poor woman to deal with that bastard, so I turned around and came back to help her." He walked over to take a closer look at the corpse. "He don't look no sweeter dead than he did alive, does he?" He backed up a step then and straightened. "So she finally done it." He looked up at a still-puzzled sheriff and chuckled. "Laid him out among the taters, didn't she? I swear, she finally done it. Looks like she drove that knife plumb through him. Good for her! I'da done the same thing, as long as that son of a bitch beat on that poor woman." He looked up from the corpse. "You say she's gone? Wonder where. What are you doin' out here, Toby?"

"I'm the new sheriff," Toby, said, and pulled his coat aside to show his badge. "We let Jim Crowder go. Beauchamp thought Joel McAllister was out to kill him, and wanted me to look into it."

"Ha!" Fuzzy snorted. "It's the other way around, don't you mean? Beauchamp's been tryin' to kill McAllister ever since he showed up here. Only trouble is, Joel McAllister was more bear than any of those no-good gunslingers Beauchamp kept sendin' up on that mountain to kill him."

Toby was dumbstruck for a few moments by Fuzzy's accusations. "Do you know what you're talkin' about? You tellin' me that McAllister wasn't doin' the rustlin' and killin'—it was the other way around?"

"That's the God's honest truth about it. Beauchamp was out to get McAllister's claim, and he didn't care how he got it done. I shoulda told somebody about it before, but there weren't nobody to tell but Jim Crowder, and that woulda been the same as tellin' Beauchamp himself."

"Why the hell didn't you go tell Jonah Newberry, or Marvin Thompson, or me?" Toby asked.

"Scared," Fuzzy replied. "My life wouldn'ta been worth spit. He'da had Mike Strong kill me in a second."

"Ronald Beauchamp," Toby pronounced, still astonished at this unexpected turn of events. "It's hard to believe he could do what you're sayin'."

"Well, ain't it kinda funny that there ain't been nobody killed anywhere on Beauchamp's property? If you go lookin' for bodies, they're all on McAllister property, includin' Boone McAllister and his woman, and the woman and child that came with his brother. I swear, I can't paint you no clearer picture than that."

"It's hard to argue with that," Toby confessed. "I guess I'll go on back to town and give the council the news. They're gonna find it as hard to believe as I did. I don't know if there's anything anybody will wanna do about it—don't know if there's anything we can do about it." He felt he should do something, but he didn't know what. "I reckon we oughta bury Beauchamp. What are you gonna do now? You stayin' here for a while?"

"Might as well," Fuzzy said. "Ain't got no place else to go."

"I need to get on back to town. How 'bout you buryin' him? Would you mind?"

"It'd give me great pleasure," Fuzzy replied grandly.

Chapter 17

Red Shirt was sitting in his tipi when he heard some young boys shouting Joel's name. "Jo," they called out, having shortened it. "Jo is back!" they alerted the village. Red Shirt put aside the pipe he had been making and hurried outside to greet his friend. He was surprised to see a woman following him on a second horse. Eager to hear the story, he ran to the center of the circle of lodges to meet him. When he got there, he saw that Walking Eagle and Crooked Arrow, along with many others, had come to greet Joel as well. They stood waiting while the horses walked up from the stream. As they came closer, there arose gentle murmurings among the gathering when they saw the bruised and battered face of the woman.

Walking Eagle was the first to speak. "I see the white warrior has returned," he said in an uncertain tone. "Were you successful on the warpath?"

"You might say that," Joel replied as he stepped down from the saddle. "But you don't have to worry about the soldiers coming to your village. The man, Beauchamp, is dead, but not by my hand."

"Ah," Walking Eagle responded. "That is good news. The white man's law is not looking for you, then?"

"They've got no reason to look for me," Joel said.

Walking Eagle looked relieved. "Then welcome back, my friend."

"Yeah, welcome," Red Shirt said then, having politely held his tongue to let the chief speak first. "Tell us what happened. Who this woman?" He nodded toward Lena, who was still seated on Boss Beauchamp's black Morgan gelding, hesitating to dismount before she was sure she was welcome.

"Lena Three Toe," Joel said. "I told her she would be welcome in Walking Eagle's village. She's had a hard time of it, and had no place to go, so I brought her here."

Yellow Moon stepped forward then and offered her hand to help Lena down. "Welcome," she said. "You must be tired and hungry. Come and we will prepare food for you."

Lena looked at Joel, as if asking if it was all right. "Go along with Yellow Moon," he said. "I'll take care of your horse."

Red Shirt stepped forward to help him pull the saddles off the two horses and carry them, along with a canvas bag filled with some clothes and personal items that belonged to Lena, to his tipi. They turned the horses out with the Indian herd, leaving their bridles on to identify them quicker, no longer feeling the precaution to tie them up next to the tipi.

"I'm hopin' one of the women will take Lena in," Joel told Red Shirt as they led the horses out to the meadow where the Shoshoni horses were grazing.

"Already done," Red Shirt said, "when Yellow Moon take her. You tell me now what happened."

Joel related all that had taken place since he rode off to kill Beauchamp, and why the Ute woman came to be with him. "I've been thinkin' a lot on the ride over here, and I've been makin' some plans on what I'm gonna do now that we don't have to worry about Beauchamp and his gang of killers. I'm gonna build another house on that piece of land Boone filed on. I'm plannin' on raisin' some cattle and horses on that mountain, and open that mine up again. I was kinda hopin' you'd help me do it."

Red Shirt started to shrug but stopped and grinned instead. "I help."

"It's a deal, then," Joel said, and offered his hand. Red Shirt took it and pumped it up and down in an exaggerated handshake, causing Joel to remark, "That oughta make it official. There's one more thing I've gotta do before we get started. I'm goin' into Silver City and have a talk with the sheriff and that city council to make sure they all know that's my land and I intend to keep it. I'd like to convince all of 'em that I'm peaceful and plan to do business with 'em."

"I go with you this time," Red Shirt said. "I not sure you come back last time."

Joel laughed and said, "All right, if you want to. We'll go in the mornin'. Ain't no use in losin' any more time. We've got a lot of work to do if we're gonna make a goin' operation outta that place."

Before leaving the next morning, Joel told Lena why they were going and that if all went well, they should be back in two days. She should know by then if there was a place for her in the Shoshoni village, but if there was not, she would be welcome to go with him and

Red Shirt. She seemed at ease with the situation, so they saddled up and rode out.

As they crossed over the stream, Joel saw White Fawn standing alone a few dozen yards upstream watching them. He touched his finger to his hat as a salute, but she turned and walked away without responding, leaving him at a loss as to what he had done to cause her icy reaction to him. It was just going to keep her on his mind that much longer.

Since Silver City was too far from the Shoshoni village to get there before nightfall, they camped that night in the barn on Joel's property. He figured the business he had in mind would be better conducted in daylight. They rode into the north end of town a little before noon, walking their horses slowly up the middle of the street until reaching the Miner's Rest and the sheriff's office across from it. Everyone they passed along the way stopped to gape at the pair, causing Joel to wonder if maybe he might be riding into an enemy camp. It was too late to reconsider now, so he pulled the Henry from his saddle scabbard just in case when he dismounted. His last meeting with Jim Crowder had not ended well.

Toby Bryan looked up from his desk when the door opened to find it filled with the formidable figure of Joel McAllister. His initial reaction was to hope everything Fuzzy Chapman had told him was true, because the expression on Joel's face was not friendly.

"McAllister," Toby said.

"Blacksmith," Joel returned, surprised to find him in the sheriff's office. "Are you the sheriff now?"

"I am," he said. "Toby Bryan's my name." He guessed that Joel had forgotten it. "What can I do for you?"

That explained why he had been riding with Beauchamp on the trail to Blackjack Mountain. "I've had some trouble up at my and my brother's place, and I wanna make sure you and the folks here in town know that I'm a peaceable man. As far as I'm concerned, the war between my land and Beauchamp's is over, and I didn't start it in the first place."

The sheriff smiled and got up from his chair. He extended his hand, and said, "I'm glad you came in. I think we know the real story behind that war you had. Fuzzy Chapman told us the whole thing. Beauchamp had us all fooled for a long time." Joel shook his hand and Toby went on. "We'll welcome you to our community." He paused, then continued. "Say, I thought I got a glimpse of the woman who cooked for him lyin' on the kitchen floor, but she wasn't at the house when I went back the next mornin'. You know anything about her?"

"Maybe," Joel replied, hesitant to say too much in case they were looking to hang Lena for the killing.

"I was just wonderin' if she was all right. I know she's the one who killed Beauchamp, but I know that it was self-defense. She ain't in no trouble."

Joel nodded thoughtfully. "Well, I can tell you that she got beat up pretty bad, but she's gonna be all right. Can't say where she's goin', just that she's gone."

The answer seemed to satisfy Toby, and Joel decided it best to be cautious, just in case. They stood there for a few moments of awkward silence, neither man sure if there was anything more to say.

"Well, I reckon I'll be on my way, then," Joel finally said. "Are you still shoein' horses?"

Toby chuckled. "Yeah, I'm just sheriffin' till we find somebody wantin' the job permanent. You wouldn't be interested in the job, would you?" The idea seemed like a good one to Toby.

"I ain't gonna have the time," Joel answered as he went out the door, where Red Shirt stood holding the horses.

After camping overnight in the barn at the ranch, they splashed across the stream by the Shoshoni village late the next morning.

"I got something I've gotta do," Joel told Red Shirt. "You go on in. I'll be there in a while."

He wheeled the gray then before Red Shirt could question him, and loped into the meadow where the horses were grazing. Red Shirt shrugged and continued on into the village. He had learned to like coffee as much as his partner, and he was ready for a cup then.

He had just gotten a fire going and was about to go to the stream to fill the pot when he heard the sound of high-pitched yelps coming from many of the people in the village. He looked back to see Joel riding into camp leading seven horses on a line behind him. Astonished, he ran back to the circle of lodges in time to see Joel pull up in front of Walking Eagle's tipi, dismount, tie the lead end of the rope to a stake in the ground, then climb back onto the gray and ride away, leaving the seven horses behind.

Red Shirt threw his head back and laughed. "He listen when I tell him he need wife."

A small crowd gathered a short distance from the chief's tipi in hopes of seeing Walking Eagle's reaction to the proposal. It was not uncommon for a father to let the gifts remain outside his lodge for a long time, even overnight while he considered the offer, while an anxious suitor waited and watched to see if the horses were taken away. In the event they were, he knew that his marriage proposal had been accepted, and he was spared the embarrassment of having to go to retrieve the horses himself.

From Red Shirt's tipi, Joel could just see the horses outside Walking Eagle's lodge, so he sat with a grinning Red Shirt, drinking the coffee he had made, only getting up once in a while to see if the horses were gone. His answer was short in coming, for he saw Walking Eagle come out of the tipi and look the horses over. As Joel watched, Yellow Moon came out then, and the two talked for a while, before White Fawn came out, marched over to the stake, and untied the rope. Then, in what looked to be no uncertain terms, she handed the rope to her father and pointed toward the pony herd in the meadow. Walking Eagle dutifully led his new horses away to the cheering of the people gathered close by.

Unaware that Red Shirt had come out behind him, Joel was startled when the Bannock warrior suddenly slapped him on the back.

"You not free man no more. We make big family now."

"Maybe so," Joel allowed. "I ain't been able to get her out of my mind, so I might as well have her in my tipi."

Feeling the need to splash some cold water on his face, Joel knelt by the stream in the same spot she had come to talk to him before he went after Strong and Zach. He knew what he had done was rash, and he wondered if he would live to regret it. In the last few weeks, it seemed that he had never had time to think about anything but killing and keeping from being killed. But the few moments that he had thought about her were troubling to him. There was so little that he knew about the girl, other than the fact she was impulsive and strong-willed.

"Joel." He heard her call his name.

The sound of it was soft and lilting. He turned to find her standing there. When he turned, she came into his arms, and he knew at that moment all he needed to know.

Read on for a look at
another exciting historical
novel from Charles G. West

WRATH OF THE SAVAGE

Available from Signet in March 2014.

Second Lieutenant Bret Hollister swallowed the last of his coffee and got to his feet. He took a few seconds to stretch his long, lean body before walking unhurriedly over to the water's edge, where he knelt down to rinse out his cup. When he stood up again, he glanced over to catch the question in Sergeant Johnny Duncan's expression. Knowing what the sergeant was silently asking, Hollister said, "Let's get 'em mounted, Sergeant. We need to find this fellow before nightfall."

"Yes, sir," Duncan answered, anticipating the order and turning to address the troopers who were taking their ease beside the stream. "All right, boys, you heard the lieutenant. Mount up."

He stood there holding his horse's reins and watched while the eight-man detail reluctantly climbed back into their saddles. When the last of the green recruits mounted, Duncan climbed aboard and looked to the lieutenant to give the order to march.

A sore-assed bunch of recruits, he thought, although not

without a modicum of sympathy for their discomfort. Not one of the eight men had ever ridden a horse before being assigned to the Second Cavalry just three months before. Duncan knew that the reason they had been assigned to this detail today was primarily because of their greenness. He also knew that the reason he had caught the assignment was because Captain Greer felt confident he could nursemaid the raw troopers and maybe the lieutenant in charge of the patrol as well.

Bret Hollister might make a good officer one day, Duncan speculated, depending upon whether he stayed alive long enough to wear off some of the polish associated with all new lieutenants coming out of West Point. He had only been with the regiment a year and a half, right out of the academy, and as far as Duncan knew, he hadn't distinguished himself one way or another. This rescue detail would be the first time the sergeant would report directly to Hollister, so in all fairness, he supposed he should give the young officer a chance to prove himself.

Hollister had been posted to Fort Ellis in time to participate in the three-pronged campaign to run Sitting Bull and Crazy Horse to ground. That campaign resulted in the annihilation of General George Custer's Seventh Cavalry at the Little Big Horn. By the time the four hundred troopers from Fort Ellis had made the two-hundred-mile march to the Little Big Horn, they were too late to reinforce General Custer. So the only combat experience Lieutenant Bret Hollister had was in the burying of slaughtered troopers of the Seventh and relief of the survivors under Major Marcus Reno. It was hardly enough to test the steel of the young officer.

Duncan's thoughts were interrupted briefly by the order to march, but his mind soon drifted back to his dissatisfaction with being assigned to nursemaid a green patrol commanded by a green officer. It was especially aggravating when the rest of the regiment was preparing to move out to intercept a band of Nez Perce intent upon escaping the reservation. He didn't like being left behind by his company and regiment, the men he had soldiered with for more than two years.

"Damn it," he muttered, "orders are orders."

"Did you say something, Sergeant?" Bret asked, reining his horse back a bit.

"Ah, no, sir," Duncan replied. "I was just talkin' to myself."

Bret smiled. "Better be careful. Talking to yourself might be a sign of battle fatigue."

"Yes, sir," Duncan said. *Don't know what the hell you'd know about battle fatigue,* he thought. Then he reprimanded himself for his attitude. *Best forget about my bad luck and think about why this patrol was ordered out.*

The admonishment made him feel a little guilty, for the patrol was an important one. Reports of two separate raids by renegade Sioux and Cheyenne on homesteaders along the Yellowstone River had come in to the post just hours before the regiment was prepared to march to intercept the Nez Perce. From the report of the young man who had ridden to Fort Ellis with the news of the attack, both families were massacred. Duncan figured the Indians had too great a head start for there to be any reasonable chance of overtaking them. He supposed the real purpose of the patrol was to show some response from the army, even with only an undersized patrol of eight privates, one sergeant, and one officer.

Because of the nature of the mission, and the need

to travel light, the men had been ordered to leave all personal items and clothing behind at Fort Ellis. Each man was issued four days' rations and told to take only one blanket, one rubber ground cloth, one hundred rounds of ammunition, no cooking utensils except one tin cup, and four days' horse feed. Those marching orders told the sergeant that they were expected to return to base as soon as they confirmed that the hostiles were no longer in the area.

Duncan had persuaded Captain Greer to let them seek out Nate Coldiron to help track the Indians responsible for the raids, just in case the trail was hotter than the young man reported. One day of their rations would already be gone in the time it would take to find Coldiron, but it couldn't hurt to have the old trapper along. He was a hell of a hunter, and Duncan thought the patrol might be out longer than four days, in spite of their orders. If that was the case, he was confident that they wouldn't go without food.

Coldiron, a cantankerous old trapper and former army scout, had a cabin on the east side of the Gallatin River, at a point where a wide stream emptied into it. Duncan had been to the cabin once before, when Coldiron had agreed to lead a scouting mission a year earlier. He knew he could find it again, so he led the small patrol west from Bozeman to intercept the Gallatin River, the point from which they were now departing. As best as he could determine, the stream that flowed by Coldiron's cabin was about twelve miles south, so the patrol set out to follow the river.

The farther south they traveled, the nearer they drew to the rugged mountains that hovered over the narrow river, the rougher the country became. Along the way, they passed many streams that fed down into the river, all looking enough alike to make it difficult to identify one particular one, especially after a year's time.

"Are you sure you'll recognize the stream we're looking for?" Bret felt compelled to ask Duncan. "It's not easy to tell one of these from all the others."

"Oh, I'll know it when I see it," Duncan assured him. "We ain't gone far enough to strike it yet."

It was toward the later part of the afternoon when they finally reached what Duncan referred to as Cold-iron Creek. "This is it," he proclaimed, and pointed toward the top of the mountain. "It goes straight up that mountain. Coldiron's cabin is about half a mile up."

Bret could see why Duncan had been so confident in his ability to identify the proper stream. It emptied into the Gallatin between two big rocks. He followed the winding stream up the slope with his eyes until it disappeared into the thick foliage of the tall trees. Above the tree line, the steep mountain peaks stood defiantly, discouraging the casual climber. "It looks pretty rough. Maybe we'd better dismount and lead the horses up there."

"It looks rough," Duncan replied, "but there's a game trail followin' the stream up the hill, and we can ride it if we take it slow. It's just hard to see it from here. I'll lead the way."

He didn't wait for the lieutenant's order, but started up through a thick stand of fir trees that bordered the river. Bret fell in behind him with eight unenthusiastic troopers following him, complaining about the occasional branches that slapped at their faces.

"Quit your bellyachin' and keep up," Duncan called back over his shoulder, admonishing the men.

As Duncan had said, they soon struck a game trail

that circled around from the north side of the mountain and started up the slope beside the stream. Bret couldn't help thinking how far removed he was from the cavalry combat training he'd been drilled in at the academy. There had been very little time spent on the basics of Indian fighting. He was convinced that it was certainly a worthwhile patrol. But what were the odds of tracking a war party of Indian raiders that had a two-day head start? Not very high in his estimation. Then he reminded himself not to question orders. He didn't want to start complaining like the privates following him. His thoughts were interrupted then by the sounds of a rifle cocking and a booming voice.

"Somethin' I can help you soldier boys with?" The question was followed almost immediately by an exclamation. "Well, damn me—Sergeant Johnny Duncan! I thought you was dead."

"Not by a long shot," Duncan replied. "Where the hell are you?"

"I'm right here," Nathaniel Coldiron replied, stepping out from between two boulders on the other side of the stream.

Bret Hollister would never forget his first sight of the old scout. From behind the boulders a man closely resembling a grizzly bear emerged, pushed through a thicket of berry bushes and crossed the stream, oblivious of the water. Clad entirely in animal skins, he wore no hat. His long gray hair, tied in a single braid, hung down his back, almost to his belt. A full beard, more gray than black, covered the bottom half of his broad face. The beard was so thick that until he opened his mouth to speak, there appeared to be no hole there at all.

"What you doin' up here, Duncan?" he asked as he

eased the hammer down on his rifle—a Henry that looked unusually small in his oversized paw.

"Lookin' for you," Duncan answered.

"What fer?" Coldiron asked, all the while casting a critical eye on the officer and enlisted men behind the sergeant.

"Got a little job for you," Duncan said. "That is, if you ain't got too old to do some trackin'."

Coldiron snorted scornfully. "If you thought I was, I don't reckon you'da drug your tired old ass up here lookin' fer me." He nodded toward Bret then. "Who you brung with you?"

Standing patiently by while the two old acquaintances greeted each other, Bret spoke up before Duncan could answer. "I'm Lieutenant Hollister. We came looking for you in hopes you might be able to track an Indian war party that massacred two white families over on the Yellowstone near Benson's Landing."

Coldiron nodded thoughtfully, openly distrustful of most army officers—and of all officers as young and green as this one appeared to be. "I heared about that raid," he spoke after a pause. "Two families got burned out. That was two nights ago. And you're lookin' to track 'em?"

"We're looking to try," Bret replied. "Those are my orders."

"Orders is orders. Ain't that right, Duncan?" Coldiron glanced at the sergeant and laughed as if he had made a joke. "That's a mighty cold trail you're lookin' to follow."

Bret began to lose his patience with the seemingly sarcastic brute. "That's the only trail there is. If you don't think you can help us, then I expect we'd best not waste any more of your time."

Coldiron chuckled and winked at Duncan. "Don't get your fur up, sonny. I didn't say I wouldn't help. I'll go over there with you and take a look around—see what's what."

"Fine," Bret replied. "That's all we're asking, but let's get one thing straight from the start. My name is Bret Hollister. I'll answer to Lieutenant, Hollister, or Bret, but don't ever call me 'sonny' again. Is that understood?"

Coldiron's head recoiled, surprised by the young officer's spunk. It was only a moment, however, before he chuckled heartily. "All right, *Lieutenant*, that's understood."

Also amused by the lieutenant's defiant attitude, Duncan said, "I reckon we'd best get started as soon as possible—cold as that trail is—and it's a pretty long ride if we have to go back the way we came." He looked up, trying to find the sun through the treetops. "It ain't gonna be long before dark in these mountains."

"I expect you're right about that," Coldiron said. "Ain't no use to start out till mornin', anyway. We ain't goin' back the way you came up the Gallatin. We'll cut across through the mountains, and if we try to make it in the dark, we're liable to break a leg or somethin'. Besides, I got things to take care of before I can go. I gotta check my traps for certain." He turned to start up the slope. "You boys follow me and I'll carve off some deer haunch to cook for supper, unless you druther have that salt pork and hardtack the army gave you." His remark stirred a quiet murmur of anticipation among the eight troopers as they followed up through the steep path to Coldiron's cabin.

Afraid the horses might stumble as the path steepened even more, Bret had the men dismount and led them the last fifty yards to the small clearing where the cabin sat, backed up against the slope. Coldiron had obviously built his small abode using logs from the trees he had cleared. Bret wondered if he had had help with the construction, but from the look of the man, he seemed capable of doing the job by himself. A short distance beyond the cabin there was a sizable meadow where the huge man's two horses were grazing. Sergeant Duncan and the men took the horses there to graze overnight while Bret volunteered to help their host build a fire.

"Them Injuns take anybody alive?" Coldiron asked when Bret brought an armload of wood from a pile near the cabin.

"Not according to the report by the thirteen-year-old boy who rode to Fort Ellis," Bret answered. "They killed everybody and set fire to the homes."

"Like I said," Coldiron replied, "I heard about the raid. I didn't hear about nobody bein' took alive, either."

"That's what I was told," Bret repeated.

"That kinda surprises me," Coldiron said. "Sometimes they'll carry off a young woman."

"The Sioux and Cheyenne have been known to take women hostages plenty of times before," Johnny Duncan commented as he walked up, having overheard the last remarks. "I don't see why these Sioux would be any different."

"Blackfoot," Coldiron said. "They was Blackfoot. They ain't Sioux or Cheyenne. They most likely were movin' too fast to bother with captives."

"Huh," Duncan grunted. "How do you know they were Blackfoot? We were told they were Sioux. Them and some Cheyenne renegades have been attackin' some farms along the Yellowstone for the last two months."

"The Injuns that hit Benson's Landing was Black-foot," Coldiron stated matter-of-factly. "I seen 'em when they came down the river last week. I figured they was lookin' to steal horses or raid homesteaders, but there ain't no homesteaders on the Gallatin, so I reckon they moved on. They was a long way from home, if they were from that bunch up near the Judith. I thought that mighta been them comin' back when you soldier boys came ridin' up my trail."

"Maybe so," Duncan allowed. "Don't make much difference, though. Injuns is Injuns. Where's that haunch of deer meat you was braggin' about?"

Coldiron chuckled again. "Still on the deer," he said, and pointed to a tree by the stream on the far side of the cabin where a carcass was hanging from a limb. "I was just fixin' to butcher it when I heard you boys comin' up my trail, soundin' like a freight train. I hadn't kilt it more'n fifteen minutes before that."

His comment surprised Bret. "We didn't hear a shot," he said. "If we were that close, I woulda thought we'd have heard the shot."

"Most likely because you boys was makin' so much noise comin' up through them bushes," Coldiron said, then waited for a few moments before explaining. "Coulda been 'cause I shot it with my bow, though." He looked at Duncan and laughed heartily. "If one of your boys can give me a hand, I'll go saw us off a haunch. Wouldn't be a bad idea if we smoked a supply of meat to take with us. We don't know how long it'll take to catch up to that raidin' party."

Duncan nodded toward Private Weaver, motioning for him to follow Coldiron.